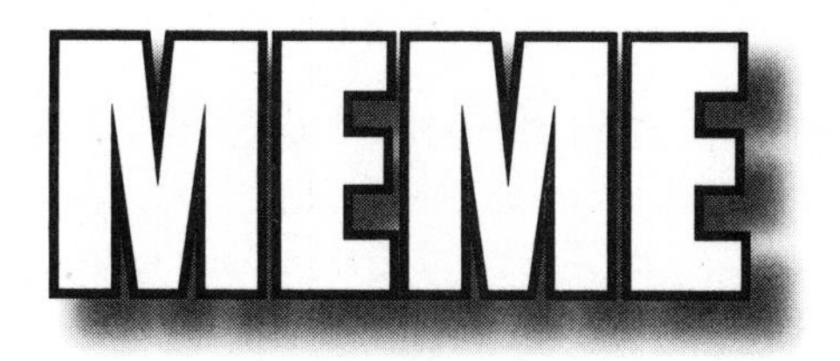
MEME

BY Aaron Starmer

DUTTON BOOKS

DUTTON BOOKS
An imprint of Penguin Random House LLC, New York

First published in the United States of America by Dutton Books,
an imprint of Penguin Random House LLC, 2020

Visit us online at penguinrandomhouse.com.

Library of Congress Cataloging-in-Publication Data is available.

Printed in the United States of America

ISBN 9780735231924

1 3 5 7 9 10 8 6 4 2

Edited by Julie Strauss-Gabel

Design by Anna Booth

Text set in Arno Pro

To Catharine . . . for everything

"When you plant a fertile meme in my mind you literally parasitize my brain, turning it into a vehicle for the meme's propagation in just the way that a virus may parasitize the genetic mechanism of a host cell."

—RICHARD DAWKINS, *THE SELFISH GENE*

"Go fuck yourself @RichardDawkins."

—MULTIPLE PEOPLE ON TWITTER

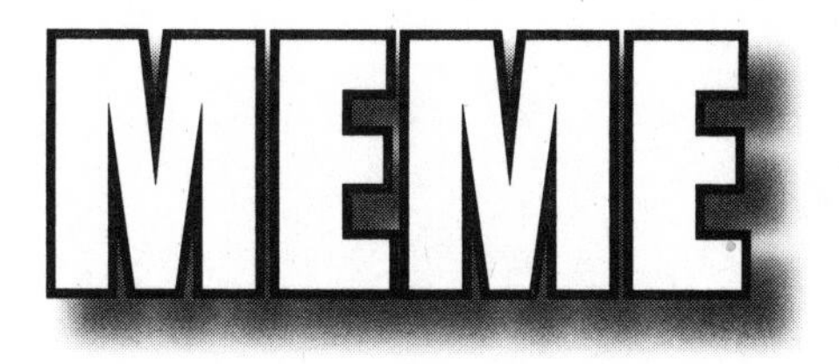
MEME

SUNDAY, OCTOBER 30

ONE DAY AFTER

LOGAN

WE BURIED COLE WESTON LAST NIGHT, on the hundred acres behind Meeka's house.

"Are you sure you want him back here?" I asked her. "Where your parents might snowshoe over him, or something might dig him up? We could still use the firebox."

"This is my choice," Meeka said as she gazed into the waist-deep grave we'd dug on Friday night, out past the orchard and next to the mossy stone wall where Cole had threatened us. "I need to know exactly where he is. If it makes you feel better, you can bury him deeper."

It did make us feel better, and with four digging, we deepened the hole to our ears, very nearly the standard six feet under. Cole's body was encased in a Thule car top carrier. Big enough for an entire family's skis . . . or one teenager. We lifted the makeshift coffin from the tractor and set it next to the grave. I opened it a crack, barely enough to slip in the bag with our old phones, our only links to this, a failsafe if anyone considered betrayal. Then we pushed it into the ground, piled on the dirt and rocks until the hole was full and we could smack it flat with the backs of shovels and kick leaves over the surface.

In silence, with the rest of us standing and clinging to the tractor's frame, Meeka drove back through the mud and dark.

Outside the barn, we stripped off our coveralls and bagged them up with everything else that Grayson would throw in the firebox at his family's sugarhouse. Meeka had filled a pressure sprayer with water and a little bleach and we sprayed down the tractor, and then we all stripped naked and doused each other with the stuff. No one was embarrassed or confused. We were horrified, or at least I was, but not about the nakedness. We'd taken things as far as they could go.

There's a good chance we'll get away with this. A long, snowy winter would help. Plus some time to let it all sink in. It's crazy how fast it's gotten to this point. We're not even into November of our senior year. Up until the end of summer, Cole and Meeka were together. The rest of us were hanging out and hooking up, but they were *serious*. Plural. They spoke in the language of *we*, and about the future.

When we move in together. When we get married. When we have kids.

That third one nearly came true in July. Apparently, there was a broken condom that Cole neglected to mention. A scare. Crying. Arguments about money. And then, four days later than expected, blood. Relief.

By the end of August, the relationship was over. It happened in private. Only the two of them knew what was said, but it was enough to turn them against each other. And Meeka went from planning a future to regretting a past.

That's when Cole got dangerous.

"Are we evil?" Holly asked me last night as we drove away from the barn, the rocks from the dirt road dinging the underside of my Hyundai.

"No," I said. "He was the evil one. Would you have rather it been Meeka? Or us? Or other people?"

"Of course not. And I know, I know, I know we didn't have a choice."

"That's right."

"I know that."

"I doubt I'll sleep for days," I said, flipping on the high beams just as something skittered into the woods in front of us. "I'm not happy about any of this."

"Are you crying?" Holly asked.

"A little."

She was crying too. I could tell from the tremble in her voice. "This will always be a part of us," she said.

"But we'll get over it," I replied.

No one is going to miss Cole. We're counting on that. Sure, he used to have other friends, guys like Gus Drummond, but they don't hang out anymore. He used to have us.

He doesn't even have a family. Ever since his brother, Craig, took off to work the oil fields somewhere in the nowhere of Canada, Cole had been living alone in their trailer. No dad, no mom, no one.

Meeka says the last time Cole talked to his dad was in middle school, when the wispy-bearded guy passed through town on his way from Montreal to Florida. He was driving a pickup with who knows what stashed in the truck box, and he stopped by to tell his sons "not to fuck up your lives like certain people do."

It was a not-so-subtle dig on Cole's mom, Teri. A sweet woman who worked the register at Carlton's Bakery, Teri had struggled with addiction for years. Alcohol and painkillers at first, but by the time we were in high school and stuff like fentanyl was getting big around here, she dove in and never resurfaced. In the winter of our junior year, she passed away. Heart attack was what the obituary said, but we all knew it was the drugs that did her in. She had that bad skin, those mossy teeth, the dead eyes. It was inevitable.

Meeka worked at Carlton's on weekends and had known Teri. Teri had even revealed a secret to her. "*I had another kid,*" she whispered early one Sunday morning as they crouched down to fill the display case with chocolate croissants. "When I was a teenager. I gave her up for adoption."

"Wow," Meeka replied. "That must've been . . . difficult."

Teri sat on the floor, stared at the wall, and said, "Tell me it was the right choice."

It was an awkward and unreasonable request, and Meeka was split between two decisions: push the woman away or hug her. She chose to hug, and as Teri wept in her arms, Meeka said, "It was the right choice. Kids like me have it way better than we would've otherwise."

When Teri died, Meeka told us she was surprised by how devastated she felt, so she wrapped her arms around Teri's son. Their grieving bound them together.

Meeka and Cole said they loved each other early and often, but when things got bad, Meeka knew it had never been true. They *needed* each other, maybe. They needed too much of each other, I think. But for different reasons, and that's what really broke them up.

After the breakup, Cole decided to not return to Plainview High for senior year. His grades were terrible, and college didn't seem like an option. He had a bit of money, though. Not from a job, but somehow he was paying for all the computers and gadgets he had stuffed in his trailer. He could afford takeout for almost every meal. Lots of Subway and pizza, but even that adds up after a while.

Cole wasn't dealing—I mean, he saw what drugs did to his mom—so Meeka suspected he was scamming old people out of their money. You know, like those con artists from Russia or Nigeria? Only Cole was smoother. He was fluent in both English and lies. Plus, he was from Vermont, and people naturally trust people from Vermont.

Whenever I was in Cole's trailer, there was this constant humming in the background and lights flickering on the switches of power strips, which were hung from hooks like flowers left to dry. The windows were covered in newspapers to keep the light out and there were always at least three screens glowing. Cole had mountains of tech. I don't know if he knew anything about coding. What he knew was how to find stuff.

He was always keyed into the latest viral video *before* it went viral. "Check this out," he'd say to me, and thrust a laptop in my face, and there would be some weird person yelling, or dancing, or, more often than not, getting hurt. His favorite was this video of a kid singing, "Walk like a man, talk like a man, walk like a man, my son," in the shrillest, most tone-deaf voice imaginable.

"Gets me every fucking time," he'd say, wiping tears from his eyes. It was a bit funny, I guess, but only the first time. After that, it seemed sad.

But it was infinitely better than most of the other things he'd watch. Disturbing stuff. With a few keystrokes, Cole could cue up a video with some shrouded guy chopping off another guy's head in the desert. Or worse, if you can imagine worse, and I hope you can't.

"Look at it, Logan," he'd squeal, chasing me around the trailer with a laptop. "You know you wanna see this shit. You know you want it to haunt your dreams."

I'd close my eyes and try to block out the images of death. My mind couldn't handle stuff like that. So it's fitting, in a way, that it's the image of Cole's dead body that I'll never have the luxury of blocking out. I'll be haunted, like he always wanted me to be. But trust me, I'd be more haunted if he had lived.

MONDAY, OCTOBER 31

TWO DAYS AFTER

HOLLY

DO THEY KNOW I'M A MURDERER? See it in my spine when I hunch over my desk? Feel the flutters from my chest vibrating through the halls? God. God. God. When I look at the door, do they sense that I want to escape, to run and to never stop running? When I duck into the bathroom, do they think it's because I'm sick? Or do they know exactly why I need to hold my head and catch my breath? Will they whisper, *"Don't worry, we understand, it's okay."* Are they happy about what I've done?

I did it. *I* did it. There were three other people involved, but I made a choice to be involved, so I am to blame. It only happened because of my actions. The pills came from me. The idea came from me. I wasn't coerced and I shouldn't convince myself otherwise. Even though I want to. Need to.

All day, I walk from class to class and somehow I don't cry. People smile, I smile back, and it seems to trick them. *Happy Holly, Happy Holly, perpetually Happy Holly*. That's my Halloween costume this year: my old self. I answer a few questions in all my classes because that's what I'd normally do. I make it through Monday, the second day since we did it. I wonder how long it will take me to stop counting the days.

After school, I go to soccer. Obviously. If I ever missed soccer, they'd call 911.

"Do you think you'll break it?" Tanya asks me during stretches.

Tanya's always talking, and this time she's talking about the single-season state scoring record. That's regular season only; counting playoffs is unfair to girls on terrible teams. For twenty-five years, the record has stayed put at forty-seven goals. Well done, Harwood striker Kim Friggett. She's probably a mom now, with kids of her own who play soccer. But I bet it's my stats she's paying the most attention to. I've got forty-five goals with two games left to go. I really only need one game. A hat trick will break the record for me, and I've had my share. Kim Friggett must know that. She probably also knows that the competition is tougher now than it's ever been. And even if my total stayed at forty-five, I'm still way better than she was. Sounds conceited, but it's the truth. Not that I'd ever say it out loud.

"I'm not thinking about breaking anything," I tell Tanya as I lean forward to stretch my hip flexor. "Finishing the season strong. Only thing on my mind."

God, I wish that were the case. Throughout practice, even as I cut and pass and scream for the ball, my mind keeps going over every detail of Saturday night. Every awful moment.

The drive up to the trailer. The knock on the door. The smug look on Cole's face when Logan told him that Meeka wanted to see him at the barn. The wink to assure him we were on his side. (Of course, we weren't. We would never be on his side.) The drive to the parking lot where it was supposed to end. The calculation of it all.

Who were we that night? How could we do those things?

We did those things.

We crushed the pills and dissolved them in a bottle of Wild Turkey. Then we placed the bottle under the passenger seat so that when

Logan sped up on the hilly section of the Malvern Loop, it rolled to the back and hit Cole's boots.

We did those things and those things worked.

"Hello there, stranger," Cole said when he picked up the bottle.

"That's for later," Logan called back, counting on the fact that Cole was going to drink it anyway. A given. I turned the music up because I didn't need to hear the actual drinking. That would be like hearing a knife going into someone.

"It's later now," Cole said after a few seconds, and even though I couldn't hear it, I know he did more than drink. He chugged. Then he thrust the bottle forward to offer me some.

Rather than touch it, I put my hands in my lap and told Logan, "Should be about five minutes, tops."

"Good," Logan said as he slowed the car and guided it into the rail trail access lot.

"Five minutes for what?" Cole asked, and he took another swig.

Logan didn't say a thing. He stopped and put the car in park as I struggled to breathe.

SATURDAY, OCTOBER 29

THE DAY OF

GRAYSON

COLE WAS HEAVING HIS GUTS OUT in the lot for the rail trail when I pulled up in my Jeep. Saturday, October 29, eight o'clock sharp. Right on time, I'll have you know. Logan was sitting on the hood of his Elantra, all bug-eyed like he was watching a snake eat a rat. Holly was in the car with her hands over her face and music thumping loud.

Cole saw me and groaned, "What's this fucker doing here?"

Then he puked. Splatter all over the gravel. I had my rifle wrapped in a towel in case we needed it. I wanted to grab it and—*Pop!*—be done, but Holly wanted to keep things "clean."

Clean. What a joke. Kid was a mess, puke running all down his shirt. I walked up to Cole and told him, "*This fucker* is here to watch you die."

I would've kicked him in the ribs if he weren't suffering plenty already.

"Shut up, Gray," Logan said. "Cole doesn't know."

"He doesn't know?" I said. "What's the point of making him OD if he doesn't know?"

Cole was on his hands and knees by that point, hacking into a puddle. It was rippling in the headlights. Kinda pretty. Still sitting on his hood, Logan craned his neck, tried to get a look into my Jeep, probably checking to see what I forgot to bring. Typical, and wrong. I brought everything I was supposed to. I'm not the forgetful one in this bunch.

"The point is to end things," Logan said, then he stared at me. "Not to be cruel."

"Really? 'Cause if that were the case, then I would've shot him," I said, and I crouched down and brought my mouth close to Cole's ear. "The *point* is to get the last word. That's right. We're killing you, Cole."

"Come on, Gray!" Logan bitched.

I ignored him, kept my eyes on the dirtbag in the mud puddle. "'Cause you are a sick, sick fuck, Mr. Weston," I said. "And you will never threaten anyone again. Hear me? We are smarter and braver than you ever were or could ever be."

Cole licked his lips and swallowed, panted, and looked up at me. Boy was pissed. So scared too. But he didn't say a thing, probably couldn't. Didn't have control of his body by then. His arms gave up—*Splash*!—and he fell facedown in the water. That's when he went into a spasm.

Holly must've seen it all through the cracks between her fingers, because she turned off the headlights and the blackness got thicker. I could hear splashing and this low sound coming from inside of Cole. Honestly, hearing the water and that hiss and moan of his body was grosser than watching him die. I've killed my share of deer, but none of them made sounds that were as animal as what came out of that kid.

Remember: *A human is an animal.*

I used to think that was bullshit, that a human is a human, nothing else. I've wised up. I know now that a human is the most animal of animals. Think of our weird skin, hair, and nails. Our balls on the outside. Plus, humans have this need to kill anything that gets in our way. Doesn't matter where we're from. Asia. Africa. Europe. Vermont. We're all killers. Even if the act of killing sickens most of us, we'll still do it.

Also the dying. When we die, we're disgusting beasts.

Cole thrashed in the puddle and I yelled, "We did this to you! Meeka too! Especially Meeka! You said you wanted to take us all out! We beat you to it, you fucker!"

Cole lifted his head from the water and wheezed out, "I never said that." Those might have been his dying words. If he had other ones, I didn't hear them. He whispered them to the water, or to the cold air as he flipped over and slipped away.

That was the end. Things got still and quiet and even darker. Clouds rolled in and blocked out the sliver of moon and made the night as black as I ever remember it being. I think it spooked Holly, and she flicked on the headlights again. We all got a good look at Cole on his back, half in the puddle, not moving.

I stepped toward him and Holly got out of the car, so the music got out too. This depressing song filled the air, some chick wailing about her shitty life. Logan hadn't moved from the hood and didn't move until Holly put a hand on his back. That's when he slid down and they joined me next to my Jeep.

Holly took a deep breath, got all focused, and asked, "You've got the bungees? The tarp?"

"I checked and it's all in the back," Logan told her, almost like it pissed him off that I was doing things right.

"Should we call Meeka and let her know it's over?" I asked.

Holly's eyes went so big, I could see the whites on all sides, and she said, "No calls! No phones at all except the old ones.

How many times do we have to say this? You don't have yours on you, do you?"

"Of course not," I told the nervous wreck. "I'm not stupid. Slipped my mind for a second. That's all."

Logan had already pulled the tarp from my Jeep and was shaking it out. Looked like he was getting ready to pitch a tent.

"Coveralls first," Holly told him, and she fished them from the back. I know she saw the rifle. Pissed her off too, I'm sure. Who cares? That wasn't important. Important thing was that Cole was dead. I put my hand in front of his mouth and nose, careful not to touch any puke. Cold. Still.

"No breath. Worked like you said it would."

That meant it was time to move, be done with it. We each ducked behind my Jeep, changed into the coveralls, and tossed our clothes in a trash bag and then in Logan's trunk. Then we rolled Cole up in the tarp and wrapped the bungees around it, tight as we possibly could so we could fit him in the roof box we'd bought with cash at a yard sale in New Hampshire. Logan put in 110 percent, made sure everything was extra tight, and I was going to make a joke about how he must've learned his wrapping skills when he worked at that burrito place, but even I wasn't messed up enough to make jokes.

What I was . . .

No, what I *am*, is a hero.

THURSDAY, NOVEMBER 3

FIVE DAYS AFTER

LOGAN

THESE ARE THE THINGS I worry about.

1. **The body:** It's buried, and when we made the hole deeper, we found old bits of metal and tools from someone who probably farmed the land at least a hundred years ago. That was only halfway down. So I'm not worried that someone will dig it up by accident. And that Thule car top carrier is hard black plastic. It's never decomposing. So I'm not worried the bones will find their way to the surface. I still think we should've cremated him in the firebox, though. It was Meeka's final call, with the logic that if we do get caught, then none of us will be able to make up stories about what happened. There will be physical, biological evidence. Not to mention the phones.

2. **The phones:** We each had old phones—two Galaxys, two iPhones—collecting dust. Basically outdated backups that we never used. We charged them up and erased all the content. As soon as we arrived at Meeka's with the body, we gathered in the barn and laid the phones in a circle on a crate. Then we recorded our confession, each of us huddled over the crate, looking down. When we were finished, we put them in a dry bag from Grayson's kayak. Then later I

slipped them in the car top carrier and we buried them with Cole so that if anyone does ever find the body, we're all implicated. It seemed like a good idea at the time. Now I'm not so sure.

3. **The temptation:** What if one of us goes out there and digs the phones up? It was backbreaking work with four of us digging, so it'd be really difficult, though not impossible, to do it alone. Holly is a great athlete, so she might have the stamina, but would she have the time? Meeka was the one who wanted Cole buried there, so I don't see why she'd do it. And Grayson? He's proud of what we did. I half suspect he might want us all to be caught so he can brag about it. Which leaves me. I'd be a liar if I said I haven't thought of going out there with a shovel. But the frost has hit harder than usual. It dropped to twenty-two degrees last night, and next week isn't supposed to get too far above freezing. I'm not sure I'm up to the task. For now.

4. **The thing in the road:** Something skittered away from my headlights when I was driving Holly home afterward. She didn't notice it, and when I told her about it, she said it was probably a possum. But at the time, I thought it might be a kid. And as I replay the memory, it's seeming more and more like a kid. A kid in a white jacket, zipping across the road and into the woods. I know that sounds crazy, but I used to sneak out of the house sometimes when I was young, to go exploring dark roads with friends. Maybe this white-jacketed boy saw the headlights and thought it was his parents searching for him. Maybe he saw my license

plate, the make of my car. It doesn't mean he witnessed the murder, but it's still not a good thing.

5. **The future:** Even if it was a boy and he did see something, I'm pretty sure we'll get away with this. The plan hasn't been perfect, but in this case, it only needed to be good. It'll be weeks until anyone realizes Cole is gone. He hardly talked to his brother. In Cole's words, he and Craig had "a holiday-only relationship," and Thanksgiving is three weeks away. The sandwich girls at Subway might notice Cole isn't stopping by anymore, but are they really going to tell anyone? Why would they? When someone does finally check out the trailer, they'll see that Cole was a kid who spent a lot of time on 4chan and Reddit and who knows where else and they'll follow his browser history and see all the dark stuff he was into and they'll figure out that there's probably about a thousand different fates he could've met. But will they actually suspect foul play? Without blood or a body, it seems unlikely. He was eighteen, no longer a minor, in charge of himself. Not to mention, an addict's son. So who cares? They'll move on.

Five days Cole's been in the ground and I'm trying my best to move on too. It's Thursday, and the weekend is visible on the horizon. Halloween has come and gone and there have been no ghosts haunting us. We're not in the clear yet, but we're getting there. At school, I've been keeping an eye on the others, and they seem to be making it through okay. Holly is a bit wobbly, but she can always blame that on soccer, on a historic season taking its toll. But, really, what would we have to do to make a person take any of us aside and ask us if we'd murdered our former friend and buried his body in the woods behind one of our houses?

We'd have to tell someone we did it. That's it and that's all.

"Hey, Es," I say as I turn the corner on my way to the gym and spot Esther Green closing her locker.

"Logan the Legend," she says in a deep voice.

"Hardly," I reply.

"Come on. How much have you raised so far?" she asks.

Not to brag, but she's talking about the good I'm bringing to the world, a fund-raiser I put together that will provide micro-loans to help disadvantaged people get socially or environmentally conscious businesses off the ground.

"Fifty-eight thousand, last I checked," I tell her.

"Hell yeah," she says, and puts a hand up. Even though it's totally a bro move, I high-five, and I love how small her hand feels against mine.

"It'll help a few people realize their dreams," I say. It sounds cheesy, but that's what it's all about. When I started it as a project for econ, I thought I'd raise a few hundred dollars from relatives and give it to the local family center. But it's taken on a life of its own.

It's even got a name: Logan's Heroes, which is a reference to an old TV show called *Hogan's Heroes* my pop-pop used to watch. Vice Principal Goldstein warned me that some Jewish people might find the name offensive, but I wasn't sure why. According to Wikipedia, the show was about guys outwitting Nazis, and I'd think Jewish people would be on board with that. I mean, Cole thought the name was "So gay!" and if Cole didn't like something, then chances were that the thing was fair and noble. He was the opposite of tolerant.

Homophobe and anti-Semite: two more boxes on his résumé of evil you can check off.

"You hit up any of those people in the Hollow for money?" Esther asks. "I heard there's a guy who's so rich, he has a private zoo!"

"I'm exploring all options," I say, though I have to admit I haven't been soliciting amateur zookeepers. However, I make a mental note.

"We blew all our 'discretionary' funds at Osheaga in Quebec a few months ago, but my mom read that article about you in the paper, and she wants to donate as soon as we have some extra cash," Esther tells me.

I'm used to people talking about that article. It was only in the local paper, but everyone read it. Fantastic exposure, even though I'd like to update some of the information.

"That's so sweet of your mom. But please tell her that I'm no longer using the Indiegogo site that's mentioned in the article. She can go directly to LogansHeroes.org to donate."

"Roger that. My mom says, 'That Logan kid is doin' right by the young generation.' Isn't that something?" Esther remarks with a dramatic sigh. "Doesn't mention her daughter as the future of this country. But Logan Bailey, that's a boy who's going places."

"To gym," I tell her. "I'm going to gym."

"What about Becca's? Hitting her party tomorrow?"

"Now that I know she's having one, I am."

She smiles. She wants me to be there, but that doesn't mean she wants *me*. The rumors about me and Holly are many and confusing. We're not a thing right now, but I can't blame people for thinking we are. I know it makes other girls keep their distance.

FRIDAY, NOVEMBER 4

SIX DAYS AFTER

HOLLY

I'M ON MY WAY TO BECCA'S PARTY with Meeka. Our lives will always be connected because of what we did, but she doesn't care to talk about it. That's what I need. Meeka drives past the Round Church, which is lit with floodlights. She points to a dog.

"Fluffy fella there is the type I want," she says.

It's a Bernese mountain dog, and it's sniffing around the church garden while its owner sits on a bench checking his phone. They're giant things, Berneses. Fuzzy and huggable and adorable. I understand why people like them, but all I can think about is how big a pain it would be to pick burdocks from their tails.

"You must still miss Skipper," I say. Skipper was her family's golden who they had to put to sleep last year. Cancer of the stomach. So sad.

"He was a good pooch all right," Meeka says. "Old Diaper Breath."

"Diaper Breath, huh? There are a couple of guys I know who could go by that nickname."

"Fuck!" Meeka says. "Who? Not—"

"Not Logan," I assure her. "That boy loves his Altoids too much."

"Then who?"

"Forget it."

"You can't tell me there are at least two guys out there with diaper breath and expect me not to grill your ass on it. This is important information for girls to share."

"Fine. Noah."

"Fuuuck!" she howls as she pounds her fist on the wheel. The horn beeps and it surprises me how much it makes me jump.

"I know, I know," I say. "He's too hot to have bad breath."

"I'll bet he'll be there tonight," she says, and her eyebrows go up and down. "I'll talk to him, get really close, and if I catch a whiff, I'll faint. Fall right into a bowl of guac."

"No you won't."

"Ya think?"

It's never wise to call Meeka's bluff. Meeka rarely bluffs.

"Fine," I say. "Do what you want, but it means I'm not going to tell you who the other guy is."

"Diaper Breath numero dos?"

"It'll be your mission to figure it out."

Meeka puckers up. "I'll be kissing a lot of frogs tonight, then."

I almost call her a slut, in a joking way, but then my chest seizes up.

Cole.

He used that word constantly. He'd always say, "Hey, if girls can call each other sluts, then I should be able to call girls sluts. And if black guys can call each other—"

"It's Caden," I blurt out. "He's the other one."

Meeka's nose scrunches up and she says, "Booo. You're no fun. And anyway, I've kissed Caden."

"What?"

"Sure," she says. "Freshman year. In the gondola. His breath was fine then."

"Well, maybe he'd had a tuna sandwich the day I kissed him."

"And when *was* this day?"

I dip my head. Sheepishly I admit, "Yesterday. After practice. In the parking lot by the fields."

"He kissed you?"

"More like the other way around."

"Holly!"

I rub my eyes and say what I haven't been able to say but have been feeling all week. "I needed to think about something else for a bit. Anything else."

Meeka's head tilts. Her eyes are wide, taking all of me in. "You told me we would be okay," she says, and she gives me her right hand.

I kiss it because I know that's what she wants. Because it makes me feel closer to her. And I nod.

"We are okay."

GRAYSON

I CAN'T BELIEVE I've known these kids for so long. Back to kindergarten for most of them, some of them even earlier. Five or six of them went to the day care that Mom ran out of our house, so they've seen me get my diapers changed. Not that anyone remembers that, but that's the level of familiarity we're working with for a lot of us. Connections run deep.

As parties go, this isn't bad. Becca doesn't want any spills or smells in the house, so we're out back. It's cold here on the patio, but there are a few heat lamps that make it bearable. Lots of hotties out here adding to the heat too, sporting Patagonia vests and beanies. Nice.

There's a keg. Always a good sign. Problem is, it's some craft shit Bornstein got from his cousin. Gose, it's called. Tastes weird, like lemonade and dishwater. I hope it's got a ton of alcohol in it, because if I'm not drunk soon, I'll have to find a bottle of something strong and duck into the woods for a bit.

These kids are all so happy. They're laughing about every little thing. That shouldn't make me mad, but I kinda feel like grabbing some random guy and punching him so I can wipe the smiles off everyone's faces. What can I say? I'm a real asshole. At least sometimes. And some of those times, I deserve to be.

"What's up?" Paul Baker says as he crashes his Solo cup against mine.

It makes the beer spill onto my hand. Cold, but I don't care. I take a gulp and say, "Getting wasted off this, whatever this is."

"This!" he shouts. "This is the best gose in the country, son!"

He pronounces it *goes-ah*, which could be the right way to say it, but it only makes the stuff sound even worse. "Still tastes like piss," I say.

"I don't know. A ninety-four on BeerAdvocate. Pretty legit."

"You're the expert."

Paul is the type of kid who will pull out his phone and check the ratings of movies, food, almost anything you're enjoying. Or, in this case, hating. He's got some old-ass Tumblr where he posts his own movie and TV reviews and other shit. Why? I don't know. We've all got stuff to make us feel important.

"We're in a golden age of beer," Paul says, sipping his like it's wine. "Bask in it."

"If you say so," I tell him, and I finish my cup without tasting, pour it directly down my throat.

If I didn't know him better, Paul would be a good candidate for that punch in the face, but I do know him better and I sort of like him, despite the know-it-all attitude. The kid actually asks me questions about myself. A rare thing.

"So how are the sculptures coming?" he says.

"They're coming," I say, because that's about all I can say. For one, I'm not really a "sculptor." I nail, I carve, sometimes weld. I don't really *sculpt*. So I don't talk about it that way. Also, I haven't touched any of my pieces in weeks. Not since we started our planning.

"I like the one you did of the eagle," he says.

"Osprey," I tell him.

"Right, right. Massive bird. The one you made looks like it

could carry away small children. You should sell it, you know? You could make some scratch."

There's no denying the osprey is one of my better pieces. I made it from reclaimed wood, hacking at it with a hatchet and a saw and then nailing and gluing it together. It has a six-foot wingspan and I mounted it on top of our sugarhouse. Kinda works like a scarecrow, except it scares mice and rats away. Also reminds me of summers kayaking on Champlain, so it's got sentimental value. That's not to say if someone offered me serious cash, I wouldn't part with it.

"We'll see," I say. "I'm keeping it for now."

I put the cup to my mouth to drink more and remember it's empty, but I keep it against my lips to play it off as Esther Green walks by. She's got this silky way about her that maybe goes along with being clever. I don't care who her parents are, or if people call her trash; that girl knows that she knows more than the rest of us.

I follow her, because she's pied-pipering the hell out of me. I don't say shit to Paul, just toss my cup and start walking. I'm not looking where I'm going and I bump into this kid, Gus, who's standing by a potted mum.

Gus Drummond, yeah, of all the luck. This scruffy motherfucker was Cole's best buddy from way back. As if I need another reminder of what we did.

"Sorry," I say.

And you know how that little stain responds? "You'll be sorry all right," he says under his breath. "Stupid duck."

Did he just call me a duck?

"Ha," I say back to him. I literally say the word "ha," because shit like that isn't even worth laughing at. He must've put on some beer muscles tonight, but trust me, the kid is harmless. All obsessed with fantasy books and Minecraft shit. Only time he's thrown a punch is in a video game.

I fake like I'm going after him and he flinches, then scurries away. No surprise there. Holly would be pissed if she saw this, what with Gus being Cole's friend from way back. But it's probably been two years since he and Cole have even talked. I'm not worried in the slightest about him. Kid can't even swear right. *Stupid duck*? Ha.

I'm back to trailing Esther, at least until she stops by the firepit and I'm standing right behind her. She senses me there and turns around, puts a finger out and pokes my chest.

"Not cool, Gray," she says.

I grin and ask, "What?"

"Sneaking up on me."

"Wasn't sneaking. You were going where I was going."

"Keep telling yourself that."

A fat kid from Southfield, who I only know as Rumson, tosses a log on the fire and sends a bunch of sparks in the air. Pretty—the opposite of rain. They dance and disappear, and when I'm done watching them, I notice that Logan is there too. All intense, staring across the fire at me. I put my hand to my forehead and flick off a tight salute, the type my sister, Greta, learned in the marines. The way Greta does it, it's like she's saying "Yessir!" and "Fuck off!" at the same time, which is what I'm going for, even if Logan doesn't realize it.

He answers with a little nod. I have to admit, he's been handling himself better than I expected. Hasn't been hounding me about anything. He's letting time go by and that's what we need. The further we get from it, the better. It rained yesterday and washed away any puke or hair or skin or whatever evidence was still left behind in the rail trail lot. At the grave, the leaves are probably matted down, and when the snow comes, it will look like any other spot in those endless woods.

"You two all right?" Esther asks.

That's when I realize Logan and I have been staring at each other for too long, so I cluck my tongue and say, "Mr. Charitable owes me twenty bucks is all."

"Do I, now?" Logan says with a huff.

"Lemme guess," Esther says. "You're one of Logan's Heroes. Gonna open a pie shop. Two young men, making the world a better place. Through pie."

She's not being serious. She's flirting. I'd like to say she's flirting with me, but . . . yeah, that ain't it.

"Twenty bucks is 'cause this bitch owes me money for a Thule roof box," I tell her.

That gets a reaction from Logan. It's like I took a piss on his leg. "I don't have a clue what you're talking about," he says.

"Just fucking around," I say, and I turn to Esther. "You know Logan is the sorta guy you can trust. He'll do anything for his friends. Anything."

"Good to know," she says. Then she kisses her fingertips, blows us both a kiss, and walks back to the house.

Logan stands on the other side of the fire, mad as I've ever seen him. I wink and walk away.

HOLLY

I'M GETTING SICK in the upstairs bathroom. It is so very nasty, but I have to admit this is a really nice remodel. Dull slate and shiny chrome. I can't imagine Becca's parents—God, *anyone's* parents—would be happy to know what I'm doing to their perfect porcelain. But they probably won't ever know, will they? I can clean this up. I can clean up anything.

Meeka is sitting on a stool, the type that toddlers use to reach the sink. "You can come back to my house," she says. "Sleep off all that booze."

"I don't want to be there or anywhere near that place," I say as I take a breath.

Besides, what is there to sleep off? I had one drink, a splash of screwdriver in a plastic cup. Which was enough to push me over the edge. How did I become so sensitive? Am I literally falling apart?

"I understand," Meeka says as she traces the lines between the tiles with her foot. "You know you're always welcome, though."

I massage my brow and tell her, "People will start saying I was drunk the night before a game. What was I thinking putting *anything* in my body?"

"You wanted to be calm," she replies. "You wanted to be normal."

"I've never wanted normal," I tell her.

I wipe my mouth with some toilet paper and lean back against the wall. The baseboard radiator is on. It's warming my back, which feels good, but I wish it would burn me. Mark me. Punish me.

There's a knock on the door.

"Beat it, peasant," Meeka yells. "We're making babies in here."

This doesn't make me laugh like it might've in the past. It makes me think. Would Meeka be a good mother? It's a weird thought, but as I look at her, I want to say . . . maybe. She's loyal, fiercely so. I know she'd do anything for me. I can't imagine her with an actual baby, though. Not because she's seventeen. There are plenty of girls in our class who I can imagine as mothers. Meeka is different. I'd like to say it's because she's more mature than them, but that sounds counterintuitive. Let's say it's her priorities. She's got so many other things she'd like to do with her life first. That makes me wonder why she was wasting her time with Cole. Will I ever stop thinking about Cole?

I lunge for the toilet and my body heaves, but nothing comes.

As Meeka rubs my back, she says, "Since you're not up to it, I'm going to make a few decisions for you."

"That so?" I mumble.

"'Tis. Okay, this is what's happening. You are going back out there. You are going to say your goodbyes and get in my car. I am going to drive you home and you are going to get into bed. You are going to sleep. You are going to wake up in the morning and you are going to go to your game and you are going to score three goals. No, four. Actually, five. Five spectacular goals. You are going to shatter that record. It's what you deserve. It's who you are. A fucking shooting star."

She helps me up, hugs me, and we push through the door. Jed

Barrow is waiting outside. He shakes his head in exasperation. We were in there for a long time.

"The babies are officially made," Meeka says, and she punches him on the shoulder as we pass.

We weave through the crowd, giving half hugs to the kids we like, with Meeka doing all the talking, squeezing my cheeks and saying things like "We gotta get our lil' darlin' wested up for tomorrow, so she can score wots and wots of goals."

As we circle around the house, we see Logan. He's next to the driveway, sitting down with his back against a tree. Alone.

"Hey," he says.

"Hey," we both respond.

"You out?" he asks.

"You bet," Meeka says.

Then we don't say anything else for a few seconds, until Logan breaks the silence.

"Good luck tomorrow. I wish I could be there, but . . ."

"Don't worry about it," I say. "It's a stupid game. A stupid number. That's all."

"No, it's a big deal," he says. "And you deserve all the credit you get."

That's a compliment, but somehow it sounds like a threat. Maybe I'm hearing it wrong, but the word "credit" doesn't sound good.

"Thanks?" is all I can manage to say.

"Have fun," Meeka adds. "Be good."

Logan tries to smile, but it doesn't work. It's painful to watch, so I don't.

Past him, in a patch of trees, I spot someone else. A boy, peeing. His blue Carhartt, splattered with bits of white paint, tells me it's Grayson. The four of us, together again. Okay, not really together, but in the same place. Only for a few seconds, though. Long enough to make me remember our confession as I rush to Meeka's car.

Huddled over the phones, the four of us said it one by one. First Grayson, then Logan, then me, and finally Meeka. The same words except for our names.

"I, Holly Morse, along with Grayson Hobbs, Logan Bailey, and Meeka Miller, have buried this recording with Cole Weston because we are the ones who caused his death. It is not a crime because we did it in self-defense. Cole Weston was a dangerous young man. He threatened Meeka. And he threatened the rest of us. It was only going to get worse from there. He had access to guns. He was great at hiding things, and the police would have never found any evidence, so they would have never been able to charge him with a serious crime. That is, until it was too late. Cole assured us of this. We believed him. So we stopped him. It was self-defense. For ourselves and our town. For the future we all want and deserve."

LOGAN

I'M DRIVING HOME by myself. Not that I expected to be leaving with Esther, but Grayson destroyed any slim chance I had of that. Probably a good thing. Random hookups are a bad idea for any number of reasons. If I want to get anywhere with Esther, I should ask her out properly. Be respectful. The opposite of the Cole approach.

Not that Cole ever actually used *any* approach. As far as I know, Meeka is the only girl he'd ever been with, and he more or less fell into that relationship. Still, he talked a big, and foul, game.

"Every girl is a slut, deep down," he once told me and Grayson. "All you have to do is find her weakness and you can bring the sluttiness out of her. You don't even have to treat her nice. In fact, it works better if you treat her like garbage."

So disgusting. And it certainly wasn't the only time he talked like that.

There was this one rainy Sunday last May, and we were all bowling together. Grayson was checking out Gayle Jasper, who was working at the alley. She was a graduating senior with a mane of red hair and a family name that, to be honest, carried some baggage.

"Give her two Mike's Hard Lemonades and she'll be blowing you

back there behind the pins," Cole whispered to Grayson, though I was close enough to hear.

Grayson chewed at his thumbnail like he was thinking about it.

Meeka, who was a little farther away, asked, "What are you guys talking about?"

"Oh, just girls with . . . questionable morals," Cole said. "Present company excluded, of course."

It made me so uncomfortable, and I couldn't stop glancing over at Gayle to make sure she couldn't hear us. Meeka put two and two together.

"*For fuck's sake,*" she said softly. "The rumors about her aren't at all true."

"About who?" Holly asked as she returned from the bathroom.

"If anything, it's the opposite of what guys tell you," Meeka went on. "She didn't put herself in those situations. I heard she doesn't even remember what happened."

"No one forced her to drink," Cole said. "That's on her. And how convenient that she 'forgets' what happens. And the guys, who were plenty drunk too, all remember. Why's that?"

"Trauma maybe?" Meeka said. "PTSD? Heard of it? Call me when you experience something traumatic and I'll—"

Meeka closed her eyes. She must've immediately regretted what she said. She didn't say she was sorry, though.

"Whose turn is it?" Holly asked as she nervously checked the monitor above our lane.

Then Cole placed a hand on Meeka's shoulder and said, "You're right. She feels victimized. And it's a shame she's suffering through those feelings."

Meeka took a long, deep breath and then put her hand on top

of Cole's. She squeezed tight, like she cared. Or maybe she was angry. I wasn't sure which.

Grayson cleared his throat, grabbed his ball, shuffled down the lane, and promptly rolled a strike. The sound of the pins and his triumphant howl pulled us away from the conversation and we didn't return to it for the rest of the night.

It was a good night after that. We had fun.

Was it a boy or a possum? I drive the dark roads looking for either, hoping for any moving thing to test against my memory. The woods are as impenetrable as velvet curtains and yet I keep searching. As much as I don't want to, I go by the rail trail lot, around the Malvern Loop, and past Meeka's place, retracing our route, hoping something will pop out and skitter across the road. When fog rolls in, I can't even fight the darkness in front of me. My headlights barely cut through and so I drive slow and my heart goes fast. I want to be home in bed. I keep driving and I don't see much of anything but the fog. Thankfully I know my way.

When I get home, Mom is still up. It's not a surprise because she watches a lot of movies. Or if there's a big news story going on, she flips from news channel to news channel. Tonight, she's watching something old, in black and white, with violins on the soundtrack. She turns it down when she hears me walking past the family room.

"Hey, bud," she calls out.

"Hey," I say, and I poke my head in.

"Good party?"

"Eh."

She pulls Dad's book off the armchair and places it on the coffee table, which is her way of asking me to sit down. I want to tell her I'm going to bed, but it's nice to have someone to talk to for a moment who actually cares about how I'm feeling. Even if I can't tell her how I'm feeling.

I flop into the seat and rub my eyes.

"Better not be drunk," she says.

"Tired," I reply.

"You were safe?"

"I drove as slow as humanly possible."

She pauses the movie on the blond heroine, who's all curls and winks. "Was Holly there?"

"Yeah, but I hardly talked to her."

"She's such a great kid," Mom says, and I know she's not saying it because she wishes I was still dating Holly. It's almost like she wants to be a teenager again herself so she can be Holly's friend. Not that I blame her. Everyone loves Holly, especially the people who don't really know her well.

"I wish I could sleep for a week," I tell Mom.

She smiles proudly and says, "There's no rest when you're trying to change the world."

It's eleven thirty on Friday night and I have to be up at five thirty so I can go with Dad to Montpelier and have a "business" breakfast with some state senator who's supposed to help me find political support for Logan's Heroes. I'm thankful for this. There's no question about that. I realize how privileged I am to have a dad who can actually set up a breakfast with an elected official. But it doesn't mean that these things aren't still physically and mentally exhausting.

I know. It beats working at a fast-food joint, which I can confirm because that's something I've done. And even though it was probably as good a fast-food job as a teen could get—it was an organic, locally sourced burrito place called Rita's Ritos, after all—the hours sucked, the kitchen was always boiling hot, and the customers were hardly ever appreciative. Working food service will teach you a lot about the world. Dad told me that, and I learned how right he was my first day on the job. It's not something I ever want to do again. The nonprofit life is the one for me. So if that means waking up early and talking to stuffy people over crepes to achieve my goal, then I'll count myself as blessed.

I'm in bed, arms crossed over my chest. The temperature is dropping but the heat hasn't kicked on because oil prices are inching up and there's no reason to keep a house above sixty degrees at night. At least that's my parents' attitude, and I really can't say anything about it until I'm "the one buying the oil."

I pull the covers to my chin and I recross my arms underneath. I imagine the covers are a layer of pebbles, covered in a layer of dirt, covered in snow. Mom left the porch light on and its glow creeps across the lawn and into my window. Outside, a few flakes are falling.

I've averaged about three hours of sleep each night for the last week. I don't think my body can handle so little for much longer. At best, I might get five hours tonight.

I close my eyes.

SATURDAY, NOVEMBER 5

SEVEN DAYS AFTER

HOLLY

THE GROUND IS FROZEN and the ball skip, skip, skips across midfield and onto my foot. Good first touch and I'm off. A lot of turf in front of me but no D nearby, so I give the ball some space. Sprint sprint touch, sprint sprint touch.

Kaci streaks down the right wing. She's open, but there's no chance. Her foot's been a brick all day. Shots too high, crosses too wide. Riley calls for the ball, but I don't see her and she's rarely where she needs to be. I'm taking it myself.

The stopper is on me.

Quick stepover and her feet are in concrete.

Like that, I'm at the top of the circle.

"Holly!"

"Holly!"

"On your right, your right!"

They're delusional. I'm in the box, I've come this far and . . .

Drop a shoulder, chop the ball, sweeper's beat.

Me and the goalie. Fake left, then pop it with the outside of my right foot.

Pop, skip, side net.

Hat trick.

Forty-eight. Forty-eight. Forty-eight.

My record. My record. For as long as—

Cole.

There are patches of time when he's out of my head. Adrenaline will chase him away. But as soon as it fades, he's back. He's all I think about for the final minutes of the game. As we clear the ball and stall, as we exercise restraint. No reason to keep the pressure on now that I've got the record. Now that I've got the record, Cole is all that matters.

That's my true legacy. Cole.

When the final whistle blows, the score is 4–0. Hartsville is a terrible team, but I didn't think they were *that* terrible. My first two goals came so quickly, and even though the third one didn't come until eight minutes left, it came. Like we all hoped it would.

We line up, say our *good game*s and slap hands. Then my girls are all around me, hugging my shoulders, patting my back, yanking my braids. They don't dump water over my head—too cold—and they don't tackle me because, yes, we won, but we still won't make the playoffs. This is my moment. It's hard to get *too* excited about another person's moment. It definitely doesn't inspire my teammates to pile on top of each other like we won states or something.

When the congratulations die down and everyone is putting on their jackets and warm-up pants, Coach Murphy walks me out to midfield. She hands me the game ball.

"Don't worry. There will be the awards at the last game and the banquet after that, but I want you to have this now," she says.

"Thank you," I reply. I tuck the ball under my arm. The crowd on the hill is thinning out. No sight of Grayson up there, but he rarely comes to games. Dad is still in his beach chair, and when he notices I'm looking his way, he pumps a fist. Mom is standing, hugging Meeka and whispering something to her. They smile at each other and then Meeka turns to walk away. She doesn't wave—or I don't see her wave—but I bet a text is coming soon. She usually texts after games. Often slightly vulgar, overly dramatic videos declaring her adoration. My phone is still in my bag, preparing for the onslaught.

"I'm sorry," Coach Murphy says.

I blink and turn back to her. "For what?"

"That we couldn't give you a better run."

"We'll win the last one."

"Sure, we'll give it our best, but 7–9–2 is not the way I wanted you to go out. You've carried us. You've done so much. More than I could've ever asked."

She's right, of course. I've scored most of our goals this year. Assisted on most of the others. There was a game where I scored five and we still lost, which is basically impossible in soccer. There's nothing I can do to bring us above mediocre.

"Everyone did great this season," I say.

Coach Murphy rolls her eyes. It's a total mean girl gesture, probably part of her repertoire since she was in high school, but I appreciate it. Obviously, not everyone did great. But what's the point of saying that out loud? The season is pretty much over.

She leans in and hugs me. She doesn't speak. She holds on to me for a long time. Eventually, she has to let me go. In every way. One more game and then I'm done with this.

Someone starts turning off the field lights, so we go our separate ways. Coach Murphy heads to the hill to greet the remaining crowd and I find my bag and have a moment to myself. I sit on the bench, peel off my cleats, and wipe them down with a small towel from my duffel. Then I slip on sneakers and lace them loosely. I close my eyes. I take a deep breath and resist the urge to scream.

About ten minutes later, my parents are talking to Coach

Murphy at the top of the hill while I'm in the parking lot waiting for them. The lights are dim here, so I don't see Riley approach until she's almost next to me. She's holding her phone up, taking a blast of pics. I have no idea why.

"I'm so sweaty right now," I say, covering my face. The sweat is freezing, and I must look hideous.

"But you're a star," Riley says.

"Yes, Vermont's most famous girls' high school soccer player." I open the hatchback on Dad's car and toss my bag in. "You do realize we're the second-smallest state? Population-wise, that is."

"Who's the smallest?"

"I don't know," I say, because this wasn't something I'd actually researched, only something I'd heard. "A Dakota maybe?"

"Well, you're bigger than Vermont and the Dakotas combined," Riley says as she holds up her phone. "You're internationally renowned."

"I doubt that. Some girl will break the record next year—"

"I'm not talking about soccer," Riley hoots. "You're a meme!"

Then she shoves her phone in my face and there's a picture filling the screen. I grab it to get a closer look because what the fuck? *What the fuck? WHAT THE FUCK?*

I drop the phone on the pavement. The screen shatters and so does my entire world.

SUNDAY, NOVEMBER 6

EIGHT DAYS AFTER

GRAYSON

MY PHONE IS BUZZING and it wakes me at nine a.m., way too early for a Sunday. What the hell is wrong with people? Notifications keep coming and coming. Not a huge surprise because the thing was dead all night and I only plugged it in when I got home at . . . three, maybe? Who knows? I haven't had a curfew since last year and I never keep track of time when I'm out drinking with Larson and those guys.

Bzzzzz.

Come on!

I can't read most of the notifications without my contacts, so I stumble to the bathroom, splash some water on my face, and slide them in. I feel the throb behind my eyes and think, "Shit, that was a lotta Jäger, wasn't it?" And like every other weekend morning, I vow to never drink again. Exactly like I did yesterday morning, when I was hungover from Becca's party. Ha.

I'm noticing a lot of stuff from Meeka. Mostly question marks and links. I follow one and it takes me to a Facebook post with a ton of likes and comments. It's a picture of me, Meeka, Holly, and Logan with our faces in a circle, looking straight at the camera. Even with my head aching and my eyes still blurry, I know what this is from.

Our fucking confession.

I tap it, but it's not a video. It's a still. A fuzzy one, so probably a screenshot. Our four faces are all twisted up in four stupid expressions like we're in pain or constipated or, I don't know, a bunch of mouth-breathers. There's writing on it, those big white letters with black outlines that people slap on old-school memes.

THE MEETING OF THE DERP COUNCIL HAS BEEN ADJ . . .

. . . DERP

It would be kinda funny if I didn't know where the pic came from. But I do. So it isn't.

I message Meeka.

WTF!

You see it? she answers.

How?

Come over. Now.

I'm wondering if I should get in touch with Logan or Holly and then I realize that it might've been one of them who leaked the pic, and even if I don't understand why they would've, I should figure out how they *could've* first.

Meeka is better than me at figuring things out. Plus, I trust her more. I mean, the body is on her property. Why the hell would she try to mess things up?

I fill a travel mug with the burnt coffee left over in the carafe from Dad's morning fix and I hop in the Jeep and it's cold as fuck but that's okay. The soft-top is flapping and the duct tape covering some cracks is peeling off and letting in air. Helps wake me up and straighten out my head.

When I get to Meeka's, she's sitting on a rocking chair on her front porch, legs crossed, feet covered in brown boots that are lined with fur. She hops down and she's hugging me as soon as my shoes hit the gravel.

"You tell me the truth and you'll only have to tell me once," she says. "Was it you?"

"The picture?" I ask. "No. Hell no."

"Good," she says, and she kisses my cheek.

"So it was Logan, then?"

Meeka looks up, all lost. "No idea. It doesn't make any sense. Why would he?"

"Why would Holly?"

She grabs my hand and leads me across the yard to the barn. She pulls the big doors shut as we walk in and then she hops onto the hood of a Trans Am her dad has been "restoring" for close to five years. Not the sort of car I could see Mr. Miller ever driving, but hey, we all have things that turn us on.

"You guys thought you had a good plan and I know it wasn't supposed to be easy, but . . ."

Meeka's voice fades into nothing and it looks like she's going to cry, but she's good at keeping that stuff locked in. She holds it together.

"I hear ya," I say, and I slide onto the hood next to her. I wait for her to lean into me, and she does, and that's when I put my arm around her. "Remember. You're here. Alive. With me. As it should be. Because of what we did."

She shakes her head. "The phones were buried. We know they were in the ground."

"Logan dug them up," I say. "That's the only explanation. He's trying to fuck us. For whatever reason."

"I don't think so."

"How do you know? Have you been out there?"

She thinks about this for a moment, then nods. "You know the stone wall out there? Right next to where we buried him? Did you know we were sitting on that wall the first time Cole and I kissed?"

I did know that. Cole had told me once. He kissed Meeka there, then a few months later, he threatened her there. And last week, we buried him there. The symbolism isn't lost on me.

"I'm not asking about the stone wall," I say. "I'm asking about digging."

She shakes her head and says, "Digging isn't the issue here."

Got it. I don't press her because she sounds so sure. Instead, I focus on the data. If no one went out there digging, then that means the phones are still out there, buried deep with Cole. I don't know a lot about how iPhones, or Galaxys, or any phones, for that matter, work. I don't know if there's a way to hack into them using other phones or computers, even while they're, like, turned off and underground. But Meeka is smart, so maybe she does.

"Do you think Logan hacked in?" I ask. "Does he know how to do that?"

Her heels tap the grill of the car and she looks at her phone but she doesn't say a thing. Then she holds the phone up and snaps a quick pic of—I don't know, the barn door?—and she taps it a few more times before finally talking.

"Someone fucked up. Maybe not intentionally, but someone fucked up."

LOGAN

I'M STARING AT THIS MEME with all four of our ridiculous and terrified faces and a caption that says: WHO FARTED? And what I'm thinking is: "WHO MADE THIS?"

It's all I've been thinking since Holly forwarded it to me last night. Obviously, whoever created it has seen our video. And since they've seen our video, then that's it. We're done. Through. Game over.

It's nine in the morning and I haven't slept a wink. I've been stumbling along the path of this nightmare for hours. There are other versions of the same pic with different captions, fonts, and layouts. The meme has already made the rounds on Facebook, but that's the realm of our parents. I can't believe the meme could've started there. Nothing ever starts there. No, it must have been born on Reddit or 4chan or 8chan or some other site where the sad and friendless hang out and all these memes originate.

But I can't find a beginning. Using a reverse image search, I find a few Reddit threads with titles like *Check out this fellowship of doinks* and *Meme the fuck out of these turds* posted over the last day or two. They're sprinkled with Photoshopped pics and snarky comments, most of which I'd rather not remember. It's like middle school all over again. I won't even mention the chans. They're cesspools of porn and violence and I have to turn away as soon as I open the first few threads.

There's no debating that the picture is unflattering. But if you've ever done a screen cap of a video, any video, you'll easily find unflattering frames. What I don't get is why it caught on. And I can't for the life of me figure out who brought it to Plainview High. It's not like there's anything in the picture identifying who we are or where we're from. It seems to have reached here almost immediately.

I message Holly: **Where did Riley get the meme?**

She writes back: **IDK. On my way to Meeka's. Come too.**

The first time I ever went to Meeka's house, it was the summer after second grade, for her birthday party. She was turning eight. We weren't necessarily friends back then, but she'd been in my class and so I was invited. I think I might have given her Legos.

It was a laid-back affair, with cake, presents, playing in the yard around her house, and a walk past the barn to a pond where we all went swimming. Meeka had always been friendly, but this was another level entirely. She was *exceedingly* happy to have us all there. She kept saying things like "Do you want a tour of the house?" and "Do you want to sit on the tractor?" and "Do you want to see where the rabbits live?"

If we were older, it might've come off as desperate. But for a kid, it was impressive. She had a gorgeous old house with built-in cubbyholes, multiple lofts, and—I assumed, though I didn't see them—secret passages. It was on a picture-perfect farm with antique equipment that probably didn't work, and didn't have to, but was rusty in all the right ways.

Plus, Meeka's parents were cool. They'd lived in Boston when they were younger and had that city confidence about them. Yet they also fit right in around here—all trucker-hatted, earthbound, and friendly—even if the older generations might've called them flatlanders.

When I got home, I asked Mom, "Is Meeka's family rich?"

Mom said, "I'm sure they're comfortable, but that doesn't really matter, does it?"

"I guess not."

"She seems like a nice girl."

"She is. She's really awesome. But why are her parents . . . not her parents?"

Mom paused for a second, then said, "Did one of the kids say that?"

I nodded.

"They're not her biological parents," Mom explained. "And that's why she looks different from them. But that also doesn't matter either, does it?"

It did, in a way, matter. At least I assumed it did. Being adopted, I mean. Only I didn't understand exactly why it mattered. So all I said was, "They have a really cool tractor and a really cool pond and a really cool barn."

Mom kissed my forehead and replied, "I'm glad you had so much fun. I hope you can go back and play there again someday."

GRAYSON

I'VE SEEN HOLLY'S TITS. I've seen Meeka's. I've seen Logan's dick, but only for a second. My eyes didn't linger.

On the night we decided to do it—in the barn where I'm sitting right now with Meeka—the four of us, butt naked on a blanket, pledged our allegiance to kill an asshole. Holly started it. She took off her shirt and said, "Are you with me?"

Unexpected? Yeah. Understandable? Kind of.

Cole scared the hell out of Holly. She was sure he'd follow through with his threats and absolutely sure we had to follow through with some rough justice. And she was motivated—boy, was she—in *everything*: school, sports, guys, name it. She always had to win, and she had to beat Cole.

So she stripped off her clothes.

It may sound insane, but being naked showed us she was committed, that she had nothing to hide. She needed to do something, and she was daring us to join her. It was a fucked-up game of chicken. Worked, though. Because Logan went next, then me, then Meeka. All our shirts off, and before we knew it, everything else too. By the time we were down to nothing but skin and hair, we were all in. There was no sex—nothing even close. It wasn't about that.

Try it sometime. Get naked with a bunch of people and make a promise or two. You'd be surprised how it sticks. In our case, promises turned into a plan. Holly promised to snatch some pills without her mom noticing. Logan would do the talking and driving, convince Cole to get into his car and make sure he drank the whiskey. I would bring the gear and burn the evidence. We'd cart the body to Meeka's house, where we'd all dig and we'd all bury. Later, we decided we had to bring our phones and confess, which was the stupidest part of the plan.

"Those fucking phones," Meeka says to me now, as we sit on the hood of the Trans Am. "I never would've guessed this could happen."

I stare at the spot where the blanket had been, where we'd all sat bare-ass and shivering. And then the door opens and there's Holly and she's crying.

"We're so screwed," she says.

"Honey, I'm so sorry I didn't get back to you last night," Meeka says. "I lost my phone in the couch cushions and Mom had one of her parties, so I was waitressing for her till midnight. But when I found out this morning, I was on it."

Holly balls her fists like she's about to punch both of us, but instead of punching, she paces. "What's to figure out? We have to dig him up. We have to burn him. We have to—"

"No," Meeka says as she moves to Holly with her hands up and open. "We have to figure out what happened. So when I ask you something, I don't want you to take it the wrong way."

"What?"

"On your old phone, did you forget to turn off your cloud?"

"What?"

"It's a question for both of you. Did you have a backup on your old phone that went to a cloud?" Meeka asks. "I know we all wiped the data, but did you turn off the backups?"

"Doesn't matter," Holly says. "The cell services were all off, transferred to our new phones ages ago."

"True," Meeka says, "but not the Wi-Fi. The Wi-Fi signal reaches the barn. The video could have been automatically uploaded to your cloud, even if the phone didn't have cell service. And if it's *on* your cloud, then someone else could take it *off* your cloud."

My mom likes the Rolling Stones and they have a song called "Get Off of My Cloud" that starts earworming in my head. So yeah, I know the lyrics to some old-ass song, but I don't have the first fucking clue about clouds. I mean, I know it's like a virtual place where your files get stored. Backups and all that. But there has to be an actual physical thing somewhere that has all your shit on it, right? Seems right, but I don't really know for sure.

I don't tell the girls that. I just say, "I turned everything off."

"Sign into your cloud to be certain," Meeka says as she pulls out her phone. She taps quickly and then holds it up. "See. Nothing from that day."

Holly taps at her own screen like she's doing Meeka a favor, stabbing her finger and rolling her eyes. She holds up the screen for both of us to see.

"Check my iCloud stream. October twenty-ninth is all clear. I'm not an idiot."

I pretend to sign into mine, but I'm not sure where to start. The two of them watch me, and I try to play it off. "Umm . . ."

Meeka grabs my phone before I can make a total ass of myself. "What cloud service do you use? And what's your password?"

I grab it back. "I'm not giving you my password."

"Fine," she says. "Sign in yourself. Make sure the video isn't in there."

I think I use . . . Dropbox?

I try my most obvious password. Nope.

Try another and . . . nothing.

I'm thinking about resetting the password, when Holly says, "If you're too stupid to open it, then you're probably too stupid to have set it up in the first place."

That earns her a cold, hard glare, because if she's stupid enough to say something like that to me, then she's not smart at all. Besides, my third try at a password—an old one with Gram's name—works and I'm in. I hold up my phone.

"Fuck you very much," I tell Holly.

She shrugs.

"What's on there?" Meeka asks.

I give the files a glance. "Mostly porn," I say.

"Oh Jesus, Grayson," Holly says.

"It's the truth," I say. "That's all I've ever used this for. To store some porn I wanted to, you know, revisit."

Meeka rolls her eyes and asks, "But nothing from that night?"

"Not a thing," I tell them. "I'm not the one who fucked up."

Meanwhile, Holly is tapping her phone like a maniac. "Well, I'm changing my password anyway. And I suggest you two do the same."

A quick breeze blows up some dust and we all turn. The door is open again and this time it's Logan standing there, all sweaty and red.

"I got here as soon as I—"

"Log into your cloud, check your photos on October twenty-ninth," Holly says. "Then change your damn password!"

He freezes and squints. "I didn't share anything, and if you think—"

"Do it!" Holly screams.

Logan holds up a hand—a total dick move, like he's saying "shut up, bitch"—and it's obvious why he and Holly aren't a thing anymore. But when he checks his phone, his mood changes.

"Oh, wait," he says.

"What?" Holly asks.

"There's that other service," he says.

"What other service?" Holly asks.

Logan puts that hand up again, and checks his phone again, and then his voice sounds like a little boy's. "Oh crap."

"It's on there?" Meeka asks. "The video?"

Logan lowers his phone and takes a good long look at his shoelaces. He nods.

Fuck.

HOLLY

NO ONE KNOWS my passwords. No one. There are some things you don't share, even with the ones you love.

No one could guess my passwords. No one. They're random letters and numbers that I always memorize. Do I write them down? Of course I don't. That's not something I would ever do.

Logan, on the other hand, shares his passwords with his girlfriends—I know that firsthand—and he probably has a piece of paper with them taped on his desk, like some grandpa who refers to the internet as the World Wide Web.

Jesus, Logan.

"Who has your passwords?" I ask him. "Who have you been sharing your passwords with?"

"No one," he says.

"Not *exactly* true," Meeka says, and she turns to me for confirmation.

"Well, I obviously didn't do it," I say. "Is it Esther? She's part of hack club, isn't she?"

"It isn't Esther," Logan assures me. "I don't know her like that. And yeah, I might've shared a password or two with you back in the day. But no, I've never shared them with anyone else."

"No one else?" Meeka asks.

"Well . . ." Logan says. "No. No one else."

"Why the hesitation?" Meeka asks.

Logan shrugs.

"Jesus, you didn't share passwords with Cole, did you?" I say.

"Cole is gone," Grayson so helpfully reminds us. "There's no Cole to worry about anymore."

"I didn't share any passwords with Cole," Logan says. "But he did recommend it."

"A password?" I ask.

"The cloud service I used," Logan says. "On my old phone."

"What?" I ask, because seriously, *what?*

"You were supposed to wipe the old phone," Grayson says. "Even I knew that."

"I wiped all the pics and stuff," Logan says.

"But not the apps?" Meeka asks.

He shrugs and says, "Didn't seem necessary."

Meeka throws her hands up. "Oh well, now fuck us all to—"

"But I never gave Cole my passwords!" Logan screams. "He only recommended the cloud service. Told me how to install the app. That's it."

"Show us," I demand.

"Like I told you, I only had the app on my old phone," he says. "But . . ."

"But?" the three of us respond at the same time.

"There's a web interface," Logan says as he holds up his phone to show us a web page.

And again, at the same time, we all grimace.

"What the fuck is that?" Grayson says. "That shit looks like something I would make."

Okay, I'll hand it to Grayson. He beat me to the punch. Because this page looks about as unprofessional as it gets. Simply terrible.

"It's bare-bones," Logan tells us. "That's why it's free. I didn't want to pay for some cloud service when I could have one for free. It made sense financially at the time."

"Oh, for fuck's sake, Logan," Meeka says. "It's called GOTCHYA. How could you think that it's reputable?"

"How could you think anything that came from Cole is reputable?" I ask. "Everything associated with that kid was infected. His viruses had viruses."

"GOTCHYA worked great. A little slow, but it had twice the storage of Dropbox and it was free. I'm going to be running a nonprofit someday, so these are decisions I take seriously," Logan says.

"Here's the thing," Meeka says calmly. "Cole always wanted access. And if you fell for one of his—"

"I didn't fall for anything!" Logan protests, and he's on the verge of tears.

"You did," Meeka tells him, and she puts a soft hand on his tense shoulder. "And so did I. More than I want to admit. If you ever signed into anything on one of his computers, Cole would keep you logged in. I learned that tidbit a little too late."

"And when exactly did you learn that *tidbit*?" I ask, because that isn't exactly a tidbit. This is huge. Enormous.

"A few days before . . . *you did it*," Meeka says, whispering the last part. "He was messing with my iTunes and Netflix. Some really passive-aggressive shit. Making playlists with songs about guys who kill their girlfriends, adding super-gross horror movies to my queue. I confronted him. He admitted he'd stolen a ton of data from people. He was proud of it."

Are you kidding me? Talk about important information to share with your friends. "Why the hell didn't you tell us?" I ask.

Meeka shrugs. "Because I figured he could have all the data in the world, but it wouldn't make a bit of difference in a few days. You had your plan. You said you were going through with it. It didn't matter."

"Shit," I blurt out, and suddenly I'm pounding my fist on the hood of her dad's car. "Shit. Shit. Shit."

And Grayson adds a "Fuckin' shit" for good measure.

Meeka's head dips and her eyes turn up, like a guilty dog, but she doesn't apologize.

I take a deep breath to steady myself. I open my hands, stretch my fingers. "Okay, so Cole could get into Logan's bootleg cloud. Probably because he had the password. Who cares? That doesn't matter at this point."

"He never had the password!" Logan whines.

"He probably didn't need the password," Meeka says with a sigh. "I'd bet every dollar I have that GOTCHYA isn't even a real cloud service. Knowing Cole, it's something he created. He had all sorts of things like that. Little traps. Stuff to amuse himself. He once rigged up a motion detector, or some Bluetooth thingy that could recognize my phone. Whenever I'd walk into his trailer, it'd send me a text. 'Hey, bae!' or whatever. He thought it was cute. I made him take it down because I thought it was creepy as fuck."

Uh . . . yeah. Über creepy, and totally on brand for Cole. As was conning his "friends."

"You said this GOTCHYA cloud was free?" I ask Logan. "How much storage space?"

"Two terabytes," he says.

"That's the size of a *really* big hard drive," I tell him. "My iMac only has a one-terabyte drive, and it's new."

"What are you saying?" Logan asks.

"She's saying that all that shit isn't floating around in the sky," Grayson says. "It's sitting somewhere."

"Basically," I add, mildly impressed that Grayson keeps barking up the right trees. "But it's more complicated than that. Typically, a cloud service shares its information over a few different servers in different locations. And no reputable service would offer that much space for free. Assuming Meeka is right, and this is something Cole set up, then I think it's probable that there's a single server somewhere that hosts all of Logan's files. A honeypot for all his secrets."

"Which means someone else must have access to that honeypot," Meeka adds.

"Where is the honeypot, then?" Logan asks.

"I know the first place to check," Grayson says as he digs into his Carhartt pockets and pulls out a pair of yellow leather wood-chopping gloves. "Let's go."

"Where?" Logan says.

Grayson slides the gloves over his hands as he says, "Cole's trailer. We have to see if that thing is still there."

"What thing?" we all ask.

"His Heart."

That trailer. That disgusting trailer.

The earthy filth, the electric noise. The stench.

The last time I was inside it, it smelled like pets—multiple pets—but as far as I knew, Cole didn't have any. He lived alone. Okay, mice were probably there, but they don't smell that bad. The odor was in the curtains. In the frayed carpet, in his sheets.

The last time I was inside was a week before Meeka and Cole broke up. She brought me along to help her collect things she'd left behind. She didn't tell me the breakup was imminent. She didn't have to. They'd been fighting for weeks, ever since the condom scare. Every time they "got back together," she did it with the enthusiasm of someone taking the last sips of cold soup.

Even though Cole didn't know it, things were through.

"Laundry day!" Meeka hollered as we busted into the place. She started grabbing any clothes she could find—hers, his—and stuffing them into a trash bag. At the same time, she was stuffing the bag with other things that belonged to her. Or ones she thought should belong to her. Not that Cole noticed. He was sitting on his bed, immersed in a book, the light of his Kindle cast over his bloodshot eyes.

"Love you, meerkat," he called out. "Add a little more fabric softener this time if you could. Pretty please with kisses on top."

"What're you reading?" I asked.

"Everything," he said, without looking up.

"As in?"

"How everything works. What our fragile lil' world depends on."

God, I hate when people read on Kindles. Perhaps you can't judge a book by a cover, but you can judge a person by one. With Kindles, people can lie about what they're reading. Or, like Cole—patronize. Why didn't he just tell me the title of the book? Was he embarrassed? No. It's because he assumed that I would never know what the book was, let alone understand it.

"It's about physics, in other words?" I asked. "Quantum theory? The laws of the universe?"

Cole shook his head. He pointed to a bright red cube that sat on a table. "You know what that is? It's my Heart. And it beats because of two simple things. Ones and zeroes, baby. True and false. That might sound simple, but you know what it's capable of? It's a cavalry. It turns boys into men and men into warriors. It's a beacon poised to spark a revolution."

"You're talking . . . video games?" I asked, because honestly that's what I thought it might be: some special gaming console.

"You're so naïve."

I threw my hands up in the air. "I'm trying to figure out what the heck you're talking about, Cole."

"You probably think guys like me are cowards, don't you?"

"Well, if the VR headset fits," I said, which made Meeka snort.

Cole simply sneered and said, "We're only lying in wait, biding our time. But we're ready to change the world. And mark my words, we will change the world."

"First you'll have to change your sheets. But good luck with the world too, pal."

He turned back to his Kindle. "I don't need luck. Just the ones and zeroes, the only things a guy can count on these days."

The only things? That felt like a slap in the face to Meeka, but I really didn't care. She was done with him and so was I. No more cryptic rants. No more casual misogyny. My plan was to cut off all ties as soon as the split was official. I didn't care if Grayson continued to hang out with Cole, because Grayson was always a free agent. But I planned to make sure Logan stayed away. The breakup was an inevitability, so sides had to be chosen. Cemented.

As soon as her bag was full, Meeka said, "Hate to run."

Cole still didn't look up, but he blew her a kiss. "Thanks, meerkat. I was almost out of undies. Will you be back later?"

"Sure," Meeka said, which was the most unsure "sure" in history. Then we were gone.

The cheap springs snapped the trailer's door shut like a mousetrap we'd barely escaped. When we reached the car, Meeka heaved the bag into the back of her BMW X5. Then she put her hands on my cheeks and said, "Be thankful for your privilege."

That was the last time I was inside the trailer.

The last time I was even near the trailer was the night we did it.

And now we're going back.

LOGAN

THE TRAILER STILL GLOWS and hums. It makes my head throb even more than it already did. If someone has been here since Cole stepped out, they haven't changed anything noticeable. It's exactly like it always was. When we enter, it's into chattering and flashing chaos.

Cole didn't believe in screensavers. Something about the barrage of images and text was like caffeine to him. I have no idea how much he slept, but it couldn't have been much. I can't say what specific games or sites he liked best, but I know he loved the infinity of stuff. He needed the world constantly shooting at him, going at light speed.

Screens are packed with messages, like platoons of ants marching across bright flat deserts. Speakers chatter softly. A game is on pause, the image of an explosion blooming. A video clip is playing on a loop, his favorite one, showing that shrill kid singing "Walk Like a Man." Thankfully, that one is muted. The stink in here is worse than ever—it's as bad as roadkill—and we all wince when we first enter and catch a whiff.

"Should we dump the trash?" Grayson asks. "Anyone comes in here and they'll know he's been gone a long time. No one can live with a stink like this."

"You'd be surprised," Meeka grumbles as she stands in the

doorway. It's obvious she doesn't want to step any farther inside, and I can't blame her.

"Don't worry about the smell," Holly says. "The important thing is that we touch as little as possible. They'll always have ways of knowing the last time Cole was here. Evidence we can't cover up. That's ultimately unimportant. The important thing is to make sure the police never know *we* were here. Keep your hands to yourself. Unless absolutely necessary."

We've taken precautions. Gloves, hats that the girls can tuck their hair up into, dust masks. We know our fingerprints and DNA are probably already in the trailer, because we've all been in the trailer before, but we don't want to leave anything fresh.

And yet I worry about osmosis. There's so much to see in here that I can't help but wonder about what's uploading to my brain. Maybe I'm filling my subconscious with images that will implicate me. The half-solved Rubik's Cube on the oven? The rubber horse head mask draped over the back of the computer chair? Maybe they mean something. If I end up being questioned about Cole's disappearance, I might let something slip that seems inconsequential, but will place me in this very trailer after Cole left it. I should probably close my eyes, but then I might fall asleep on my feet and crash into a web of computer cables.

I hate this place so much.

Grayson points and says, "There. That thing."

The trailer is a perpetual mess, but there's one corner of a table that's pristine. Set in that pristine corner is a red cube. Though everything else is dusty and grimy, it shines, radiates even. There's a blinking blue light and a few buttons on the front, and a few cords running out the back. Cole called this thing his Heart.

We'd discussed the Heart while we were walking the quarter mile to the trailer from the abandoned lumber mill where we parked our cars. We'd all noticed the Heart before, during our various visits to the trailer. We weren't sure if it was a small server, some sort of computer or gaming console, or a hard drive. It was difficult to say because there were no labels on it, and while Cole had always been quick to point it out and brag about how important it was to him, he had also been unwilling to tell us what it actually did.

That was typical. He liked to taunt and troll. And we all assumed the same thing: The Heart contained secrets—Cole's secrets—whether they were in the form of programs he used or files he created or downloaded. Now I'm thinking it contains my secrets too, that the stuff from my cloud ended up there. It would explain why Cole was always drawing my attention to it. He was mocking me, keeping his treachery in plain sight. Gotchya! He had me dead to rights and he probably figured there was nothing I could do about it.

Only problem was, I did do something. We all did.

But someone else did something too. The big questions are: Who did something, and what exactly did they do?

"The Heart is still here," Holly says. "That's good, right?"

Meeka nods, takes a deep breath through her mask, and finally leaves her post by the door, making a beeline to the table. "He would've boned this thing if he could've. I tell you, the way he looked at it . . . he never looked at me that way."

"That's exactly how he always left it?" Holly asks. "Confirm to me that nothing's been stolen."

"Nothing's been stolen," Meeka says as she reaches forward to touch it. "Yet."

Holly lunges and pushes Meeka's hand down. "Please!" she

says, and her mask goes cockeyed, revealing half of her snarling mouth. "No touching."

"Chill," Meeka says as she pulls her hand back. "I don't know if forensics people can tell old DNA from new DNA, but there's so much of me in here already that it shouldn't matter if I touch anything. And why should it matter if I move anything? The trailer is a sty."

All true, but Holly still insists. "No touching. That's what we agreed on."

"Well, at least we can breathe easier," Meeka says. "Because no one has stolen Cole's Heart."

She laughs a little, but it doesn't seem to be at her own joke. It's a nervous laughter, flavored with a hint of relief. I don't want to throw water on that relief, but someone has to state the obvious.

"Do I have to remind you all that no one had to *physically* take anything to access whatever information is on there?"

"That's right!" Grayson replies, as if this were the most mind-blowing revelation. "They could've hacked the shit out of it!"

Holly rolls her eyes and says, "Everyone loves to talk about 'hacking,' but do you know the first thing about it? Do you really think it's as simple as saying 'Hey, I'mma hack that guy' and then start tapping a few keys and you're in? How do we even know that device is networked? If it was so important to Cole, then leaving it vulnerable to exterior threats seems pretty damn stupid."

Maybe Cole *was* pretty damn stupid—he fell for our trap, after all—or maybe . . .

"What about Bluetooth?" I say. "Or things you're not even considering? I'm sorry, but what do *you* know about hacking? We've already proven that even though we're smart, it doesn't mean we can spot all our vulnerabilities."

"*Your* vulnerabilities," Holly reminds me.

Okay, fine. I deserve a little salt in my wounds. But picking on people doesn't get us any closer to figuring out who's exploiting my mistake.

"My mom writes all her important shit on paper," Grayson says as he crouches down next to the refrigerator. "Goes right on a Post-it stuck to the fridge. No one's gonna hack a Post-it."

Holly moves closer to Grayson. She's obviously playing defense, getting ready to swat his hand away if he reaches for something. It's a tiny fridge, the type that college kids have in their dorm rooms, but it's still big enough for magnets to hold up photos and mail, things posted as reminders. There's a faded receipt from Best Buy, but I can't read what it's for. There's a postcard from somewhere thick with palm trees. There's a photo—I think it's what you call a Polaroid—of a woman. It's blurry, but it looks like Cole's mom, Teri.

Teri's half-cocked smile hits me harder than I'd expect. Like everyone, I was devastated when she died. Because she wasn't a bad person. She was . . . damaged. The single good thing to come out of her death was that at least she didn't live to see what became of her son. An awful thought, I know, but I can't help it.

My lungs seize for a second. I can hold back the tears—and I *will* hold them back—but the tears might help. My body needs something to keep it going.

"We didn't come here for a Post-it. We came here for *that*," Meeka says, and she reaches a hand forward again and this time she snags that little red box. I almost cheer for her. Holding it and bending forward, she studies the tangle of cords behind it.

"Unplug that shit and let's bounce," Grayson says.

But Holly, as enraged as I've ever seen her, hip-checks Meeka, causing her to drop the Heart back onto the table. Frankly, it's a bit shocking. Holly is not a violent person, and this is clearly violence. It's basically assault.

"What the—?" Meeka says as she gains her balance.

"Don't touch it!" Holly barks.

She doesn't listen. Instead, Meeka moves back over and grabs the Heart again. She can wrap her fingers around one side of it. It's bigger than a human heart, but not by much. Maybe horse heart size? It's still plugged in, but the cords are long enough that she can present it to Holly without unplugging it.

"Take it," she says.

Holly hesitates for a moment, and then peels it from Meeka's gloved hands like it's contaminated. "You shouldn't have done that," Holly tells her as she carefully examines all sides of the thing.

"There's a lot that shouldn't have been done," Meeka replies. "But this is where we are. So unplug it. Bring it home. Find out what's on it. Or destroy it. You started this. Now see it through. Or else things are only gonna get worse and worse."

Let it be clear: *We all* started this. But Meeka has a point. Holly has been the lead decision-maker, which is a role she's always been comfortable with. It's something I've always been comfortable with too. Until now. Now Holly is freaking me out a little.

Her teeth clenched, Meeka pushes past me and Grayson, and sits down in a mesh camping chair near the door. I notice there's a folded tarp beneath it, like the one we wrapped Cole in, and I don't doubt she notices it too. Reminders of what we did, everywhere. She closes her eyes and lowers her head. She's done with this, with us, with everything.

"What the fuck was that?" Grayson says to Holly.

"No kidding," Holly answers. "She's being so reckless, huh?"

"I'm talking about you," Grayson says. "Meeka's right, you know."

"About what?" Holly asks. "That we should see what's on that thing? What if it's password-protected? What if it's teeming with viruses that will infect whatever I plug it into, or leaves some sort of digital mark behind, something we can't see but detectives can find?"

"Smash it to bits, then," Grayson says. "Or bury it with Cole."

"It stays here," she says, and Holly places it back on its neat little corner of the table.

"But we haven't figured anything out," I protest. "Who the hell has been in my cloud? Who's seen the video? We've got nothing."

"Damn straight, because there's still some guy out there somewhere," Grayson adds. "And he still has us by the balls."

"First, how do you know it's a guy?" Holly says. "And second, we're the ones who are holding the metaphorical balls in this situation."

Meeka perks up. Her posture straightens and her eyes open. Her eyebrows are fully cocked.

"Keep telling yourself that," Grayson says.

Holly nods confidently. "I will. Because let's not forget an important fact. This person knows what we're capable of. Which means they're probably scared. In fact, I bet they're terrified of us."

I'm not sure if I should call it irony or coincidence, but the moment Holly speaks, an image appears on the scrolling feed of one of Cole's laptops. It's us, our four faces.

The meme.

It's there for a few seconds and then scrolls up and off the screen. But that's long enough for me read the caption.

SQUAD GOALS:
SNIFF SOME GLUE

GRAYSON

WE'RE AT THE OLD LUMBER MILL, standing in the muck next to my Jeep as Holly's and Logan's cars squeal and splatter their way out of here. Meeka puts a hand on my back. She rubs.

"Thank you," she says.

"For what?" I say. "We didn't find shit."

"For being there. When I needed you. That was the last place I wanted to be."

There's a glow down the road. Cole's trailer. "I can go back by myself and get that thing," I tell her. "The Heart. You were right. And what Holly said was BS. It's too important."

"Maybe," Meeka says. "But what was the other thing she said? About having this person by the balls?"

"It's definitely a dude," I say. "Chicks don't fuck around like this. Spreading a meme is some cocky little shit's way of thinking he's being clever and sneaky. Chicks aren't sneaky like that."

Meeka snorts and says, "Oh, Gray, don't ever change."

I'm not totally sure what she means by that, but I shrug it off. Meeka's always saying stuff that can either be taken as an insult or a compliment. Best to take it as neither.

"Think about it, though," she tells me. "This . . . guy . . . has a reason to fear us. Let's make him fear us. Or fear you. You're the scary one in the bunch."

Again, I don't say shit.

"That's a good thing, by the way," she says, and she grabs my wrist and holds it up so my arm is in a flexing position. "You're friggin' tough, Gray. No one at school would ever think of messing with you."

"Yeah, but this guy doesn't go to school with us," I say, pulling my arm back.

"Are you sure about that?" she asks.

"Why would he? Memes are, like, a national thing. International."

"Yeah, maybe, but even though memes spread quickly, it's been what, eight days? If the meme started somewhere else, it got to Plainview High around Thursday. So maybe it took five days to reach our shores. At the most. Probably less than that. Especially fast for a picture that's nothing special."

"Maybe someone who knows us was dicking around on Reddit or whatever and found it. It's possible."

"*Possible* is far different from *likely*. So what's the likely scenario?"

"That . . . ?"

"The meme wasn't found by someone in our school. It was *created* by someone in our school. Someone Cole knew, and probably knew well."

This makes some sense. No one needed to hack Cole. "So what you're saying is that Cole gave some dude all the stuff that's on the Heart?"

"Not necessarily," Meeka says. "Maybe the Heart has nothing to do with it. Red herring, as they say. Maybe this other guy has controlled access to GOTCHYA all along. And Cole was nothing but a salesman for his phony cloud service. Cole convinces Logan to use GOTCHYA, the other guy pays Cole a commission, and now the other guy can sell Logan's identity. Or steal money from Logan's Heroes."

"But the other guy saw the video," I say. "Why not turn us in? Why fuck with us like this?"

Meeka shrugs. "Because people are jealous and want to embarrass us?"

"I don't know . . ."

"Really? Think it through. I hate to say it, but we're simply better than most. Smarter. Cuter. More talented. Since we merged with Foxbury, there are now what . . . two hundred kids in our class alone? That includes plenty of people who know us even though we don't know them."

"I know a shit ton of people," I say, because I do.

"Yeah, but not everyone. That's the problem with popularity. The faceless, nameless kids who walk the halls or sit in the back of classrooms are the ones you have to watch out for. They lust and they plot. The dumb among them are usually harmless. But the smart ones? Better be careful."

Sounds like she's talking about kids just like . . .

"Like Cole," I say.

"Like Cole."

Makes a lot of sense, actually. In mysteries—real mysteries—it's never the complicated answer. It's always the obvious one.

"So Cole sells Logan out to another kid at school, right?" I say.

"Why not?"

"And that guy goes into the cloud, sees the video, makes that meme, and spreads it?"

"Got another explanation?"

"No. But I'm not buying that he did it because he was jealous of us."

"Fine. Then why?"

The answer is right in front of me: Meeka's BMW.

"Blackmail," I say.

My family does all right—at least we have been since we upgraded our site and started shipping orders nationally about five years ago. Logan's folks do okay too. But Meeka? Holly? Their parents have real cash. Christmas at their houses is insane. New skis every winter. Cashmere everything. Checks in amounts more than I earn in a year. So when it comes to blackmailing, they're definitely the targets. If it were only me who did this, my ass would already be in jail.

"Okay," Meeka says. "I guess I can see that."

"But I can't figure out what he's waiting for," I say. "Why isn't he reaching out and asking us to pay up?"

And Meeka says, "Hard thing to know when we don't know who he is. But I have a pretty good guess."

Suddenly I do too. It's better than a pretty good guess. There's only one person it can possibly be. The same little dude who tried to throw down with me at Becca's party. Who called me a "stupid duck." The one who told me I'd be "sorry."

"Gus Drummond?" I say.

That's right. Gus *Fucking* Drummond. Of all the people. It seems nuts to say it, but then I think about it. Really think. It makes sense. More sense than anyone else. I mean, he and Cole were boys for a while, before I became friends with Cole. Always gaming or talking DC vs. Marvel or whatever. Nerd shit. That's not saying it was bad shit. Hey, I like *Call of Duty* and Avengers movies and all that too—but they were intense about it.

Also memes. The two of them were always fucking around with memes.

But that was mostly freshman year. Then they quit hanging out. I never heard anyone trash the kid, so I always figured he wasn't much trouble. But who knows? Maybe Gus is a bigger dick than Cole. Maybe he's one of those jealous kids Meeka is talking about. Maybe he cares more about getting paid than getting justice for an old pal. Yeah, he seems harmless, but how do I know for sure? All I know is that he's our guy. I can feel it all the way down to my core.

Meeka nods because she's feeling it too. "I knew you'd get there."

"It makes sense, right?"

"Oh yeah. Tons. But I wasn't going to say it first because he seems like such a puppy dog."

"Yeah, but puppy dogs can still bite. So what do we do about our boy Gus?"

"We let him know we know."

"Like, call him?"

"No. Like face him. Make him know this is real life."

Okay. Tomorrow, then. School. I know the perfect place.

HOLLY

BREATHE. Breathe. Breathe.

I'm getting through Sunday supper like I've gotten through every Sunday supper of my life. Smiles. Big bites. Pure stamina.

Carter and Oran are making faces from across the table. On any other day, it wouldn't bother me. Kids will be kids, right? But Carter recently got Dad's old iPhone—no cell plan, only data—and he uses it to message with his friends. I'm wondering if he's seen the meme, and if he's shown it to Oran. Are they mocking my face in it? Is that what this is?

"I'm glad you've finally found something you're good at," I tell them.

"What?" Carter asks.

"Being ugly," I say.

"Boom!" Oran says, and he starts cackling. He may be the younger of the two, but he's the more sadistic one. People sometimes call him my "carbon copy," which I don't see. At all.

"I'm talking about you too, buddy," I tell Oran.

"Okay," Oran says with a sneer. "Then you look like a baboon butt!"

"Not another word," Mom says.

And Dad says, "Yeah, quit it or else," but it's more for Grandpa's sake than anything. If Grandpa weren't here, Dad would ignore all of this, focus on scarfing down his food so he could get back to watching football. But Dad feels like he has to show his father that he's in control of the madness. Funny thing is, Grandpa doesn't seem to care. He's all about the potatoes right now.

"Lovely mash, Heidi," he tells Mom. "Are these reds? Or russets?"

"Yukon Golds," Mom says. "With a splash of cream and a touch of cauliflower. It was your son who cooked them."

"That so? Still delicious," Grandpa says to Dad as he takes down another forkful.

I'm not hungry, but this is my favorite meal. Roasted chicken, mashed potatoes, apple slaw. So I eat, because not eating would seem weird. I've gotten through enough of it that I can see a window opening up. I can make my escape.

But Mom delays me with a question. "So, now that you've had time to reflect on it, how does it feel?"

I know she's talking about the record, but my answer is about the other thing. "It's not nearly as big a relief as I'd hoped."

"It was never meant to be a relief," Dad says, his mouth partly full. "Success is simply an outcome you earn."

Is he trying to be deep? I suppose so, though I wouldn't put that quote on motivational posters. "I'm looking forward to not thinking about it," I tell them.

"I'm looking forward to dessert," Grandpa announces, and he scruffs Oran's hair. "Right, pal?"

"Peanut butter pie!" Oran shouts with a fist up. "Peanut butter pie!"

As delicious as that sounds, I use this as my cue to exit. "Save me a slice. I've got homework to finish."

I kiss Grandpa's dry forehead as I pass, and he pats me on the cheek. Then I hurry to the back staircase and take the steps two at a time. When I'm at the top, I suck in another big breath.

Okay. Okay. Okay.

From the back of the linen closet, I snatch Grandpa's laptop. Actually, it's hard to call it *his* laptop because he's never used it. He never even opened the box. We bought it for him as a Christmas present last year. Mom thought it would be good for him to be on Facebook so he could keep up with the world. Grandpa disagreed.

"They still print the newspaper and they still make stationery, pens, and stamps, don't they? Therefore, I will not be needing one of these contraptions."

Even for a grandparent, he's old-fashioned. But then, he's older than most. Eighty-four, an entire generation separated from the tech-friendly seventy somethings my friends call their pop-pops and nanas.

Since he didn't want the laptop and everyone in my house already had their own—and since Mom had gotten it cheap in Williston on Black Friday and didn't think it was worth returning—we exiled it to a shelf behind some old towels, in hopes of regifting it.

Happy early birthday to me.

With the new laptop tucked under my arm, I jog the length of the upstairs and head down the front staircase, then down to the basement. Our house was built five years ago, and our basement is more or less a fortress. The foundation is so thick that you could pile ten houses on top of it and it wouldn't crack. It's as well insulated as a cave. It stays cool in the summer and warm in the winter. It's carpeted wall-to-wall. It's all part of our builder's energy-efficient plans. This also means that you can say anything you want down there and nobody is going to hear. You can play an action movie on full volume. If you're up in the kitchen, not even the faintest sound of an explosion will reach your ears. There's one way in and out, so it's the only place in this house where you're guaranteed a certain amount of privacy.

I settle into Mom's comfy reading chair in the corner. I plug in the laptop and power it on. It prompts me for all sorts of information. I enter a fake name, fake email address, etc., and when it asks me to connect to a Wi-Fi network, I have no choice but to select our own. Our neighbors' houses are too far away to piggyback onto their networks, even if I did know their passwords. I'm taking a small risk, but as soon as I'm done, I'm going to reformat the drive and restore all the defaults, so I'm pretty sure I'll be in the clear.

Even though I feel like an idiot for doing this, I open an incognito tab on Chrome and I start to type a question into the search bar.

How do you make . . .

The autofill presents some thoroughly odd options.

French toast? No.

Slime? Really? Gross.

Buttermilk? Even grosser.

Why are these the top searches?

A meme, I type. *How do you make a meme?*

Obviously, I'm not the first person to ask, because there are a ton of results. Most of them link to sites where you can upload your own picture or redo popular memes with your own text. Whether any of the sites will help me narrow down who did this to us is a long shot.

I need another plan of attack.

I need to see the meme again.

Riley posted a version to her Instagram page. Obviously, it's her passive-aggressive attempt at payback for my breaking her phone in the parking lot. "Not a big deal. It's insured and I wanted a new one anyway," she told me at the time, but there was no way she isn't holding a grudge.

As soon as I get the meme on my screen, I realize that I haven't looked at this thing close enough. Whenever I've seen it, I've turned away, like it's a dirty picture. Which it is. The dirtiest. But if I'm going to have any hope of figuring out who first spread it, I have to study it. So that's what I do.

The version Riley posted has the unfortunate caption FOUR HEADS . . . HALF A BRAIN.

Which is stupid. Between Meeka, Logan, and me, you've got three of the top ten students in our class. Everyone knows this. Okay, so maybe Grayson has a half a brain, but we've got—

THEDLOM

There, in the bottom corner. A word. It's like a signature or a watermark. Faint, but clear enough to read, especially when I zoom in. There's no doubt about it, it says THEDLOM.

Thedlom?

Is that a word I should know? Like bedlam?

Or is it a reference to something?

I do a search. The first hit for "Thedlom" is a site called The-Cavalry.net, but that doesn't look right. The next is a Twitter account. I don't have my own Twitter account, but I can click through to it anyway. @THEDLOM's avatar is a picture of a tongue with a flame on the tip, like it's a candle. The bio simply reads: *Hot memes from a cold land.*

The feed is almost all retweets of memes from other accounts, and it looks like Thedlom follows a bunch of other meme-focused accounts, but if—

Wait. What am I doing?

Incognito tab or not, this is too much exposure.

I go to the settings to clear the cache and browsing history, but that's probably not enough, so I open the disk utility to start reformatting the drive.

As it reformats, I put a hand on my chest and feel my heart pounding.

That was sloppy.

I should never have even thought of compromising my family like this. I need to find out more, but not here. Not where an IP address can be traced back to our house.

Tomorrow. School.

LOGAN

SOMEONE IS SUICIDAL. How could they not be? Don't they realize that things could get very dangerous for them?

Yes, this is me admitting that Holly is right. This person—girl *or* guy—who started the meme knows what we did. How could they not be afraid?

I also agree with Meeka. That red box, Cole's Heart, is of vital importance. Even if that's not where the files from my cloud are, it means something. And maybe no one has accessed it yet, but they will soon. The police. Or his brother, Craig, when he's back for Thanksgiving and wondering where Cole is. And, given Cole's penchant for spying and stealing, who knows what they'll find on there. We have to nip this thing right in the bud. But how?

Dinner is over and Mom and Dad are cleaning the dishes while I'm sitting at the breakfast bar, staring at GOTCHYA. I'm not stupid. I deleted everything in it. And it no longer links to my photos or other files. But I haven't deactivated my account yet. Because I want to understand exactly how it works.

I have to be humble and I have to accept something. I need help and I'm not going to get it from the others, because I need someone who actually understands what's possible in terms of hacking, passwords, clouds, all of that stuff.

I need Esther.

Esther, along with being absolutely radiant, is president of the hack club at school. Cole used to say it was a club for poseurs and wannabes, but I think that was only because he was jealous. Those kids are legit, and I don't doubt half of them will get scholarships to Ivys and end up in Silicon Valley changing the world. Or at least that's what I hope happens for Esther. She deserves it.

I don't have Esther's number, and while I'm sure I could figure it out, it's probably best for me to keep this communication face-to-face. Luckily, she doesn't live far away.

"I know it's a school night, but I was hoping to go over to my friend Esther's," I tell my parents.

Dad moves his eyebrows up and down and says, "Friend . . . with benefits?"

He thinks it makes him a cool dad to joke like this, but it mostly makes him creepy.

"Mike!" Mom yelps, and she throws a dish towel at him, but not in a *well, aren't you a rascal?* sort of way. She's legitimately pissed.

He puts his hands up in surrender. "That's how kids talk."

"That's not how kids talk," I say. "And it's not like that with her. She's interested in Logan's Heroes."

It isn't technically a lie because she told me she was last week. In fact, she's the exact type of person I should be funding. Smart, motivated, tons of potential, but also in a tough spot.

"Homework done?" Mom asks.

"Yes."

"Let him go," Dad says. "Did I mention how impressive he was with Senator Barnes yesterday? A real professional. Just perfect."

"So you told me," Mom says, but she's clearly on the fence.

I clasp my hands together and tip my head and do my sweet

little angel face that always makes her eyes roll but her mouth curl up in a smile. Which is exactly what happens this time, before she says, "Fine. Go ahead, Mr. Perfect."

Perfect.

That was also the theme of the meeting with Senator Barnes yesterday morning.

"The books have to be perfect," she said to Dad as I picked at my omelet. I could barely keep my eyes open, but that hardly mattered to the state senator. She was talking almost exclusively to Dad, treating him as though he were the one running Logan's Heroes. Dad kept deflecting the conversation back to me, saying things like "Logan is practically a one-man show." But Barnes wasn't having it. She probably figured I was some spoiled brat and it was my parents who were pulling the strings. I don't necessarily blame her. There are a lot of kids like that.

To prove I'm not one of those kids, I'd channeled my last ounce of energy into telling her, "I'm taking college-level accounting courses and I've already consulted with some lawyers and my uncle is a CPA. If things get to a certain level, then we can hire him."

She finally focused her eyes on me. "Clearly, you've thought some things through, and that is commendable. But people are going to be watching you closely, so we need you to make sure that as the money becomes available, every cent is accounted for. Yours is not the only reputation that will be on the line."

She was right, obviously. And even though I wasn't going to tell her this, I had already taken steps to make sure the funds would be safe and accounted for. I had ended the Indiegogo campaign almost two weeks ago, after we first started planning our

Cole solution. I figured if the funds were secure in the bank, then my work could carry on even if I got caught. If it remained in the Indiegogo account, then someone would probably find a loophole and return all the donations. Which would be a disaster.

I set up another campaign directly on LogansHeroes.org for new donations, but the $58,000 I raised has been transferred over to the Logan's Heroes bank account, which I opened on my eighteenth birthday in September. My parents and uncle have access, but I am the one who actually has control of the funds.

"It's all handled," I'd assured Senator Barnes. "I wouldn't do anything to jeopardize my mission to help the vulnerable and downtrodden."

Esther lives downtown, in a ramshackle house across from the Price Chopper. It's a sad place, sprawling and crumbling and divided into multiple illegal apartments. I'm sure some sketchy stuff goes on there. I doubt Esther is involved, but I worry she might end up being collateral damage.

Her parents are, quite frankly, a mess. They're a couple of wayward souls who make ends meet by collecting some rent and selling hemp and CBD products at festivals. I think they followed Phish for a while and sold their stuff at shows—that's where Esther's name comes from, a Phish song—but then they bought that crappy house back when it wasn't quite as crappy and they've had friends and "associates" move in over the years. Ski bums, musicians, and artists mostly. Not bad people necessarily, but not model citizens either.

And yet these are the citizens I'll be dealing with for Logan's Heroes—the luckless and underprivileged dreamers of the world. I'm trying to be more comfortable around them. Even if I weren't popping in on Esther, making a house call at a place like this is a good idea. It shows I'm motivated, and that I care. People rarely make house calls anymore, and that's understandable. I'm as attached to my phone as anyone. But I also know that showing up at someone's door, forging an actual human connection, is vastly more important than any digital communication.

So I pull into the driveway and park next to a rusty van. The yard is littered with cans and the walkway is a strip of dirt leading to the rickety front porch. At the door, names and apartment numbers are written on cardboard and tacked to the siding. The cardboard is warped from moisture and the names are barely legible.

It doesn't really matter because there's only one doorbell. I ring it and I wait.

There's music playing above me, something loud and vaguely familiar, music from the 1960s, the stuff grandparents listen to.

I try the bell again because I worry I didn't press hard enough and suddenly the music cuts out. Then there's a voice above me, hollering.

"Hey!"

There's a white guy with blond dreadlocks sticking his head out of a top-floor window.

"Hey," I say back.

"You here about the . . . stuff?"

"No. I'm here for Esther. Is she home?"

"She was, fam. Made us all waffles earlier. But I think she bounced for a bit."

"Back soon?"

He shrugs. "Probably. You're welcome to wait in her room."

"Where's that?"

"Aw man, you don't know?" he says as he flips his hair back from his face. "Straight through the door, down the hall, past the kitchen. All the way in the back."

I'm ready to enter, but I pause. Something bothers me.

"You don't know me," I say.

"Should I?" he asks, and then he laughs a goofy, throaty laugh.

"It's not about that," I say, and I step back from the door. "You don't know me, but you're fine with me walking right in. Some random dude. You give him the keys to the castle."

The guy laughs again. "Good point, buddy. But then who am I to decide who gets to come and go? You've got free will. You could've busted into the place, guns blazing, and I wouldn't have been able to stop you. But no, you rang the bell. Tells me you're legit."

"Legit *what*?" I ask. "Criminals can ring doorbells."

"Buddy," the guy says with that laugh again, and I can hardly hear him because he's snorting and coughing the words out. "Look at you. A'right? Look at the whole thing you got going. You're fine, fam, you're fine."

The thing I got going? Does he mean nice jeans and a button-down shirt? There are plenty of guys in town who are preppier than I am. Just because I don't smell like I bathe in bong water or I don't wear Carhartt head-to-toe, it doesn't mean I'm not capable of—

Stop it, I tell myself. Slow down and keep your wits. I can't let a guy like this bother me.

Instead, I calmly explain to him, "I want her to be safe. She deserves that, don't you think?"

"Indeed," he says. "But sorry, my man, all I'm doing is living here. People come and people go. And Esther knows plenty of guys I don't. Usually seem like upstanding dudes. But scout's honor, if someone seemed sketch, I'd take the necessary measures."

"Yeah, well, I hope so," I say, and I linger for a second, waiting for him to respond, but he doesn't, so I keep talking. "I'm Logan, by the way. I'm not comfortable waiting in her room, so can you tell her I stopped by?"

"Brogan," he says. "Got it."

"No, *Logan*," I say.

"Messing with you, fam," he says, and taps a finger on his temple. "It's a pneumonic device. Helps me remember your name. I'll tell her. No worries."

Then he pulls his head back in, closes the window, and turns his light off. Music begins playing, and it's even louder than before.

This time it's Bob Dylan, and he's singing about how someone "aches just like a woman." I know it's him because his voice is so distinctive and my grandpa listens to him sometimes. But as I walk away from the dim yellow porch light toward my car, it's not that song that's suddenly stuck in my head. It's the one that goes:

Walk like a man, talk like a man,

Walk like a man, my son . . .

MONDAY, NOVEMBER 7

NINE DAYS AFTER

HOLLY

MONDAY MORNING COMES like Monday morning always comes. Cold, unwelcome.

I'm sick of trying. Trying is all life ever is, right? Trying to be honest. Trying to be happy. Trying to turn yourself into the person that people think you are.

Trying.

All that SAT prep got me more than a 1500. Because it taught me there's another definition of the word. In adjective form, "trying" means stressful. Difficult. Fraught. Which sounds about right.

The first two periods of school are trying. I can't stop wondering who has seen the video, who is out there letting us walk free, who is dangling the ax above our heads. And when will it drop?

The meme is lurking around every corner of Plainview High. Riley, who first showed it to me, isn't the one who brought it here. I'm confident of that. The girl can't even find her car in the student parking lot. No, she got it from someone, who got it from someone, who got it from someone, and on and on.

And now people are huddled up and whispering in the halls. They're pointing at me. They're passing phones back and forth and having a ball. In calc, Prachi Mukherjee tells me that Paul Baker, the school paper's editor in chief, has a clean copy of the image—meaning without captions, but with the THEDLOM watermark—and you can pluck it from his Tumblr. Over the weekend, that's exactly what everybody did. Then they made their own stupid versions of the meme.

"Where did Paul get the clean copy?" I ask Prachi, because I'm dead certain it didn't start with him. He's a goofball and an attention whore. But he's not that cold. Or calculating.

"I asked him the same thing," Prachi says. "And he told me that he's 'a principled journalist' and will never reveal his sources."

Even if he did admit where he got it, how can I know the person who gave it to him didn't get it from someone else? What I need to know is who's seen the video. Accuse the wrong people and suddenly everyone is curious. The house of cards falls.

And there are so many potential suspects! By Sunday, Paul had opened up his sad little Tumblr so people could post their own versions of the meme. It's been an absolute free-for-all, with my classmates competing to see who gets the most notes for making fun of me. There are Instagram-friendly memes with white frames and little black text. Old-school memes with black frames and big white text. Others with Snapchat effects: dog noses, rainbows, the usual. Some that integrate our faces into other popular memes. Crude animation, fart sounds, anything offensive you can imagine.

And what am I doing about it?

Nothing. I'm stumbling through my day, smiling, enduring.

What *should* I do about it?

Something.

Doing. Doing is so much better than trying, right? I need to do something. I've been wanting to do something since I sat in the basement last night, laptop in my lap, feeling absolutely helpless.

At the start of third period, which I have free, I go to the computer lab. I usually focus on homework, but now, against my best judgment, I slide up to a computer in the corner. I open a browser and check out Paul Baker's Tumblr.

I scroll through the parade of memes. They're posted anonymously, or with avatars that hide the true identities of our mockers. And most aren't even remotely clever.

One says DUCK, DUCK, DUCK . . . GOOSE. Because we're sitting in a circle? I'm not sure. But that's about as tame as things get. Most are downright cruel.

HEY LOOK! IT'S ASSHOLE, BITCH, SLUT, AND PUSSY! another says, and I have to ask why I'm doing this to myself. It's torture, but each one reminds me why I'm torturing myself. They all have that same signature, the same source.

THEDLOM.

Someone sneaks up behind me, so I quickly switch tabs to a BuzzFeed quiz.

"Working hard, superstar?" Mr. O'Reilly asks.

Mr. O'Reilly is overseeing the computer lab this period because Mrs. Lee is sick. He's usually nothing more than a gym teacher. I haven't had him since freshman year, but he still goes out of his way to compliment me. To stop me in the halls. To constantly remind me that he's paying attention. I'm not going to flirt, but I have to be friendly so that he'll happily move along when I basically tell him to mind his own business.

"Oh, you know me," I say. "Trying to figure out which member of One Direction I'm supposed to marry. Standard lady stuff."

He shoots me a thumbs-up. He wants me to know that he gets the joke. That he's not dumb. That he knows I'm "not like the other girls," which he probably thinks is a compliment. He doesn't laugh, though, because his sense of humor is much crasser. He's probably in his forties. He acts more like he's eighteen. Or maybe thirteen. He's not above a fart joke.

"Congratulations on the record," he says. "We're all so proud of you."

"It's no big deal," I respond, because it isn't. Or it hasn't felt like it is ever since that ball hit the net.

"You can say that it's no big deal, but it means something. You'll always remember these days. Trust me."

That's certainly true. Good god, I wish I could forget the entire last month.

"Can I ask you for a favor?" I say.

"Quid pro quo, Clarice," he responds with a weird sneer. Sounds Latin, but I take Chinese, so I don't know what he's talking about.

"Is that supposed to mean something to me?"

He rolls his eyes and says, "Kids. No appreciation for the classics. It's from a movie."

"I don't have much time for movies."

"That's a shame. Sounds like you work too hard. You need to loosen up. Smile more."

His hands are looming now, near my shoulders, like he wants to massage them. He's waiting for me to lean back. It's so inappropriate. Forget being friendly, because I am never, ever smiling for this man.

"That favor?" I say, stone-faced. "It's privacy. I'm really busy. When I get home, I'll watch a few *motion pictures* so I can keep up with your dusty quotes. But for now, I need to get back to what I was doing."

He pauses and then leans forward. I flinch. But he doesn't

touch me. He grabs my mouse and opens the tab with Paul Baker's Tumblr on it.

"If you want to get back at them," he says, "then fight fire with fire. Take their pictures. Put your own jokes on them. Skewer those insensitive toads."

Then he slaps his hands together and rubs them, like his work here is done. He pivots on a heel and struts to the other side of the lab. I shiver, hoping it shakes the grossness off the moment. Then I shift my seat and turn the monitor toward the wall to shield it from views. And I stare at the memes again. I hate to admit it, but he's given me an idea.

Like anyone, I've seen more memes than I can remember. The standard cute animals and babies. The Photoshopped movie stars. The stock photos. The repurposed cartoons. The SpongeBobs and Arthurs, etc. The goofy pictures—like ours—of regular people that other regular people make fun of. The video clips, the GIFs, the things I'm told are going to define my generation in the way that, I don't know, shopping malls and ugly sweaters defined my parents' generation.

That's taking things a bit too far. Because most kids are passing time when we share these things. We don't really care. Barely any of these memes are actually funny. The majority don't even make sense. The only thing they have in common is that they're all some sort of inside joke. My parents don't understand the ones I enjoy, and vice versa. That means they require knowledge. They're a language. And whoever started this speaks that language.

I know what I have to do.

I open another tab and go to one of the sites I found last night. It's called MemeMonster.com. I click on a link to "Find Classic Memes!"

I search for one I remember from middle school. It's called "Overly Attached Girlfriend."

A picture of a smiling white girl with bulging eyes pops up. She seems normal enough, maybe a tad overexcited. But this image has become synonymous with a certain type of person: a clingy, unreasonable, unstoppable psychopath.

People who know memes know this image and what it means.

There's a prompt for text, so I start typing. I want to say I don't have any idea what's possessing me to do this, but I know exactly what's possessing me. It's not about fighting fire with fire, like O'Reilly suggested. It's about sending a clear message.

At the top of the image, I write: YOU'RE

At the bottom: NEXT!

I download it.

Then I create a Gmail account using a fake name: Nonya Bizness.

I open Twitter and create a new account using that new email. I call the account: IWillFindYou.

I use the original picture of the four of us as my profile pic so it's clear who's sending this. I can always delete or change the whole account later.

I follow Thedlom's account so that I can send a DM. Then I write the following message:

And when I do find you . . .

I attach the YOU'RE NEXT! meme to the message.

Send.

I delete the original download from the downloads folder.

I clear the computer's cache and browsing history.

I close the browser.

I look over my shoulder. No one to worry about.

I pretend like I'm doing homework.

LOGAN

MY SHOULDER resting on the bathroom door and cracking it open a sliver, I watch as Holly walks out of the computer lab. That's where she always spends her free period, getting ahead on homework so she can spend extra time at practice.

I'm never in the computer lab, because I always wait until the last minute to do my homework. It's a bad habit, I know, but I perform best under pressure. At least, that's what's worked for me so far. It might be catching up with me, though. Because I'm so exhausted. Another night that I hardly slept.

I was up for hours, visited by ghosts from Cole's trailer. The flashing screens. The dangling wires. The Heart, beating on his table—*thump-thump, thump-thump*—like something out of a horror story.

Mostly it's that video, though. The one playing on a loop, with the kid singing in a high-pitched voice.

Walk like a man, talk like a man, walk like a man, my son . . .

That kid's face has been haunting me. Because that's not just any video. It's a meme. And it isn't just any meme. It was Cole's *favorite* meme. Though I can't for the life of me figure out why.

It wasn't funny. It was sadistic. Who mocks a little kid like that?

Cole, that's who. He showed it to me over and over again, and each time he did, he laughed harder. "Look at that glorious little shit!" he'd say. "Sing, Boyatee! Sing!"

The Boyatee, that's what he called the kid. It was a pun on those lumpy aquatic mammals called manatees (*Boy*atee, get it?), which only made the mocking seem worse. The kid had a shaved head and he was chubby, almost triple-chinned; he did look a bit like a manatee. But he was a child—nine years old, maybe ten. He had puberty and growth spurts and so much to look forward to in life. And guys like Cole were turning his adolescent awkwardness into a joke.

It's more than a joke, though. I feel like it's the key to something. Because last night, I remembered another thing Cole once said to me. It was a few days after Meeka broke up with him and I ran into him at Subway. He had a couple of footlongs in a bag and the stench of booze on his breath.

"Well, if it isn't one of the traitors," he said. "Enjoying your Cole-free life?"

"It isn't like that," I replied.

As he stumbled to his Kia, he growled, "I'll have the last word."

"What are you talking about?"

"You. Meeka. The Boyatee. Always want to prove you're better than me. That's all you think about, huh?"

"No, I don't think about that at all."

"You'll see. I'll have the last word."

It seemed like drunk posturing, a pathetic moment, and I wanted to tell him I was sorry. But he was in his car before I could respond.

It wasn't until a few weeks later that I truly understood what he meant by "I'll have the last word."

It wasn't until last night that I considered the Boyatee.

And it wasn't until a few minutes ago that I decided to see if there was a connection between all of these things.

I step out of the bathroom as soon as Holly rounds the corner into the main hall. I hurry into the computer lab before anyone spots me.

When I find an available computer in the corner, I plug my headphones into it and settle in. I search "Boyatee meme," and I click on the first result.

About a Boyatee

BY KAMEELA STOKES

"I'm so much bigger than that old thing," the Boyatee tells me.

We're in the Rainforest Cafe in the Disney Springs section of the sprawling eponymous resort. I'm eating something called Anaconda Pasta, which is basically pasta primavera. He's eating key lime pie, which he chose as a "nostalgia cheat."

"Everyone is bigger than who they are online," I tell him. "It's why virtual worlds are so cruel. We minimize everyone, especially ourselves."

The Boyatee savors a bite of pie and says, "That's not what I mean. I'm talking about changing the country, the world. And the way you do that is through memes. I saw that potential firsthand. Soon it will be my time to fulfill that potential. Right after I destroy someone."

"And who might that be?" I ask.

"The person who tried to ruin everything," the Boyatee says with a smile, and he leaves it at that.

I call him the Boyatee because that's the moniker the bleary-eyed meme hounds have bestowed upon him. But he

doesn't look like the kid in the famous video anymore. Puberty hit. The weight came off. The hair came on. The eyes are the same, but that's about it. His innocence is replaced by bluster.

Even though he's given me permission to use his real name, I'm not interested in doxing anyone, especially a minor. I'm not interested in promoting the entirely problematic views he asked me to promote via this article. I'm interested in answering a few questions.

What happens to someone after the internet hordes are through with them? What happens to someone so young? How do they heal? What do they need? What do they want?

Revenge.

That's what the author explores in this article I'm reading in the computer lab. It's a somewhat unflattering profile on Fission.com from a few months ago, describing the journey of a kid known as the Boyatee.

Which is basically this. A boy living in Kissimmee, Florida, goes to see a touring production of *Jersey Boys*. He falls in love with the songs of 1960s pop star Frankie Valli. Why? Because kids get obsessed with weird things sometimes. He records himself singing Valli's song "Walk Like a Man" and posts it to YouTube. No one notices.

At first.

Then, years after he posts it, someone digs it up and throws it to the digital wolves. Remixes and auto-tunes start popping up online. In a matter of weeks, the meme completely explodes. The comment sections are ruthless.

Here's the catch. By the time he's an internet sensation, he's not that kid anymore. Not only does he look entirely different, but he's started a different life. A divorce sent him north with his mom. He gave up singing. He spends his days gaming, reading, writing. He's obsessive about a low-carb diet that keeps the pounds off. He's angry, but his anger is not directed at the people who made fun of him. It's focused on a single mysterious person.

By the time the Boyatee takes his semiannual trip to Florida to visit his father and is sitting down to lunch in the Rainforest Cafe with a journalist named Kameela Stokes—whose byline includes such articles as "They Know Your Secrets: A Day with the Housekeeping Staff of Holiday Inn" and "Black Boys with Sticks: The Men of Color Who Are Changing the Game of Lacrosse"—his plan for revenge is already in motion.

He never reveals what that revenge will entail, but the article ends with an ominous statement from the Boyatee.

"I will make you feel the pain that I have felt. You know who you are."

Revenge. The last word. The Boyatee. Cole. How is it all connected?

That's what I ponder as I drive away from school. I received permission for early dismissal from Vice Principal Goldstein, who thinks I've got some Logan's Heroes business to attend to. That's a lie, of course.

I need to be alone so I can figure this out. I will drive and think, for as long as it takes.

GRAYSON

THERE ARE A LOT OF THINGS that can hurt people in the shop. Maim, kill them even. Freshman year Drake Lawson accidentally cut off the tip of his pinkie finger with the band saw. Christ. I've never seen more blood. Still haven't, and I've seen someone die.

Mr. Lopez gave me the keys to the shop because there are tools here I don't have at home and he knows I like to work on projects after school. Good guy, Lopez, but maybe it's not the best idea letting a kid like me be alone in a place like this. Maybe it isn't even legal. I'm not eighteen until March.

Not that I'm actually going to do anything violent. The bloodiest day in here will still be that day with Drake. Gus Drummond doesn't have to know that, though.

The last bell rang a few minutes ago and that means Gus will be walking past the shop any second. Every time I'm in here after school I see his head bob past the little glass window in the door. Not sure where he's going, but it's like clockwork.

I wait in the shop, with the lights off and the door open a crack. I kind of wish Meeka was here with me, but she thought I would be more intimidating by myself. It's probably true. Sometimes you need a good cop/bad cop routine and sometimes you just need a really fucking scary criminal.

Footsteps.

I peer into the hall and I see him. He's alone. I could grab him, but I don't want to risk him fighting back. Better to bait him.

"Help!" I call out. "Help!"

The footsteps stop.

"Quick! Help!" I shout, and I step back from the door.

He *is* quick, busting through the door into the darkness, head jerking from side to side.

"Hello?" he shouts. "What's the matter? Everything okay?"

He's small. Maybe five four. I'm not huge, but I have at least six inches and forty pounds on him.

He takes a few more steps inside and I slide in behind him and close the door. I lock it. "You said I'd be sorry."

He turns around, and when he sees me, he's absolutely and completely shitless. He doesn't have to say a word to convince me. A gulp is enough. This guy is the one.

"Who's sorry now?" I ask him.

"Um . . . um . . . uh . . ."

"The answer is *you,* Gus," I say. "Or me, I guess. If you said it, you'd say the word 'me.' Got that?"

He nods, even though I'm not sure he's got it.

Doesn't matter. Only one thing does. And I tell him what it is. "Well then, it looks like I'm in charge here."

His face is frozen for a moment. He's thinking about his response. And when he has it, he whispers it. "*Looks that way.*"

"Good," I say. "Now I want you to tell me what you think we should do."

He looks over his shoulders. There's still some light coming through the windows, so it isn't pitch-black in here. The drills, the blades, the sharp things? All very visible. This might as well be the type of place the CIA uses to torture terrorists.

"I guess . . . I was thinking . . . we should come to an understanding?" Gus says softly.

"An understanding? How's that supposed to work? Because you've gone way too far, Gus. I decide what happens now."

His eyes are glued to the door and its lock. The kid is desperate for an escape plan. I've been watching his hands, making sure he doesn't reach for his phone, but I'm also watching his backpack. It's stuffed, probably with books. Heavy. If he were smart, and brave, he'd use it as a club to knock me out of the way.

He is smart. I'm sure of that. But he isn't brave.

"If I could take it back, I would," he whimpers.

"You're scared, aren't you?" I say.

He nods.

"Because you've seen it?"

He stares at me for a moment, then lowers his head into his hand and turns away. "Of course I've seen it," he says. "I showed it to everyone."

I get closer to him. "Everyone?"

His hand slides across his face to his shoulder and the strap of his backpack. I brace myself, but he doesn't swing it. He drops it to the ground.

I breathe deep.

He sits on a stool.

I don't sit, because I need to stay above him. I need to have the upper hand in every way.

"I didn't mean for everyone else to see it," he says, moving his fingers back over his eyes because he's a coward and cowards can't face the messes they've made. "It took on a life of its own."

"So, how many people exactly have seen it?"

"The whole school, I guess. More than that."

Fucking shit . . .

"The whole school has watched the video?" I say, flexing my hand, trying to keep my voice from breaking, focusing on my anger.

His fingers fall from his eyes. He's confused. "What video?"

Wait. *What?*

Wait. Are we having the same conversation?

"What exactly did they see?" I ask him.

He winces. "I made that stupid meme and shared it with Carly, who showed it to Paul, and he posted it, and suddenly everyone is laughing at you guys and making their own memes. I told them not to tell anyone it came from me, but obviously they did."

"Wait," I say, and now I grab a stool and sit down next to him so I can get close. "You don't know anything about a video?"

He shakes his head like crazy. "I mean, the pic is obviously a screen cap, but I don't know from what."

"If you don't know from what, then where'd you find it?"

He rubs his eyes. "Online."

"Where?"

"A website. It doesn't matter."

"It does. It matters."

"It really doesn't."

I jump up. I walk over to a table saw. I plug it into the wall and say, "You're gonna tell me what site."

His head keeps shaking, and he says, "I found it, okay? That's all. I found it and I made a meme out of it. I thought it might impress some people. If it—"

I turn the table saw on—*whirrrr!*—and the sound makes Gus shut his trap.

"Impress some people?" I say loud enough so he can hear me over the machine.

He's losing it completely, stuttering like a bitch. "One-one-one person at least."

I grab a ball-peen hammer off a bench. "Who?"

"He's . . . your . . . he helped create the whole Boyatee thing so-so-so I thought that maybe he'd—"

I flip the hammer once in the air and catch it by the handle. "Who?"

The saw whirs and I point at him with the hammer like it's an extension of my finger and tears start bursting from his eyes.

"Cole!" he cries.

And I throw that fucker.

I don't mean to. It's a reflex. The hammer flips through the air and—*clang!*—bounces off the cinder blocks above Gus's head.

He yells something that sounds like "*Ermahgerd!*" as he flinches and ducks.

Even though I didn't mean to do it, I can tell it worked. The kid is fucking spooked. I'm not playing, and he knows it.

But what does he know about Cole? If Gus created the meme to impress Cole, then he definitely doesn't know he's dead. That means I have to pretend Cole is alive. I can't slip up and use the past tense.

"I guarantee that Cole doesn't care about you or that meme shit," I tell him. "He's got better things to do."

Gus is still crouched over, arms on his head, when he whispers something. But I can't hear it.

"What's that?" I say.

"But . . . but . . . but Cole wanted me to make it."

What?

No. No. No.

I'm usually good at keeping my shit together. Poker. Principal's office. It's hard to faze me. But this does it. Here's hoping I turned away fast enough that Gus didn't see shock waves move across my face.

"He wanted you to make it?" I ask as I stare into a dark corner.

"Well, he told the followers to make memes of it," Gus says.

"Followers . . . ?"

"On the site. The Cavalry. I assumed you already knew that."

I don't have the first fucking clue what he's talking about. I regain my composure and turn back around. "Show it to me. Is it on your phone?"

Gus is definitely more flustered than I am. He doesn't move his hands at all. Where's his phone? A kid should be able to whip out his phone in a heartbeat. But he doesn't. He just says, "I didn't mean to hurt all of you. I want to like you. I wish you liked me. It was a stupid thing I did to feel good about myself. I'm working on that. I swear, I'm trying to be better."

Who cares what he's working on or what he's trying to be? All I want is that fucking phone. I begin patting his thigh to see if it's in one of his jean pockets. He squirms. He's freaked.

"Settle down," I say. "It isn't like that. I need to know *exactly* where you got that pic. This shouldn't be so hard."

He grabs his backpack and hugs it close to his body. My body is braced and ready in case he swings it at me. His hands dig into one of the outer pockets until he finds it.

He huddles over his phone and says, "Like I said, it was on the Cavalry."

"Am I supposed to know what that means?"

"It's . . . I . . . Cole really never showed you?"

"Lemme see," I say, and I snatch the phone from him.

He tries to snatch the phone back, but I dodge him, and move over to the table saw, which is still whirring like crazy. I set the phone on the table like I'll cut the thing in half if he tries to come close.

"If it's a . . . sex tape thing . . . then I won't tell anyone," Gus says.

"The fuck are you talking about?" I say as I turn my shoulder to him.

"The screen cap. If the video is from, you know, something like that, well, I'd never tell. I'd never embarrass you. I'm sorry for what I did. You have to know I didn't mean to hurt anyone. I'm confused is all. And scared."

I'm actually kind of flattered he'd think Meeka and Holly would be down for a little action with me, but I'm also kind of offended he'd think I'd be down for some action with Logan in the mix.

None of it matters, though. I focus on the phone.

A website called the Cavalry is on the screen. There's a picture of two guys in jeans and T-shirts and they're standing in the woods, wearing those rubber horse head masks that were all the rage a few years back. Their arms are crossed, and their stances are wide. And there's a caption:

HORSEMEN OF THE MEMEPIRE

"This is Cole's site?" I ask.

He nods. And I'm about to scroll down when—

Shit!

The shop door flies open.

The lights flick on.

Someone's here.

"Oh. Hey, Grayson. I didn't know you were working today."

It's Mr. Lopez. He's got his hands on his hips and he's trying to figure the scene out.

"Yeah, I'm working," I say. "And showing my boy Gus some tools. That's all."

Oh really, with the lights off? Lopez's face is saying. But he doesn't call me out. And Gus backs me up with a big nod, because he knows it's best not to get me in trouble. But he also knows this is his chance to bounce.

"I have to get to hack club," he says with his hand out, "so I need my phone."

What can I do? I can't look like a total dick in front of Lopez. I fork it over.

As soon as Gus has it, the kid is out the door. And Lopez is turning off the saw and shaking his head.

"Gray," he says. "This isn't a clubhouse. You can't be bringing your friends here after hours. Technically, you shouldn't even be here."

"Then I'm gone," I say, with my hands up. "And I'm sorry."

I follow Gus out the door, but the hall is already empty. He and his phone are on their way to hack club. I could try to chase him down, but I can't risk making a scene out in the open. Besides, now I've got something to work with. I don't know what, but it's something.

HOLLY

LAST BELL RINGS and it sounds louder than ever. It feels like it's shattering my insides. I'd like to go home for the day, but it's time for practice. My last practice. Tomorrow is my last game because we aren't making the playoffs. Tradition dictates that for the last practice of the year, seniors get to do whatever they want. The other seniors and I have been talking. We decided that we'd dedicate the entire session to a scrimmage, pitting seniors against everyone else.

It's eight seniors versus nine juniors and four sophomores. The numbers aren't close to even, so we're making things interesting. Every time we get a corner or goal kick, they have to pull one player off the field. Which means they can't miss many shots and they have to be extra careful on defense.

In the first ten minutes, the younger players score a couple of goals. But they also shoot a few shots wide and have miscues that result in corner and goal kicks. Suddenly, it's ten versus eight. Still an advantage, but the seniors are more skilled. And we have me.

They play conservatively, opting to kick the ball to the sidelines as much as possible, but we rattle off two hard-fought goals and so the score is tied.

They get flustered, make some bad decisions, and before we know it, their numbers are down to seven. Now we have the advantage. With such low numbers, the field is wide open.

Conditioning comes into play. I'm in the best shape I've ever been in and my blood is pulsing.

I score with a header.

I score with a volley.

I even score with a back heel.

Before they can catch their breath, they're down to five players versus our eight and now it's far too easy. All the girls who were pulled are gathered on the sidelines. Even though they're underclassmen, they're cheering for us seniors. The ones who are left on the field are exhausted, trying to keep up, but they can't.

We're too good. *I'm* too good.

Coach finally calls the game. We're winning 9–3. She tells the seniors to "take a victory lap," which we happily do. We're hooting and chanting "Seniors, seniors, seniors!" as we go, but not in a cocky way. The others chant it too. They know they'll have their turn next year. Or the year after that.

When we turn the last corner, they keep chanting and run to meet us. But now some of them are holding up T-shirts, which they must've stashed in bags during practice. It's not exactly a surprise. It's another tradition. Every year the underclassmen give the seniors T-shirts with funny photos and nicknames on them.

They give Maya one with the nickname Walrus on it and a picture of her with straws up her nose. I remember when the pic was taken. A team dinner at O'Flaherty's, everyone goofing off. We all cracked up as Maya stuck various things up her admittedly large nostrils. Straws, obviously. But also french fries and the tapered ends of half-and-half containers.

Caitlin's shirt has a picture of her slipping on wet grass and the nickname Klutz. Which she is. Ella's shirt has her in pigtails—she's always in pigtails—and the nickname Piggy. It's very obvious stuff. Probably not funny to anyone who's not on the team. But it's got all the girls laughing as they show and share. Except for me.

Riley approaches with my shirt. I can't see the picture, but she looks downright wicked. Dammit, I know what it's going to be.

The meme. It has to be the meme.

I want to say something threatening. *Put it away or I will knock you on your ass, Riley.* But that's not me.

Or is it me? Because that's when it hits me. I've already threatened someone today. Like Cole threatened us. Exactly like Cole.

Sure, I don't plan to go through with the threat, but when I created my meme and DM'ed it to Thedlom, it was most definitely a threat. What I realize now is that I didn't do it to scare someone into silence. Because that won't work.

No. I did it to make the person talk.

I did it because, deep down, I want to be caught.

Jesus.

It's like I'm scoring an own goal. What is happening to me? I have completely given up control of the situation. I need to get it back. Now. Now!

Before Riley can hold up the T-shirt and have a big laugh, I tell her, "Sorry, but I have to go."

She stops. She's annoyed. Everyone else is puzzled.

I'll do anything to get away from them. I want to bolt right this second, but that would seem too weird. So I add, "I forgot that my mom needs me to pick her up. Like ten minutes ago. Which means I have to go. I'm sorry. I'll get the T-shirt later."

And I turn away and start walking. Very fast.

The walk becomes a jog.

I can't control my momentum and the jog becomes a run.

They call out to me.

"Holly!"

"Are you okay?"

"It's only a joke!"

I block it all out and focus on my car.

I get inside, get going.

The tires don't kick up dirt and gravel, but they probably should the way I tear out of there.

I don't look back.

Yellow lines. Dead leaves. Headlights. I see it all through the blur of tears as I finally realize the inevitable: The world will soon know the truth. There's nothing at all I can do to stop that.

My life is over.

Like Cole's. Exactly like Cole's.

Jesus!

He should be alive. I shouldn't have—

I breathe. Deep and long. I can't fall for that sort of thinking.

I spend the rest of the drive focusing on breathing, on trying to keep myself calm. When I turn onto my road and see my house in the distance, I tell myself what I know to be true. Ending Cole's life was the right thing to do. The best thing to do. The only thing to do. Even if I feel awful about it.

Feeling awful is what makes me a good human. And as a good human, I know I have to confess. Be honest, but on my own terms. Help the world understand why I did what I did. Forget about Grayson and Logan. Because I am not part of that team anymore. I saved Meeka's life and now there is only my life left to save.

I will control this thing.

This doesn't make me feel less awful about what I did, but it makes me confident in what I'm about to do. I'll talk to my parents. They'll hire a lawyer, who'll help guide my confession. I'm sure we can find a way out of this. It might not be a total victory, but I'll get through. I'll get on with my life.

I take some long slow breaths as I pull into the driveway.

I pull out my phone and I open Twitter. I know my phone is not as safe to use as an anonymous computer with a school IP, but I have to do this now. My plan is to delete the account and anything else that might prove to be a liability. That way I can control my confession, but . . .

No.

No!

NO!

It's too late.

Because there's a response to my DM. Only two words show up on my notification:

Hey psycho!

There's a pic attached.

LOGAN

I TAP OUT AN EMAIL to the journalist Kameela Stokes, who helpfully included her email address in her byline. My subject line is *Boy Seeking Boyatee.*

Dear Ms. Stokes,

I am a high school student in Plainview, Vermont, who is doing a project on memes and I came across your article on the Boyatee. It was very good. I'd be interested if you have any updates on him: what he's up to now, where I might find more information about him, that sort of thing. Anything you can pass my way would be a great help.

Kind regards,
Logan

P.S. You may be interested in my important work with Logan's Heroes. I've included a link to more information below.

There's no doubt that Holly would reprimand me for using my real email and real name, but I'm not too worried about it. This is a big-time journalist who probably lives in New York or

LA. She's not going to be suspicious of some kid all the way up in Vermont who's doing a high school project. She'll either ignore me or humor me and get on with more important things.

Of course, I know she's not going to dox the kid—that's against journalistic ethics and the stated intentions in the article—but if she does humor me with some new tidbit, she might confirm what I suspect.

I suspect the obvious. That Cole is the one who turned that Boyatee video into a meme. Or, at the very least, he's the one who first spread it. Why else would he be so obsessed with the thing? I'm thinking Gus Drummond might've even been involved too. Because the height of the Boyatee meme was about three years ago. Freshman year, when he and Cole were best friends. Those guys always knew where to find the craziest stuff online. They called each other the Meme Gods of the Meme Empire or something like that. It seemed harmless enough, but I wasn't hanging out with either of them then. Maybe they were more vicious than I could ever imagine.

I know Gus a little bit. When he moved to town in sixth grade, I went to his place a few times and played Zelda. He lived in a town house, which seemed weird. I thought only old people lived in town houses, but it wasn't the first or last time I've been wrong about something. Gus, his sister, and his mom spent their days and nights in a three-bedroom unit next to the golf course. There was a community pool and tennis courts. It seemed pretty cool back then, but the idea depresses me now. They shared their walls with someone else. They didn't have their own yard. That's not a home. And I'm pretty sure they still live there.

I have a couple classes with Gus this year. Physics and English. He's pretty good at physics, but English is where he shines. I remember he said something really insightful about *The Catcher in the Rye* and how it was a hero's descent into the underworld, similar to ones in Greek mythology. Mr. Huntington was impressed, but I've always known Gus was into mythology and ancient cultures. He was the first kid in our class to read all the Percy Jacksons. His backpack was always weighed down with books on Egyptian pyramids and Norse sagas. He had posters on his bedroom wall of mythological family trees, and he always dressed as some sort of god for Halloween. His full name is Augustus, and he likes to remind people it's the name that all Roman emperors adopted.

I wouldn't call Gus a nerd necessarily, but he's always been a bit odd. Or quiet, though not in a skeevy loner way. I think he ran cross-country for a little while. I'm not sure if he still does. All in all, I'm pretty sure he's a good kid, though the fact that he was Cole's best friend makes me believe they must have had some things in common, which doesn't reflect well on him.

It stands to reason that they are the ones who caused the Boyatee's suffering. And it certainly stands to reason that they—or Cole, at the very least—is the target of the Boyatee's vengeance. I could ask Gus about it, I suppose. But involving him at this point would be foolish.

It's better to go directly to the source.

Walk like a man, talk like a man, walk like a man, my son . . .

I've been driving for a few hours and the song is still there, a full infestation. I need a break from it and I'm hoping some other music might chase it away. I tap on the radio, but it's tuned to NPR and they're talking politics. I tap it off, because it reminds me of Senator Barnes and the mountain of things I have yet to do.

I keep driving. Past the rail trail lot. Along the Malvern Loop near the back of Meeka's property. I feel like I should go until my gas runs out. It'll mean I have a little more time left without having to face whatever comes next.

I've done this before.

In the past, when I've felt overwhelmed or nervous, I'd drive, for hours sometimes. And when I'd get low on gas, I'd almost always end up outside of Holly's house. During our on-again, off-again period, I used to park along the road—about ten yards past her long, snaking driveway—and I'd message with her. She didn't know where I was, and I didn't tell her because it might've freaked her out. Being physically closer to her made me feel emotionally closer. I wouldn't call it stalking. I had no bad intentions and I wasn't peeking in her window or anything.

I don't want to be at Holly's now. I'm not sure where I want to be. My head is a—

I slam the brakes.

What the hell was that?

I saw something in the woods. Something big. And gray. Or was it white? Flashing through the trees, leaping even, like the kid. Like, I don't know what. Like a . . . monster?

I pull over and put the car in park, but I leave it running. I push open the door.

"Hello?"

Nothing. No birds, not even wind rustling the blankets of fallen leaves. I wish I had a flashlight so I could stab it through the trees. But all I have is my headlights, and all they're showing me is the road and the ditch alongside it.

I close my eyes for a second. I take a breath. My head is a festering mess. Thoughts like spiders, like rats, like . . .

I need some sleep. I need to go home.

I don't go home. I pull up to Esther's house instead.

I check my email—no response yet from Kameela Stokes. Oh well, probably won't be any response. A big shot like her must have an overflowing inbox.

I'd like to sit here for a few minutes, to luxuriate in the silence. But that's not possible. Because there's music. It's coming from a rusty van that's idling in the driveway.

There are voices too, an argument, followed by tires on gravel. The van backs into the road at a speed that's, quite frankly, dangerous. And now the music is blasting. Sounds like a jam band, which fits the vehicle. As does the driver.

It's the guy with the dreads. I don't know if he sees me, but I get a good look at him before he drives off. He's got that vibe that addicts have. The one Cole's mom had. Something about his eyes.

When I turn back to the cluttered and weedy driveway, I spot Esther. She'd been hidden by the van, but she'd obviously been there the whole time. Arguing with that . . . dude.

She's staring at me right now, and walking toward my car, and I'm staring at her and smiling, but I'm not entirely happy. While I know I came here to see her, I wish I had a few more moments alone, to sit and imagine impossible scenarios. The type where everything is normal and she's my girlfriend, where the comfort I seek from her isn't about distracting myself or saving myself. It's about bettering myself. I feel like she's the type of person who makes other people better.

Tap tap tap.

She's at the passenger-side window, her gorgeous knuckles rapping the glass. And she's all smiles. She's not mad or creeped out for me showing up like this. She seems genuinely pleased to see me.

"Logan, my good man," she says as she opens the door and slides into the passenger seat.

"Yes, I'm good," I say. "A good person. Very good person."

It's a weird thing to say and I say it weird, at least that's what the confusion on her face indicates. "Everything okay?" she asks. "Because you look a bit—"

"Exhausted," I tell her. "Too much to do."

"I hear ya. Including trying to track me down, right? It's a full-time job. Tweety told me you stopped by yesterday."

The guy's name is Tweety. Of course it is. "Yeah, I—"

"I own a phone. I've got, like, Insta, Snap, everything," she says.

"I realize that. It was . . . I was driving around and, you know, thought I'd pop by again. Sorry to scare you, but I was out here checking my messages before—"

"No, it's me who should be sorry. You shouldn't have to hear stuff like that."

"I didn't hear anything," I say, which is the truth.

"It was nothing. Tweety is . . . nothing."

I appreciate her saying that, even if it sounds callous.

"Life has its challenges," I tell her.

"Hell yeah it does," she says, and then she pats my knee, and her voice switches over to the flawless accent of a charming

Southern debutante. "But you are not a challenge, dear Logan. You are an adventure. And I'm positively flattered you stopped by. Young ladies don't have the opportunity to entertain gentlemen callers as much as we would like."

Along with being a computer genius, she stars in all the school's theatrical productions. The girl is a wonder and I'm sitting with her, alone in my car, and I could lean over and kiss her and she'd probably kiss me back and that's an amazing feeling, but not enough to knock away the other feelings crawling around inside me.

"Not sure how entertaining this will be," I say, "because this gentleman caller is mostly looking for a little tech support."

"How positively fascinating," she says with a hand on her chest, and then she goes back to her regular voice, which is even more flawless and charming. "No joke, though, how can I be of service?"

"Well," I say, like this is off the top of my head, even though I've been practicing it. "What if I had an enemy?"

"You? An enemy? Oh no, that can't be. You're too sweet."

"I'm being serious," I say. "Say there was someone who hated me, and they wanted to hurt me and Logan's Heroes. You know, like, get revenge on us. And say I had all my files and financials stored on a cloud service. Could they, like, hack into it?"

As soon as I say it, I realize that even though it's rehearsed, it sounds breathtakingly ignorant. But Esther humors me.

"If they have, or could guess, a password, then of course," she says. "That's hardly hacking."

"Okay, then what about a hard drive?" I say, because I'm still wondering about what's on Cole's Heart. "What if all the data was captured and stored on a hard drive?"

"I'd need to know more about this hard drive," she says. "Is it connected to a network?"

I shrug.

"You don't know if your very important hard drive is on a network?"

"I mean . . . someone else set it up."

"So ask that person," she says. "But if it's networked and that network has vulnerabilities, then sure, someone could hack in. There are kids in hack club that would be up to the task. Penny Kim, Gus Drummond . . . me. I'd need more information to know exactly how they'd do it, though."

I nod. "I guess I need more information too."

"This isn't about that picture of you guys that's going around, is it?"

"What? No. That's . . . we started that whole thing. You know, self-deprecation?"

"Actually, I have no idea what self-deprecation means, but then again, I'm the world's biggest idiot," she says with a wink.

"Don't sell yourself short. You're the universe's biggest idiot," I say, and I wink back.

She smiles and says, "Seriously, I do feel pretty stupid sometimes. At least compared to you."

"Don't say that."

"I mean, look at you. You're making waves. You have a purpose. And me, I can't even figure out how to get outta this place."

"Get outta where? Your home?"

"The town, the state, the whole country. It's all going to shit. It'd be great to start over somewhere with a whole new identity. That's what I need."

To be honest, I'd never needed that before. But right now, you'd better believe I'm warming to the idea.

"That sounds so much . . . easier," I say. "It's the opposite of stupid."

"If you have the money," she says. "A big ol' 'if.' It always comes down to that, doesn't it?"

I reach into my pocket and pull out my phone. I take the case off it and show her that I have ten dollars hidden inside.

"Enough?" I ask.

She smiles and says, "Almost."

And then we sit there, looking at each other and smiling. It's an amazing moment. The best. It clears my head and fills my heart and, yes, this is the time to lean in for that kiss. Now or never, right? But just as I start to, she says something I don't expect. At all.

"If you don't mind, could you tell me the best way to contact Grayson?"

I whimper, but not out loud. In my heart. And I ask, "For . . . what?"

"Just because."

"Just because?"

"Just because."

And she shrugs and my heart takes a dive off a cliff.

Did I completely misread the vibe she was giving me? Is my head in that bad of a place?

But what can I do now? I check my phone for Grayson's contact. I could give her his number. So she could do what with it? Call him or text him and hook up with him instead of me?

I know he has a Facebook profile that he never uses. He once told me the only reason he created it was so he could use Spotify.

His profile pic is of some partially clothed porn star, which he probably thinks is hilarious. I wonder what Esther will think.

"You should try him on Facebook Messenger," I tell her, and I hold up my phone to show her his profile. "He uses it all the time."

"Cool," she says. "You're a lifesaver."

Of course, the moment is completely ruined. "I should go home," I tell her.

She smiles and says, "See you around, Logan." Then she disappears, slipping out the door and back to the belly of that decrepit house.

I *should* go home. I should, but I won't. I can't wait around worrying and hoping for any emails. I have to act.

I have to go back to the trailer.

GRAYSON

A HORSESHOE HANGS above the door to the sugarhouse. Wish I could say it's made of silver or platinum or something worth some cash, but I'm pretty sure it's aluminum. Dad put it up there a long time ago and that's where it's stayed. Good luck, they say. I could use some.

I pull a cinder block over to the door, stand on it, and take the horseshoe down off the nail. Yep, aluminum. It's light as hell and I spin it around my wrist as I go inside.

I know I should be on my tablet or phone, figuring out what this Cavalry website is all about and how our picture ended up there, but I've got too much nervous energy. That shit with Gus has me all keyed up and the only thing that'll help is doing something with my hands. Besides the shop at school, the sugarhouse is where I do most of my work, at least when we're not in sugaring season.

There's this black bear piece I'd been messing around with a few weeks ago, and that's what I'd been planning to work on. But with this Cavalry shit on my mind and this horseshoe calling out to me, plans have changed.

I'm making a fucking stallion.

When I was thirteen or so, my uncle Ray taught me how to weld. I haven't done it all that much. Don't ask me to mend a bridge or fix a ship. But make an abstract metal horse? That I can do.

And that's what I'm doing. A body banged out from a rusty, holey bucket; legs from old bike cranks; a tail and mane made of spokes; a funnel for a neck; and a head from this horseshoe. But twisted to look all horsey.

I'm bending and pounding and welding and it's coming together. The sugarhouse is heating up like we're sugaring and I'm sweating and, let me tell you, this thing could be really good. Who knows? Maybe my masterpiece.

I lose track of time and Dad busts in without me noticing.

"Working hard?" he says, trying to peek over my shoulder.

"Something like that," I say, and I set the horseshoe in my lap. I haven't had time to bend it and shape it into the head yet.

He gets a good look at what I've finished and asks, "Lion?"

"Horse," I say.

He nods.

In the nod, I can see so much. He supports me, but he's jealous too. He wants to give me everything that he can give me, but he's kinda pissed off that I don't have to take the path he did. Not that he fought in wars or worked in a factory or any of that shit. From what I know, he never wanted to be anything other than what he became. This family has always been in the sugaring business and I'm the first one who wants out. And he's okay with that, except when he isn't.

You might not believe I can see all that in a nod, but I can. He's been nodding like that for years.

"Mom made pork loin," he says. "Teriyaki."

"Nice," I say. "Gimme a couple minutes to get cleaned up."

He should leave, but he doesn't. He hangs out in the doorway as I roll up an extension cord. "Everything cool?" he asks when I stop and give him the stink eye.

"Sure," I say.

"Something in your voice. You seem agitated. Or, more agitated than normal."

"I'm agitated in general, then?"

He pats his chest. "You're my son. It comes with the blood."

Dad had a small heart attack last year because of high blood pressure and he jokes about it more than he does anything helpful about it. Still covers his food with salt and works way too long and hard.

"I guess it's school," I say. "Fucking useless these days."

"Be cool, son," he says, and then he laughs. "Be cool. Stay in school."

"Yeah, it'd be just like me to drop out a few months before graduating."

Dad steps forward and puts an arm around me. He kisses my head like he's been doing since I can remember. I hated it during middle school, but these days I tolerate it as much as I tolerate anything he does. I might even appreciate it sometimes. Not that I'd tell him.

"You'll get your diploma," he says as he shoves me away to show me that he's still the stronger one in the room. "Then you'll go to New York City and hang out in Greenwich Village with all the other artists."

"Artists can't afford to live in Greenwich Village," I tell him. "Most can't even afford Brooklyn anymore."

"Did I tell you about when I went to Greenwich Village about twenty years ago?" he says, and his eyes light up. "There was a dude with a cat on his head. He was walking around. A cat, just sittin' on his head. You would've lost your mind."

"I don't know," I say. "Not much surprises me these days."

"Well, it was funny in any case. I want you to know that if things are getting you down, just remember, you got talent. More than any kid in this town. You don't have to resort to nonsense to get attention. I mean look at that . . . thing. It's gonna be a horse, right?"

The basic shape is there but, yeah, it's probably hard to picture at the moment. "The head isn't ready yet," I tell him, and I hold up the horseshoe. "Making it out of this."

"You always liked to do things backward," he says with a smile. "And you always were attracted to the disturbing shit."

Even unfinished, it's probably the best piece I've ever done. It stirs a feeling in me that I can't quite get ahold of. But *disturbing*?

"You think it's disturbing?" I ask.

He shrugs. "Life is disturbing."

As soon as he says that, I think of Cole's body. In a puddle. Dead. Puke-covered. Animal.

"What do you mean by that?" I ask.

"Cat-head dude," he says. And he laughs.

"Come on. You got me curious. What do you find disturbing in life?"

He scratches at his bushy sideburns and takes a deep breath. I have a pretty good guess what he's going to talk about. Seeing his dad die in this very same sugarhouse we're standing in now. Back when Dad was about my age and Grandpa was his age. You guessed it: heart attack.

But instead he says, "When you dig deep and find out why things are the way they are, you always find dark shit, right?

Never a happy story, or what you expect. Even things in life that seem harmless have a much more sordid history than we could ever imagine. Like, you know, that horseshoe."

"This one?" I say, holding it up again. It's almost weightless. So insignificant, basically nothing.

"Horseshoes in general. You do know why people hang them above doors, don't you?"

"It's good luck," I say.

"But why's it good luck?"

"I don't know. Just is."

"Just is, huh?" Dad says, and he winks at me. "It never *just is*. There's always a story behind things, but the stories get buried. Written over. Forgotten."

"What's the story?"

"I've never told you this one?"

The stories he usually tells are the ones about my uncle Ray—which involve beer or girls or, usually, both—but I've never heard one about a horseshoe. Maybe he told my sister, or my brother, but never me.

"Enlighten me, Old Man," I say.

He pulls up his pants by the belt loops because they're always sagging and he won't buy the right waist size or wear a belt. Then he takes a seat.

"Well," he says, and he clears his throat. "There's this old legend, right? All about a blacksmith. One morning the devil—Satan himself, you know?—goes into this blacksmith's shop. He's not in disguise. He's got the head of a man but with horns poking out from his wooly hair. He's wearing a red coat. His legs are goat legs and his feet are cloven. 'Feels like I've been walking for an eternity,' the devil says, flashing his bright teeth. 'And now my hooves are killing me. I've heard you can help.' "

Dad has always been a good storyteller. That's because he enjoys it. And I can tell he's really enjoying this story, getting into character for the dialogue, hamming it up.

"The blacksmith is a religious man, and he's no idiot," Dad goes on. "He recognizes the devil right off the bat and decides to take a righteous risk. 'I have the exact thing you need,' the blacksmith says, and he ducks into the back of his shop. He returns with his prized possession, a pair of horseshoes forged from pure gold."

"Seems like a waste of perfectly good gold," I say. "Cash that shit in and buy a wagon, ya dumbass blacksmith."

"Ah, but the horseshoes would prove to be much more valuable than that," Dad says. "You see, the devil's beady eyes light up when he sees those beauties, 'cause we all know the devil is the vainest of creatures.

" 'I must have them,' the devil says.

" 'You may not like how I put them on,' the blacksmith tells him.

" 'Whatever it takes,' the devil says. 'As long as shoes so beautiful exist, then they must be mine. No one except me must wear them.'

" 'Fine,' the blacksmith says. 'To get to your hooves, I'm gonna have to tie your legs and hang you upside down.'

"The devil agrees, because along with tons of vanity, he's got way too much confidence. He never believes that harm will come his way. You see, the devil is immortal. But just because he's immortal, it doesn't mean he's immune to pain.

"And so the blacksmith ties the devil's legs, hoists him in the air, and turns him upside down. The devil is completely helpless, and the blacksmith goes to work. He places the gold horseshoes on the devil's hooves.

"'Oh,' the devil moans in pleasure. 'Wonderful.'

"The pleasure doesn't last long, though. While the devil is distracted, the blacksmith pulls out a long, sharp nail that he's been heating in the fire and he drives it into one of the devil's hooves. *Bam!*

"'*Yaowww!*' the devil howls, because the nail goes so deep that it pierces his flesh and bone.

"The blacksmith doesn't stop. He drives another. *Bam!*

"'*Yaowww!*'

"And another. *Bam!*

"'*Yaowww!*'

"And the blacksmith keeps driving in the nails and the only thing the devil can do is scream and squirm and endure the pain.

"'I will keep doing this, until the day I die, because you, sir, are the devil and you deserve to suffer for the evil you have put upon this earth!' the blacksmith hollers.

"The devil catches his breath, grits his teeth, and says in as calm a voice as he can muster, 'But you, stupid blacksmith, *will indeed* die someday and I, most definitely, *will not*. And when you do, I will find my way down from here and I will utterly destroy your family.'

"The blacksmith hadn't considered this. He loves his family more than anything and can't imagine them suffering because of his choices. He decides to make a deal, for as vain and confident as the devil is, he is also known to keep his word.

"'I will show you mercy,' the blacksmith says, 'and let you down, so long as you make me a promise.'

" 'Until I hear it,' the devil says, 'I make no promises.'

" 'I will let you down if you vow to never harm nor bother a blacksmith or a blacksmith's family ever again,' the blacksmith says, holding another nail in the air, threatening to plunge it into the devil's hoof.

"The devil sighs and says, 'It's a reasonable request. But what if I'm in search of souls, and I come upon a house? How am I to know a blacksmith lives there?'

"The blacksmith removes the nails from the devil's hooves until he is able to free the golden horseshoes. He carries one to the front of the shop, opens the door, and steps outside. He nails the horseshoe above the door and comes back to inform the devil, 'I will tell all the blacksmiths to nail a horseshoe above their door, and when you see it, you will know never to pass through.'

" 'All right,' the devil says. 'I can agree to that.'

"The blacksmith shakes the devil's hand to seal the deal and then grabs the rope to lower him down, but before he does, the blacksmith says, 'Oh and one more thing. You're not getting any of my damn horseshoes.' "

Dad stops talking and puts his hands out like *ta-da!*

It's a good story, no doubt. And I say, "And that's why people hang horseshoes above their doors."

"So it goes, so it goes," Dad says.

Obviously, it's not a true story. Sure, I believe in God and all that, maybe even the devil, because how can you have something so good without something so bad? But I know the devil isn't strolling around, twirling a cane or whatever.

"So now that I've whet your appetite with tales of devil torture, it's time for dinner," he says. "Or you can stay out here and work. It's a hell of thing you got there, Gray."

I'm suddenly super anxious. I'm not hungry, but I don't want to be alone.

"Let's go inside," I say as I fish my phone from the mesh bag that hangs from a nail in the wall above the workbench. Before I pocket it, I notice there's a text from Meeka.

So? Gus?

HOLLY

MY BROTHERS ARE UP IN THEIR ROOMS, playing video games. Dad is in his workshop, turning wooden bowls with a lathe, which is something he does to "relax." Mom is going for one of her late-evening jogs, all clad in orange reflective gear and a headlamp. I'm back in the basement, back in Mom's comfy chair, laptop poised at the edge of my knees.

I didn't want to look at the pic on my phone, in case it had spyware or a virus attached to it. But I'm willing to sacrifice the laptop, and I'm willing to use our Wi-Fi because I don't have time to go somewhere else. I need to see this now. The risk versus reward is leaning heavily toward reward.

I click it and . . .

It's another meme. It's a picture of that blond actress from the movie *Mean Girls*. The meanest of the mean girls. Regina George, I think. The caption reads:

LIKE, WHY ARE YOU
SO OBSESSED WITH ME?

Jesus. What is it with this person? Do they think I'm not serious?

I need to respond. Since they seem to get off on this little meme game, I go to MemeMonster.com. I search for OWL memes.

There are hundreds of pics to choose from. I go with one called INQUISITIVE OWL, which is a cute little bird with a tilted head, and I enter my text:

HOO
R U
REEEEELY?

I download it. I DM it.

But a moment later I'm regretting it. Owls are predators, though adorable ones don't exactly convey a serious violent threat. Unfortunately, I don't think I can take the message back. All I can do is wait.

My cursor is poised over the notifications, and I click.

Click, refresh. Click, refresh. Click, refresh. Click, refresh. Click—

Thedlom is either on Twitter or has notifications enabled. Because a response comes after only a minute or two.

It's a picture of two hands. One is holding a blue pill, the other is holding a red pill.

The text says above the blue pill says: *Find out who I am . . .*

The text says above the red pill says: *Find out who I reeeely am.*

Okay, okay, okay.

This is a meme that self-inflated assholes use. It's basically about taking a philosophical stance. People who choose the blue pill—and that's apparently most people—choose not to see the world for what it truly is. They prefer to live in comfortable ignorance. But people who choose the red pill are willing to confront the often ugly and corrupt reality of the world.

I'm obviously choosing the red pill, even though I'm not sure what that will entail. Perhaps it's a trap, but what do I have to lose?

I send back a pic that is just red. All red, red, red.

And I wait. Refresh, refresh, infinite refresh. Until . . .

A disappointing response.

The screen lights up with a picture of Neil Patrick Harris in a suit. It says:

WAIT FOR IT . . .

The light from Cole's phone was cast across our faces as we all looked down at a picture of him and Meeka. Embracing. Like they were in love.

They weren't in love. At least Meeka wasn't. Not even when that picture was taken.

"You stole this from me," Cole said to us. The phone was lit for another second or two, then the screen went black.

We were in the woods behind Meeka's house. But Meeka wasn't there. She and her parents were at the Cape, a vacation planned at the last minute. Probably to dodge Cole, who had not been handling the breakup well.

As for why we were all there, Cole had invited us, saying, "Meet me at the bend in Meeka's stone wall and we'll talk about what comes next." Like fools, we all went. Logan, and Grayson, and I, standing there, staring at this pathetic and vengeful man.

"We didn't steal anything from you," I said. "You lost it."

"So I'm a loser, huh?" Cole asked.

"That's not what she said," Logan answered.

"It's exactly what she said," Cole told him. "But it's wrong. Mark my words. This isn't ending quietly."

"What's that supposed to mean?" Grayson asked. "Is that a threat?"

"No, that's a prophecy," Cole answered. "And there's no way to stop it."

"Prophecy of what *exactly?" Logan asked.*

Cole set the phone down next to him on the stone wall where he was sitting. "Of who the winner will be."

"It didn't work out with Meeka," Logan said. "You have to accept that."

"I have *accepted it," Cole said.*

"By inviting us out to where Meeka fuckin' lives . . . and then what?" Grayson barked. "Threatening her? Threatening us?"

Cole shifted his weight on the wall. Some pebbles cascaded down, making the sound of a rainstick. "You think I'm threatening Meeka?"

Of course we did, but it was best to be careful with our words. Cole was already eighteen. He could buy guns easier than he could buy liquor. And he had no trouble buying liquor.

"We want everyone to move on with their lives," I replied.

"Do we, now?" Cole said. "Because do you know what I'll be moving on with? What my life is?"

"You're a white man living in America," I said. "It means you've got it pretty darn good."

"And recognizing that privilege is the first step toward improving your life," Logan added.

Cole tore at some moss on the wall. He tossed it to the ground as he said, "Fuck you, Logan. And fuck you too, Holly. You think I got it pretty darn good, huh? But you would never change places with me, would you? Not in a million years."

I started to say, "Your heart is broken and—"

But Cole jumped from the wall and got in my face. "My heart isn't broken. It's this fuckin' country that's broken. Everyone pretending to be someone they aren't. Liars! All of them!"

His breath stank of booze and salami, which I would've known without even smelling it, because that was what he'd been surviving on. I stepped back and said, "Chill."

Cole pointed a finger. "Why don't you fuckin' chill, all right. Go back to your little palace and shine your fuckin' trophies. Be the fake-ass bitch you've always been. You don't care about me. You don't care about anyone."

"I care about Meeka," I said.

"Holly cares about me too," Logan added. "And I care about you, Cole. I'm worried that you're losing your way and that—"

"Holly turned you into such a whipped little pussy," Cole said to him.

"Come on, man," Logan responded. "Holly and I are only friends. We're not even dating anymore."

It'd been a while, in fact. The last and final time we'd broken up was in May. It was early October at this point. Also, I'll have it known that Logan was never whipped. If anything, I was the one compromising in the relationship. I was the who was always trying to please him, to speak on his behalf. Even months later, I was still doing it.

"All Logan is trying to tell you is that as bad as things are going, it'll get better. You have privilege. That should be encouraging. If you were born—"

"It would've been a 'privilege' to be born in a gutter. A fuckin' privilege to be given away. Then I would've been adopted by some rich Boston execs who'd whisk me off to a plush life in Vermont, right? You all adore heartwarming stories like that, don't you?"

I wanted to slap his face. This was an obvious dig at Meeka. Meeka wasn't always forthcoming about her past because she didn't know all that much about it. But people speculated, of course. About her birth mom being a sex worker who basically gave her away. Selling her, in so many words.

All Meeka ever told me was that when she was adopted as a toddler, she was undernourished, could barely communicate. And Mason and Sara basically saved her. They've always been loving and supportive parents. Which has nothing to do with her being anything other than their daughter. Forget biology. Family isn't about that.

"Everyone has their own lives, their own problems," I said to Cole. "Yours are big. I'm not saying yours aren't big."

His eyes were glistening with tears about to burst. He sniffled and picked his phone up off the wall. "You'll all have much bigger problems soon. When I'm finished, you'll all regret how you've treated me. And everyone will know who I am. For a long time."

Grayson cleared his throat. He had been pretty quiet through most of this and I couldn't tell whether he was angry or agreeing with the things Cole said. Of the rest of us, he was always the closest with Cole. They had their disagreements—loud ones, too—but they also shared some views.

"What the fuck is all that supposed to mean?" he asked Cole as he puffed up his chest. "What kind of bullshit are you slinging? You call us out here, and now what do you want from us? You want us to convince her to go back to you? Or else? Is that it?"

Sniffling, Cole said, "No. I want you to wait."

"For what?" I asked.

Cole turned away from us and started walking into the moonlit woods. I'm not sure where his car was parked. Not out by the barn with our cars. I noticed that when we arrived. It was probably somewhere along the Malvern Loop. For all I knew, he had a gun in the trunk, and he was going to march right back here with it.

"Wait for what, asshole?" Grayson hollered as Cole kept walking.

Cole didn't respond. He disappeared into the forest.

"Should we go after him?" Logan asked.

"And do what exactly?" I asked. "Hold him down?"

"Yeah," Grayson said, stepping forward. "Grab his throat and tell him we're not playing. He's gonna try to kill her, man. Us too. That's how this shit starts. You heard him, right? How he wants to make a name for himself?"

I put a hand on his shoulder and said, "He's angry. Going after him right now might make it worse. We need to warn Meeka. We need to tell the cops."

That's what we planned to do. That seemed like the right thing to do. At least at the beginning.

GRAYSON

It isn't Gus, I text Meeka.

You sure? she writes back.

Dinner is over and I'm sitting on a wicker chair on our back porch. It's chilly, but the porch is screened in and this is my favorite time to sit out here. It's dead quiet and plenty dark. I've got my phone in my lap. It's cold enough that I can see my breath in the glow of the screen, but not so cold that I can't flip the horseshoe over and over in one of my bare hands.

Dad's devil story has got me all wound up again. Not sure why—it's only a legend—and yet something about it seemed personal.

I imagine myself in thirty years, with a teenage son looking all confused about something. Assuming I get through this mess, what sort of story do I tell him? Do I tell him about Cole? About how we hung a horseshoe on our world and drove that devil right the fuck out of here?

Hell no.

But what about in sixty years, when I'm really old and have nothing left to lose. Who knows? Maybe I'll confess to every bad thing I've ever seen or done. Lay it all out there.

For now, what I've done stays between me and the rest of them. And the Gus stuff stays, well, only with me.

I don't respond to Meeka's text right away. Explaining the

whole Gus shakedown would take too long, and besides, I need to get a handle on what exactly is going on. So I plop the horseshoe down on the wicker table and I unlock my phone.

I search for "The Cavalry."

Tons of hits. There's a Wikipedia page that talks about horses and the military and all that. There's a podcast called *The Cavalry* and I listen to the first minute of it and figure out it's a dead end; meatheads talking about football doesn't have shit to do with Cole. There's some band from Kentucky that's also called the Cavalry and they play punk bluegrass and their SoundCloud clips aren't half bad—I might even check them out in the future—but they aren't what I'm looking for.

Finally, after a few pages of results, I spot a site called TheCavalry.net. I open it.

It's pretty simple looking, and I recognize it as the same thing Gus showed me. Again, along the top there's that photo of two guys wearing those stupid horse head masks, trying to look tough. And there's that tagline:

HORSEMEN OF THE MEMEPIRE

When I was thirteen or fourteen, I might've thought this was badass, but now it's pathetic. What grown person is actually impressed by shit like that?

Cole. That's who.

I suddenly realize that Cole used to forward me articles and videos from this site all the time. He was always writing shit like *this one will melt your face right the fuck off.* I never bothered to read any of them. If I'm not even taking the time to read my homework, I'm not about to settle down with some nose-picker's essay about how he can't get laid.

That's basically what most of this stuff is. The homepage is plastered with articles, but they're all borrowed from other sites. I scroll down and see titles like:

Rules for Ghosting

Cryptocurrency and Becoming Master of the New Economy

How to Bang Your Waitress

None of it is what I'm looking for and I'm pissed that Lopez showed up when he did. Gus was all ready to point me in the right direction, and now here I am, having to dig through mounds of hot garbage.

There's a search bar at the top, along with a menu. I notice there's a link for *Forums* in the menu, so I go with that. I tap it and it takes me to a page full of folders.

There's one called *Our Favorite Boyatee Memes*. Another is *MRA Talk with Emperor Augustus,* whatever that means. But it's the one at the top, the one labeled *The Dank Lord of Memes,* that makes me go holy shit.

HOLY SHIT!

Gus wasn't blowing smoke, because I know exactly who the Dank Lord of Memes is.

It's Cole! Fucking Cole!

That was his avatar, or whatever you call it. It's what he named his video game characters—top scores always went to the Dank Lord of Memes. It was also how he signed everything online—YouTube and Reddit comments were always from the Dank Lord of Memes. Probably thought it was a superhero identity, like his Batman to his Bruce Wayne.

I open the *Dank Lord of Memes* folder and it leads me to a forum full of posts, and there's a caption along the top that says:

THE FORGE OF THE MEMEPIRE

There are hundreds of posts with titles like *Meme Away* and *Meme It Long and Hard* and I'm not sure I have time to sift through all of them. But I start with the latest one. It's titled *Meme This Shit.*

It's from Sunday of last week. The day after we killed Cole.

I click it, and sure enough, there it is. That fucking picture. The one that started the meme. Our goddamn faces in a circle. It's a clean version of the picture, except for some weird word in the bottom corner: THEDLOM.

It freaks me out to see the pic in its raw form.

There's a single comment in the thread below and it's from someone who goes by the name Emperor Augustus. It says:

How about this one? Appropriate, right?

And it's the same picture, but now it has text over it. DUCK, DUCK, DUCK . . . GOOSE it says. Like the game kids play.

I understand it in that I understand the reference, but I don't *get* it. Maybe it's an inside joke? If this is where Gus found the pic and where he was trying to impress Cole with his meme, then I'm guessing Emperor Augustus is him, right? Makes sense.

And it reminds me. I saw that name, Emperor Augustus, on one of the previous pages. I click back to check it out. But when I open the folder called *MRA Talk with Emperor Augustus,* I get an error.

404 Error: The page you're looking for can't be found.

I refresh the page. No luck. I even go to my settings and clear all the caches and cookies, which supposedly makes the internet run faster and smoother. It doesn't help. Same error.

So I click back to the page I've already looked at and—

What? The fuck? Is this shit?

Another error.

Refresh. Click back. Type in the name of the site. Errors all around.

Every post, pic, page, and folder. The entire Cavalry.

It's all gone.

LOGAN

I TURN ON MY DELL LAPTOP. It's 11:50 p.m. and I'm wide awake, sitting at my desk. I didn't think it was possible for someone to be so tired and yet still so awake. But here I am. Scientists should put me in a glass room and poke and prod and study me.

Everyone in the house is asleep. I know because I crept past my parents' room and I could hear them all snoring. Mom, Dad, Toby (the dog)—all curled up together on the king-size bed. Still, I check my door to make sure it's locked. It is. Even though it's cold in here, I turn my fan to high. I can't risk anyone hearing anything, even though I'm not sure what they might hear.

I feel dizzy, but my body is also pulsing from a toxic brew of anxiety and regret. I can't believe what I'm about to do. I can't believe what I've already done.

I type in my password and I close my eyes and try to focus on the sound of the blood pumping in my head, but the fan is so loud that I can't hear anything else. I can hardly think.

I give my face a little slap to jump-start my brain. It works well enough. It keeps me on task. I reach down to grab my backpack, unzip it quickly—tearing off that proverbial Band-Aid—and plunge my hands inside.

I have it.

There in my fingers, in my shaking hands, I have Cole's Heart.

After my visit to Esther's house, I went back to the trailer to get it. I know it was a risky move, but when she mentioned wanting to talk to Grayson, I was gutted. Esther made it clear that she's not interested in me in the way I want her to be, and so my sole focus became about salvaging what I can of my future.

Everything that matters—Logan's Heroes, the goals of so many wayward dreamers—has been compromised because someone took advantage of my mistake, and if stealing this red box gets me closer to figuring out who that person is, then that was my only option.

The trailer was the same as we'd left it. I slipped in, did what the others didn't have the courage to do, and slipped out. I don't think I touched a single other thing. I hardly even looked at anything, though of course I couldn't help but notice the video of the Boyatee was still looping, like some wound that won't stop oozing.

Walk like a man, talk like—

I slap the Heart down on my desk, next to the laptop. Could this thing fry my computer? I'm willing to risk it.

I plug it into the wall, and then I plug it into the Dell.

The Heart mounts. I suppose that means it's a hard drive and I can access what's on it.

The name of it is MY HEART BELONGS TO? That's undeniably weird, but it has to mean something important, right? I double-click the icon and it prompts me for a password.

Crap.

How am I supposed to guess one of Cole's passwords? He'd make it impossible.

Or would he?

When I start typing, I notice that it enters all the letters in caps, so I at least don't have to worry about capitalization. And the name of the drive is clearly a clue. He wants me to answer the question.

So who does Cole's Heart belong to?

I try MEEKA.

It doesn't work.

I try MEEKAMILLER.

Nope.

I try variations on: MOM, MOMMY, MOTHER, TERI, and TERIWESTON.

I was sure one of these might be the solution, but no, no, no, no, no, no, and no. Luckily, it hasn't locked me out. It's almost like Cole wanted someone to guess it. I'm obviously not the best candidate for that.

Esther mentioned there were kids in the hack club who could handle things like this. It's best if I don't deal with her anymore, but maybe I should contact one of them? They might have an idea of how to crack this open and get out all its secrets.

Nope. No way. I can't involve anyone else. I can't drag any innocent parties into this mess. For my safety, sure, but primarily for their safety. I need to think of other people. All the time. Never me. This isn't about me. It's about saving Meeka, letting Holly live up to all her potential, and making sure Grayson steps out on the right path in life. Even if that's a path that puts Esther in his arms instead of mine.

That's when it hits me. Even though I sometimes slip, I'm naturally a selfless person. Cole, on the other hand, was a proud Libertarian. By definition, *selfish*. It's no wonder I can't figure out his password. It's not in my nature to think like him. So how do I solve Cole's riddle? How do I think like him? Who does his heart ultimately belong to?

I think like a selfish person. I type COLE.

Wrong.

COLEWESTON?

Crap. Nope.

Maybe I misjudged him. But who else can it be? His heart doesn't belong to Meeka or his mom or anyone else. It's only him. I stare at the screen hoping the answer will suddenly appear, but the only thing that appears is an alert.

I have a new email.

I switch over to my Gmail tab, and there it is, the message I've been waiting for.

RE: Boy Seeking Boyatee

I don't delay. I double-click. It reads:

This is a joke, right? Because I don't get it. Did he put you up to this? You Plainview kids are a strange bunch and I'm sorry if the article didn't turn out to your friend's liking. But I told him from the beginning that I wasn't going to plug his vile website. And I'm not plugging your little charity either, as well-intentioned as you might think it is. Sorry.

That was it. That was Kameela Stokes's entire response, and I am, for lack of a better word, flummoxed.

What on Earth?

I'm stuck on the fourth sentence. *"You Plainview kids are a strange bunch and I'm sorry if the article didn't turn out to your friend's liking."*

Is the implication that the Boyatee is from Plainview? And that I should know him?

I close my eyes and I feel dizzy. Colors swirl on the dark

background of my eyelids. I'm not sure I can handle any more of this. I try to replace the colors with my memories of the Boyatee video, in an attempt to recognize the kid's face, but I can't do it. All I see is color. All I can—

An idea strikes me. I open my eyes. I click over to the Heart. I try one more password.

BOYATEE.

Nothing . . .

Except a shadow, moving across the light that's cast from the laptop onto the wall.

The door is locked, the window is locked. Everything, locked. But I saw it, the sweep of a shadow. I swing around and—

Is that a dark figure reclining on my bed? I can't make out a face; it's almost like a 3-D silhouette.

"Hello?" I say.

No answer.

"Who . . . are . . . you?" I ask.

There's something there. I swear it. A body, bathed in darkness, but with a distinct shape. Round, smooth. The thing doesn't speak, not out loud. But suddenly I feel it communicating, a soundless whisper.

You know me.

"No," I say. "No. I don't know you because you're not real."

What's real? Don't you see me?

I don't hear the words. I feel them. Like you do in a dream. And as for what I see, it's shadows. The shape of a boy? The shape of a manatee? The shape of—

I close my eyes and slap my face again. "Go away," I say.

It was me.

The words are crawling across my skin. I open my eyes and

it's still there. A shadow more than a living thing, but still, maybe it is real. People believe in ghosts. And demons.

"Go away," I say, but I don't know what I'm saying it to. The thing or my broken brain. Because, yes, people do believe in ghosts and demons. But not me. Me, I'm hallucinating. That happens when you don't sleep. You see things that aren't there. You hear things that aren't there.

Me. Me. Me. Me. Meme. Meme.

The words linger in the air, like humidity, and they stick to my skin.

And I suddenly realize I *do* know who the Boyatee is.

All of us know him.

TUESDAY, NOVEMBER 8

TEN DAYS AFTER

GRAYSON

IT'S HOLLY'S LAST GAME, and I'm here to support her, sitting in a lawn chair on the hill with all the frothing-at-the-mouth soccer parents. Not really my choice. Meeka told me she was going alone, and I was worried about her, so I had her pick me up. But I made sure we came late. There's only so much soccer I can stand.

I don't know what it is about Meeka. Whatever she wants, she gets. From everybody. She's the opposite of pushy about it. It's not like she's tossing promises around. Sometimes she doesn't even ask. You want to please her, simple as that. She's super strong and super vulnerable at the same time, if that's possible. Anyone who's met her would back me up on this. Teachers, parents, kids—we all want to make her happy.

So here I am, in the thick of it. Even though I don't know what to tell her about Gus. About Cole and the Cavalry. About the posts and pics. All this nonsense spinning in my brain. Cole is dead and buried. No doubt about that. But someone out there is using his name.

Now the evidence is gone. It's all gone. And I don't just mean the picture of us. I mean the whole fucking site. Everything on TheCavalry.net is: *404 Error: The page you're looking for can't be found.* There's nothing to show Meeka, and I can't prove a thing if there's nothing to show. Obviously, she'd believe me, because I don't ever bullshit her. But she'd also believe

I fucked things up. That I did something wrong to lose the only evidence we have.

Long story short, it's best if I handle this myself. Only, I don't know how to do that. And it's ripping my insides apart.

I brought the horseshoe with me, and it's in the pocket of my Carhartt. I've been gripping it, squeezing it, hoping it will give me luck when all it's been giving me is cold metal on my cold hands. I've got no answers, nothing I can do but sit here, watching soccer and trying to keep my head together.

Our team is getting their asses handed to them 5–2. The two goals are Holly's, adding to her record. The game is almost over and she's still going like a rabid dog, chasing down every play, never stopping. Meeka cheers each time the ball touches Holly's foot, or knee, or head. So do most of the parents. They're whistling and shouting her name like this is church and she's Jesus. I'd never say Holly isn't a great player, because she is. If she could live her whole life on that field, she'd be as perfect as everyone thinks she is. But that field is a tiny place and the world is a big one.

The world is full of top athletes.

The world is full of murderers too. Serial killers. School shooters. Domestic abusers.

The world is full of memes.

Holly, Meeka, Logan, me—we aren't even a little bit special.

I remember this one meme called Bubble Girl from when I was a kid. It was a picture of some chubby little chick holding a plastic container of bubbles. She was running along, looking weird as hell. Tons of people Photoshopped it and made it look like she was running from Voldemort or a T. rex or whatever. And it was funny. I remember laughing my ass off at the little dough ball. I never made one of those memes myself because I've never been good with things like that. But I probably would've if I knew how.

That girl was everywhere for a while, but what about now? I never see that meme anymore. I can only picture Bubble Girl as a kid, even though she's probably seventeen or eighteen now. Like me. That meme lived out its life—they all do, right?—but maybe not in her head. I bet she got sick of seeing people clowning on her like that. Might have even quit the internet. Sure, there's a chance she got over it, and now laughs it off like it was no big deal, pretends to get on with her life. Doesn't mean it didn't change her forever, though. While it didn't even make a dent in anyone else's soul. We all laughed and moved on.

She's like us. She isn't any more special than any of us. Because no one cares about her anymore. And soon they won't care about Holly's soccer skills or Logan's stupid charity or my art. They definitely won't care about our meme or Cole or what we did to him. Which is so disturbing, because it's the only thing that matters right now. It's my entire life.

As the crowd cheers and groans, Meeka taps me on the shoulder, leans in, and whispers, "*I'm not buying it.*"

"Buying what?"

"It's gotta be Gus who started it, right?" Meeka says. "Who else in school could it be?"

Good question, and I don't have an answer. Could it be Gus? Was Gus pretending to be Cole? Posting on the Cavalry as the Dank Lord of Memes? It's possible. But if he goes by Emperor Augustus online, then why would he be responding to his own post? Doesn't make sense.

It's a lot more likely that he was checking out his old friend's site and stumbled on the pic. The post said *Meme This Shit*, so he memed that shit. Then shared it in school. Exactly like he confessed to.

"Gus is harmless," I tell Meeka, because I know that's the truth. "I think we gotta look beyond school. Like, what about Cole's online friends? Social media, forums, shit like that?"

I say it because now I'm wondering how many other people have access to the Cavalry. Swamp-ass gamers Cole met playing MMORPGs or some shit.

"He didn't have any online friends," Meeka says, and she says it like she's sure of it.

"Really?"

"He was a troll. Trolls don't exist to make friends," she says, and then jumps from her chair and cheers as Holly dribbles the ball down the sideline and passes it to Krystal in front of the goal. Krystal gets stuffed by the goalie.

"Awwww!" go all the parents. They're so mesmerized by the game that we could be talking about blowing up the Capitol dome and they wouldn't be paying attention to a word we're saying. At least I hope not.

Meeka sits back down and says, "What did you like about him?"

"Who?"

"You know . . . *Our Old Friend.*"

Jesus. What a question.

"Is that something you really care about now?" I ask.

She shrugs.

Come to think of it, it's not exactly a bad question. Your friends can become your enemies in a heartbeat, and then you forget why they were your friends in the first place. It forces me to think about my history with Cole.

I always sort of knew Cole, but I only started hanging out

with him sophomore year. He was giving away some old wires and scrap wood on Front Porch Forum and I took it all. When we were loading up Dad's truck, the two of us got talking about movies for some reason. Next thing I knew, we were in his trailer watching this Liam Neeson movie where he's fighting wolves, and Cole's mom was by the stove dancing to old punk songs and making us home fries. She was letting us drink PBR tall boys and laughing as we yelled and swore at the movie. It was nothing like my house, and it wasn't like anyone else's house either. The Westons weren't pretending to be anyone other than who they were, and they didn't seem to give a shit about who I was.

That's always been my problem. I don't fit with the rich kids or the poor kids and there aren't many people around here who live in the middle. I don't know, maybe that's not true, but it feels like it is. Feels like everyone has always judged me, except for the Westons.

But things changed.

After he lost his mom, Cole changed. His obsession with Meeka gave way to other obsessions. That Cavalry bullshit and who knows what else. Dark thoughts and impulses. I know people get all broken apart when they lose someone, but most don't become dangerous. Cole wasn't like that before, and that's why doing what we did was easier for me than it was for Holly, Meeka, and Logan. They didn't realize how far off the rails he'd gone. But I knew there was no getting him back. I loved who he was, and that's why I hated what he had become.

"He was a good kid," I tell Meeka over the crowd. "Until he wasn't."

"Yeah," Meeka says, and then she puts a hand over her mouth. There's a tear in her eye. Two tears.

She leans into me and all of a sudden I'm whispering, *"It'll be okay, it'll be okay."*

That's when the whistle blows. That's the game. The parents rush the field to hug their kids. I want to get going, but I don't know where to get going to. Meeka has me feeling so many things right now.

"I'm treating Holly to dinner after this," she says, and she sniffles and forces a smile. "The Little Kitchen. For a farm-to-table feast. You should come. We should talk."

"You should drive me home," I tell her.

Her face twists, like she's tasting something sour. "Oh. That makes me so sad."

Here we are again. I don't know if I can turn her down, even if I wanted to. Is it her mouth? The way it seems to be holding back secret words? It's like she's daring me to do something without even saying it. And it's always something I suddenly realize I actually want to do. I throw up my hands in defeat.

"They better have deep-fried things, because I'm not eating quinoa or whatever," I say. The Little Kitchen has been around for a while, but I've never been there. Meeka likes it, so I can guess what they serve. Every time I've eaten at her house it's all quinoa, or farro, or one of these other "healthy" grains that people stopped eating back in the dark ages when they realized rice and bread taste a shit ton better.

"It'll be delicious," she says. "Guaranteed."

I don't bother calling her out on that bit of BS because I'm committed now. And when I'm committed to something, I don't back out.

HOLLY

THE DRINKS COME OUT: seltzer for me, kombucha for Meeka, and Boylan Red Birch Beer for Grayson. We're in a booth in the corner. The waitress has already taken our order, but she lingers a bit, making small talk. "You guys have a big night planned?" and other similar questions that go right through me. We're polite, or I am, even though we all want her to move along. I think she's being so friendly because her younger sister is someone in our class. I can't remember who, and I don't care.

When the waitress finally returns to the kitchen, Meeka raises a glass. Actually, a mason jar with a little handle. It's that kind of place.

"To the champion. Long may she reign."

I don't know about that. Maybe my record will last. As for me, I'm not sure I ever want to play again. Will I even be allowed? Do prisons have soccer teams?

Meeka starts clinking her jar against my jar and Grayson's jar and I can't help but think about who's missing here. Logan. The kid loves a toast. If we get through this ordeal, he'll be the guy who's always raising a glass at weddings and saying something sappy. Making people cry or cringe.

If we get through this ordeal. That's a big "if." I texted Logan, told him to meet us here, but haven't heard a thing back. And that worries me. He's been more careless than ever. I'm not sure what other mistakes he's capable of.

"We are all so very, very proud of you, babe," Meeka says after she sips her drink. "You surprise us every day."

"*Thank you*," I say softly as my hair falls over my face. I suppose it looks like I'm being coy, but really, I'm super nervous. A few more goals to add to my total did nothing to relieve the feeling that I have ceded all my control. To a person named Thedlom, whatever the heck that means. I haven't heard back since the WAIT FOR IT meme. Which means my only option is to . . . wait for it.

Grayson slams down his jar on the distressed wood table and says, "Are we really fucking doing this?"

Meeka pulls back, lip curled, as if Grayson spit on the silverware. "Doing what? Celebrating our friend?"

"Holly deserves to be celebrated," Grayson says, and then he waves his hands around. "I'm talking about *this*. Acting normal."

"Isn't that how we should be acting?" Meeka says. "Nothing has happened yet. We should act like nothing has happened, right?"

I check the room. The Little Kitchen is pretty packed for a Tuesday night, and plenty loud. I try to focus on the conversation at the closest table. I can't make it out, and they definitely aren't whispering. Logic tells me nobody can possibly eavesdrop on us. Still, I try to keep my voice low and calm.

"But, Meeka, things *have* happened," I say. "And we need to discuss those things."

"Oh, I'm all about discussing," Grayson says.

"Without Logan?" I ask.

"I'm fine with him not being here," Grayson says.

Meeka leans forward and whispers, "*He wasn't even in school today. Not AP English. Not art.*"

"Seriously?" I ask.

She nods.

"That's not good," Grayson says.

"To say the least," Meeka adds.

"Do you think he's . . . ?" Grayson doesn't need to finish his thought.

"I don't think he would turn us in," I say, because I don't. At least not yet. He's got too much to lose.

"But if he's out there playing boy detective right now, I'm not super confident he won't fuck things up," Meeka says.

A truer statement has never been spoken. And I add my own truth to the mix. "Good thing *I've* been playing girl detective, then. Because I have a lead."

I'm not even going to ask what the others have been up to, because I'm sure I've made far more headway on this than anyone. Like group projects in class. One kid usually carries the load. And that kid is always me.

Meeka scoots closer and says, "Okay, spill."

"I plan to," I say. "But first, some ground rules."

"Oh great, exactly what we need—rules," Grayson says, because why would Grayson ever want to follow any rules?

I ignore him. I hold up a single finger and say, "First rule. We don't use his name out loud in here. In case someone is listening. We should never say that name in public again. We should call him something else."

"Logan?" Grayson asks.

"No," I say, pointing down. "The other guy."

"I've been calling him Our Old Friend," Meeka says.

"Works for me," I say.

And Grayson says, "Whatever."

I hold up two fingers. "Okay, second rule. Whatever steps we take next must be agreed upon. Logan is off doing whatever he's doing. And that's not good. We need unity."

Meeka nods. And Grayson says, "That's more than fine by me. I'm all about unity."

I hold up three fingers. "Third and final rule. Don't focus on how or where I got my information. Be thankful that I have it. Then help me figure out what to do with it."

By the sour looks they're giving me, I can tell this rule doesn't sit well. Tough luck. I'm not telling them every little detail of what I've done because they don't need to know every little detail. They only need to know the result.

"Just spill, Holly," Meeka says. "Spill."

And I respond with a single word. "Thedlom."

They don't say anything. The chatter of the crowd—like ravens cawing or raccoons snickering, like things that pick dead bodies apart—it fills their silence. Neither Grayson nor Meeka knows what I'm talking about. It's probably best to explain.

"It's a name," I tell them. "Of some meme-obsessed creeper. And I'm hoping one of you might know who he is. Do you know someone who goes by the name Thedlom? Like online. Thedlom?"

Grayson's eyes narrow in recognition. "Wait a second. *Spell it.*"

"T-H-E-D-L-O-M," I say.

And he says, "Holy fucking shit."

It's at that very moment the waitress places plates of food in front of us. "Now that's the attitude I like to hear!" she says. "Our apps are amazing, right?"

We all shut up.

LOGAN

THEY HAVE THEIR APPETIZERS.

The waitress is laying it all out. Crispy roasted Brussels sprouts and butternut squash and ricotta bruschetta. I'm betting that's what it is. It's a seasonal menu and those are seasonal staples here. I know because my family comes to the Little Kitchen a lot. We appreciate their sustainability.

I doubt the others can see me. It's bright in the restaurant, and it's dark out here in the parking lot, where snow is starting to fall, and fat, fluffy, beautiful flakes are collecting on my shoulders as I lean against my car. I'm peering back and forth at my friends and my phone, where there's a version of our meme from Paul Baker's Tumblr on the screen.

The meme says: DUCK, DUCK, DUCK . . . GOOSE.

I faked sick today and hid out at home. No napping, but maybe that's for the best. I'm thinking more intuitively and creatively. There's a buzz in my head and it's taking ideas and turning them over and upside down and inside out and showing them to me in ways I might never have seen them if I were well rested.

Maybe it's another form of hallucination, like lucid dreaming. Whatever it is, it's helped me piece together a theory. More than a theory, actually. A truth. Derived from looking at version upon version of the meme, watching videos of the Boyatee, and being open to a universe of possibilities. What I discovered is this:

The DUCK, DUCK, DUCK . . . GOOSE version of the meme is the most important one.

Why?

Because that version was posted by someone who goes by the name of Emperor Augustus.

And who is Emperor Augustus?

Well, he's the meme-loving, hack-clubbing classics expert of our school, Augustus "Gus" Drummond.

And who is Gus Drummond?

He's Cole's old friend, of course. But he's also Cole's old enemy. Because Gus Drummond is the Boyatee.

It's not as crazy as it sounds, and I have the evidence to make the case. Starting with . . .

1. **The Boyatee video:** The eyes of the Boyatee are Gus's eyes, and your eyes are always your eyes. Even with colored contacts, you can't hide that. I never noticed they were the same eyes because I'd only seen the video from afar, in the background, at Cole's trailer. I never truly *looked* at it. Until today, and when I did, I saw Gus. A younger Gus, a chubbier Gus, a balder Gus, but Gus no less. The exact same eyes. Which brings us to . . .

2. **The Florida connection:** According to Kameela Stokes's email, the Boyatee goes to Plainview High with us. And according to Kameela Stokes's article, the Boyatee lived in Florida, but left the state after his parents got a divorce. This describes Gus exactly. He moved to Vermont in sixth grade, with his mom and sister. No dad in the house. Once upon a time, I might've even known that Gus came from

Florida, but have since forgotten it. After all, that was ages ago. It doesn't matter what I knew then, because this is what I know now. I searched *Augustus Drummond Florida* and I found out that his father, Augustus Drummond Sr., lives in Kissimmee. That's basically Disney World, where the Boyatee met Kameela Stokes. So now it's time to map . . .

3. **The evolution:** Let's assume Gus made the video in fourth grade, when he was nine or ten. Then he lost some weight, grew out his hair, and ended up in Vermont two years later. Sixth grade, when I first met him. Maybe he still looked a bit like the Boyatee then, but no one would've noticed. It would be another three years until the Boyatee video went viral. Freshman year, when Gus and Cole were best friends, and a lot of our class had made it safely over the puberty hump. The boy in the video and the teen hanging out in Cole's trailer would have been different species by that point. Therefore no one would make that connection, except maybe . . .

4. **Cole:** He was Gus's best friend. And he must have found the video. Or maybe Gus shared it with him. This also doesn't matter. Cole must've betrayed his best friend, that's the important point. I'm guessing he put the video on YouTube, Reddit, 4chan, everywhere he could think of. "Check out this stupid Boyatee," he said, and it went viral. People ran with it, created their own versions, and that destroyed Gus's well-fought and well-earned self-esteem, not to mention his friendship with Cole, so Gus wanted . . .

5. **Revenge:** The flavor of the month, the year, and the century. But revenge takes time. A dish best served cold, right? Right? Right? So Gus joined the hack club and spent years learning some hacking skills. Esther even told me he was one of the best hackers in school. Talk about dedication! He got so good that he eventually hacked Cole's computer, his little Heart thing, which maybe he planned to infect with a virus, or steal from, or, I don't know, I'm not a genius at such treachery. Whatever his plans were, they changed as soon as he found my pics and videos in the Heart, the moment he watched our confession. And so what did Gus do? He took a screen cap of the video and created a meme: DUCK, DUCK, DUCK . . . GOOSE. He shared it at school and his version got lost in the sea of other versions and it drove us out of our minds and that . . . that . . . that brings us to now. And now is when someone like Holly would shout her . . .

6. **Objections:** "No, Logan, no! You're wrong, wrong, wrong! Why would Gus create the meme? How is the meme revenge against Cole? Cole is dead." It seems like a good point, but it actually proves why I'm right, right, right. Because yes, Cole is dead. We did that! We saved Meeka, and ourselves, maybe dozens of people, and we gave the Boyatee the revenge he so desperately wanted, so what does he give us in return? He gives us . . . he gives us . . . he gives us . . .

7. **Duck, duck, goose:** Yes! A children's game. Of course! Because what's the point of that game? To have your friends chase you as you try to join their circle. That's what we've

been doing—we've been chasing Gus!—and he wants to sit down and join our circle. The meme is his sly way of saying: "I know what you did, I like what you did, I won't get you in trouble for what you did, I just want to be a part of it."

Wow. I'm out of breath just thinking about it. And as I stand here with the snow falling and my head buzzing, and as I watch my friends talk and eat their appetizers, I am ready to present my evidence. I am prepared to pull Cole's Heart out of my backpack, lay it on the table, and explain, "We've got all we need now. And everything will be fine. We've got our goose. Thanks to me."

Except I know everything won't be fine, because I know what type of people my friends really are.

GRAYSON

THAT CHATTY-ASS WAITRESS is finally far enough away that we can get back to business. I push the plate of un-appetizers away from me and say, "So . . . ?"

"So," Holly says. "Enlighten us, Gray. Who do you think Thedlom is?"

"The Dank Lord of Memes," I say.

And the moment the words leave my mouth, Meeka cries, "Oh, for fuck's sake."

"Wait, what are you talking about?" Holly says, because her ass isn't as clever as she thinks she is.

"*The* D-L-O-M," I say. "The Dank Lord of Memes. It's sort of a . . . what-do-you-call-it?"

"Acronym," Meeka says. "And I don't like where this is going."

"Where's it going?" Holly asks.

"It was Our Old Friend's avatar," Meeka says. "His online handle."

"And what he used when he posted to the Cavalry," I say.

"Oh, for fuck's sake," Meeka says again.

"What's the Cavalry?" Holly asks.

"Nothing anymore," I say, and I hold up my phone, show them the page and the 404 Error.

"Come on, Gray," Meeka says. "You weren't reading that trash, were you?"

"You know the Cavalry?" I ask.

"Of it," she says, and she takes a bite of Brussels sprouts. "I mean, it's whiny red-pill, Pepe the Frog, alt-right bullshit. Why would I give that the time of day?"

"But how do you know about it?" I ask. "Because of him?"

Meeka shrugs. "Sure. I kind of blocked it out. Tried to ignore that that whole part of his life even existed."

Holly stares at my phone and says, "So this Cavalry site is . . . ? Was . . . ?"

"Nothing special," Meeka says. "There are hundreds of sites like it. Or thousands. Tens of thousands, probably."

"No," I say. "This one is special. Because this is where it started. That's where the pic first went up. Posted by . . ."

"The Dank Lord of Memes?" Holly asks.

"Bingo," I say. "But the site's been dead since yesterday. Like someone erased it."

"You said the Dank Lord of Memes was Our Old Friend, though," Holly says. "And he posted the pic? That doesn't make any sense."

"You're tellin' me," I say.

Then Holly leans forward, and her hair falls in front of her face as she whispers, "*Especially since he's been in contact with me.*"

Her tone makes it sound like it's the worst thing she's ever done. Okay, maybe second-worst.

"*Wait, what*?" Meeka whispers back, but it's a loud whisper, so it's barely a whisper at all. "What did he say?"

"Not much, but now I'm worried about something," Holly says.

Meeka lays the sarcasm on thick. "Oh, so now you're worried?"

Holly doesn't bother with sarcasm. She's totally serious when she leans forward and says, "Grayson. Tell us everything you know about this Dank Lord of Memes. Because now I'm worried that we might not have done . . . what we think we did."

LOGAN

ANOTHER DEAD BODY. That's the future we're looking at. If I go in there and tell them about Gus, what will happen? At first, they'll probably laugh at me. But then, when they see the evidence is undeniable, they'll formulate a plan—Holly scheming, Grayson following orders, and Meeka sitting back and twiddling her thumbs.

Their plan can only end one way. With Gus buried somewhere too.

It's written all over them, in how they talk and move. I can even see that right now from a distance. Grayson is gesturing wildly, undoubtedly telling some tall tale of his manliness. Holly has her fingers locked together and she's watching him intently, sizing him up, waiting to pounce. Meeka seems embarrassed. She's picking at her food and looking around the restaurant. I don't blame her.

If I go in there, they'll take the Heart from me, and they'll go after Gus. That's the type of people they are. With Cole, it was justified, so I helped. But going after Gus is not about the greater good. It's selfish.

I need to warn him. I should call him, or text him, or . . . no. He probably won't respond because he's smarter than that. He doesn't want to leave a digital trail either. He hasn't turned us in and that means he could be implicated too. An accessory after the fact is what they call it. I learned that in law class last year.

The best plan is to go to his house. I know where it is. I'll go there, we'll chat, and we'll figure this out. I'll save another life. As for the others, they'll—

Oh crap.

HOLLY

"THAT'S LOGAN," I say, standing up.

"Where?" Grayson asks, standing too.

I point to the back window and the parking lot, where a shadowy figure is tossing a backpack into a Hyundai and climbing into the driver's seat. There's a thin layer of snow on the windows and he doesn't even bother to brush it off. He starts the engine, engages the wipers, and drives away.

"Logan was here?" Meeka asks.

"And Logan left," I say as I watch his car disappear down the road.

I wonder what scared him off. I also have to wonder what the hell Grayson was thinking. He's just finished telling us a gut-churning tale about cornering Gus Drummond in the shop and threatening him with a table saw. Absolutely ridiculous. I'm surprised SWAT teams didn't kick down our doors last night after such foolishness.

Silver lining: That stupid encounter led him to the Cavalry and to the posts by the Dank Lord of Memes. Those posts are gone now, which is more than a little suspicious. But their very existence confirms what I've been thinking.

I sit back down and motion for Grayson to sit too. "Let's forget about Logan for a second and focus on you. You don't think Gus is behind this, do you?"

"I do not," Grayson says as he takes his seat.

"Um, I do," Meeka says, raising her hand. It's an accusation she was pushing throughout Grayson's story and he wasn't buying it. Neither was I, at least not her version, where Gus is a mastermind who's cooked up some elaborate scheme to mess with our heads. He's got more of a henchman vibe.

"Let's forget about Gus for a second too," I say. "Because I have a question for Grayson."

"Shoot."

"Did you check for a pulse?"

Grayson's right eyebrow twitches, almost imperceptibly, but I notice. He's worried.

"Check for a pulse on . . . ?"

"You put your hand in front of his nose," I say. "I saw it. That's the only way you checked to see if he was . . . still with us. But people can hold their breath, you know? For at least a minute."

Instead of looking offended, Grayson looks worried. And his response—"What are you saying?"—isn't laden with swears, which means he's not being defensive. He realizes I'm right. And I keep on being right.

"There was a green tarp in his trailer. Like the one we used. It was folded up under a camp chair. Logan saw it. I noticed that you saw it too," I say to Meeka.

"Yeah, so?" Meeka says. "He had a tarp. Lots of people have those tarps. So what?"

"The Thule box," I go on. "It's like six hundred liters. There would be enough air in there to breathe for at least a few hours."

Now it's Meeka who stands up. "This is crazy. You're not suggesting . . . ?"

Then I'm back on my feet again. "If someone brought some heavy equipment out there, they could've dug up that box in ten minutes."

Grayson remains seated. "Wait . . . so you're actually saying . . . ?"

"She's being insane," Meeka tells him. "How would someone know where to dig him up?"

Grayson puts his head in his hands and mutters, "Oh shit. His phone."

"What do you mean?" I ask.

"We were so focused on our phones that we didn't take *his* phone," he says.

News to me. Jesus. Jesus! "We buried him with his phone?"

Grayson nods. "Wasn't in the stuff I burned. Never saw you or Logan take it from him."

"Perfect plan, huh?" Meeka says.

My instinct is to start pacing, because that's what I do when I'm figuring things out. But we're drawing enough attention to ourselves as it is. I put my hands on the table to hold myself in place and calmly say, "Okay, so here's what happened. Our Old Friend figured out our plan when he saw something on Logan's stupid GOTCHYA account. He faked drinking the whiskey, or swapped it out with something that'd make him puke. Fooled us, in other words. He loosened the tarp while he was in the Thule. And when he was underground, he called someone. Or maybe that person did the 'Find My iPhone' thing, then came and dug him up."

"So who's the digger?" Grayson asks.

"Well, Logan told me he saw something on the night we did it," I say. "I didn't believe it at the time, but now it seems plausible. He thinks he saw a kid. Crossing the road. In the woods. Near your house."

"Kids don't hang out in the woods near my house at night," Meeka says.

"True, but what about a smaller teenager who might be

mistaken for a kid?" I say. "What about Gus? I think we have to find him. Because that's where you might be on the right track, Meeka. If Our Old Friend needed help, then who better than His Old—"

Ding.

There's a notification on someone's phone that stops me mid-sentence. It's a bell like mine, so I check my phone thinking it might be Logan. Nope. Grayson doesn't check his, because his notifications don't sound like that—they're more of a chime.

When Meeka steals a glance at her phone, she flinches. Literally jumps back from it.

"What the hell's that about?" Grayson asks.

"I . . . I . . . I . . ." Meeka starts to say. But rather than listen to her explain, I grab her wrist and turn the phone so I can see it.

There's a text.

From Cole.

DID YOU STEAL MY HEART? GOOD THING I'VE GOT ANOTHER.

"We can't make any mistakes," Logan said, his hands crossed over his lap, trying to cover himself. "We might not trust the police to fix this, but we can surely trust them to investigate."

We were in the barn. On a blanket. Empty vodka bottle. A circle of naked bodies. Logan's. Grayson's. Meeka's. Mine. Hair. Nipples. Flesh, flushed.

I was the first to take my clothes off. Why? Because I was scared. Does that make sense? I was scared, so I did something else that was scary. Like when you're in pain and you pinch yourself to redirect the pain somewhere else. Or maybe it's like when you're in pain and you want others to feel the pain too. So you don't feel alone. Does that make more sense?

Our nakedness wasn't sexual. I got a glimpse at the guys before they sat down. I saw what was happening. Zilch.

"We can, and will, get away with this," I assured Logan. "We have to be smart, though."

"Shoot him, burn him, dump his ashes in the Winooski," Grayson said.

"That's a bit barbaric, don't you think?" I said.

"You do realize what we're talking about here, right?" Grayson said. His hands were strategically placed too. That's all guys need to cover up, strategically placed hands. They have it easier in terms of nudity too, don't they?

"What about drugs?" I asked. "Like an OD."

"Cole doesn't do drugs," Meeka said.

"Then we slip it into something," Logan said. "He loves his Wild Turkey, right?"

"And once it's over, we bury him," I added. "Gentle. Respectful."

"I don't give two shits about gentleness or respect," Grayson said. "Quick. Easy. Destroy all the evidence."

"I prefer the other way," I said. "It's clean. I want to keep things clean. I might be able to get something we can use. There's . . . stuff I can take from my mom's office without anyone noticing."

This was the easiest way to convince them, but it wasn't exactly the truth. The truth was that I already had some "stuff." Fentanyl. Enough to take down an elephant. I wasn't going to tell them where I got it, though. Because Cole gave it to me. After Teri died.

"Not sure of the best way to dispose of this stuff, without it contaminating the groundwater," Cole said. "And I'm not going to the cops with it. Maybe your mom has some use for it with her practice. I sure as hell don't want it around anymore."

My mom definitely didn't have any use for it, but I held on to it. In case I got injured this season. I was willing to self-medicate if it meant I wouldn't have a doctor—or my parents—telling me I couldn't go for the record.

Luckily, it never came to that.

Poetically, it came this.

We were going to kill Cole with the exact same drugs that killed his mom.

"Why do you have to burn or bury him?" Meeka asked.

"Um . . . so that no one knows," Grayson said.

"Yeah," Logan said. "No body means no investigation. People won't miss him."

"But if he ODs, then what does it matter?" Meeka asked. "This is all so stupid. Who cares if the police find him? He could be at home, like always. Slumped in front of his screens. They don't know he didn't touch the stuff. They'll think he did it to himself."

It's not a bad point, but it seems too simple. Simple usually means sloppy.

"There are too many other factors involved," I said. "It's better if they can't find a body. And burning can still leave evidence. Bone fragments in the firebox. Burial is the only option."

"Fair enough," Grayson conceded.

"Fair enough," Logan echoed.

And Meeka threw her hands up. "Fine. Then bury him on my property. At least he'll be safe there."

We discussed more details. Timing. Cleanup. Meeka stayed quiet, mostly listened. It must have been overwhelming for her.

After a while, she said, "Well, it sounds like you've got it all figured out."

Which meant it was time to go.

LOGAN

THEY'RE FOLLOWING ME. I know it.

They saw me in the parking lot and now they're after me.

I shouldn't go to Gus's house now. That'll implicate him. I should go home, pretend like nothing happened. I should check—

Crap. I didn't wipe off the back windshield and it's covered in snow. I look in the back seat for my snow brush and that's when I notice the Heart is sticking out of my overstuffed backpack. It's almost as if it's trying to crawl home to the trailer where it belongs.

I turn away from it, focus on the road. I can't pull over now. I have to keep driving.

My headlights must be covered in snow, too, because they barely cut through the dark. I love snow, but I hate the dark. I can't stand that it's getting so dark so early. It was the end of daylight saving on Sunday, which is the absolute worst. What is it, seven o'clock? It might as well be midnight. Driving in the dark always makes me feel like I'm up to no good. Add snow to that and it also feels like I'm risking my life.

The worst of my hallucinations seems to come when I'm anxious and it's dark. That thing on my bed last night wasn't real. I suspected it then and I know it now. But what about other things? Have I been hallucinating and not realizing it?

The roadkill I drove past, which looked like a deer, was it there? Or was it conjured by my tired mind? The woman on her dimly lit porch up ahead, placing jack-o'-lanterns in a Hefty bag. Is she a real person? Do I know her? Do I know that house? I've driven this route so many times, but would I notice if there was a new house along it, a new house that looked old? I'd have to assume it had always been there, right, that it's my memory that's faulty, not the part of my brain that processes reality?

As I turn onto Gregson Drive, there's an explosion of red light that shines through the film of snow on the back windshield. At first, I think it's a fire truck, but now I see blue as well, and since the fire station is only a mile or so away, I'm guessing it's an ambulance.

I pull to the side of the road, because that's what you're supposed to do, but the vehicle doesn't pass me. It eases up behind me, and I check my side mirror, and that's when I realize it's not an ambulance or a fire truck.

It's a police car.

Or is it?

I stare at the windshield and take some deep breaths. Here we go. It's not real. This is only my brain, messing with me. It's—

Tap tap tap.

There's a badge, rapping against my window, and a man looking down at me through a veil of snow. He's smiling, which is weird, and now he's motioning downward with the badge. I can't read it, but it reflects the flashing light, which should mean it's not some fake plastic novelty.

I close my eyes and shake my head because I want this vision to go away. I don't need this now. I don't—

"Window," a muffled voice says. "Engine."

He's still there when I open my eyes. And now I have to make a choice. Do I drive away? Or do I open the window and turn off the engine? If he isn't real, then what's the harm in staying? If he is real, then there's plenty of harm in leaving.

I open the window.

"Engine," he says, flashing the smile again, which is weirding me out more than anything. But maybe that's because I've never been pulled over before.

I turn off the engine and ask, "Do you need my license and registration?"

He considers this and then finally says, "Not today. I already know who you are."

Really? Because I don't recognize him. He's young for the job—twenties, probably—and good-looking, with a square jawline and dark wavy hair, like a movie version of a police officer. If we had reported Cole to the police, we might've reported him to this guy. Assuming this guy is real.

And what would this real guy have done? Cole was eighteen. He had his independence and his rights. The police officer might've told us, "Don't worry, we'll check your pal out," but then what? He would've driven to Cole's trailer? He would have asked Cole if he'd made the threats? Cole would've denied it. Even with a search warrant, the police officer wouldn't have found anything. Then the next day Cole, drunk and angry, would've waited for Meeka somewhere, pulled out a gun and—

Yeah. We ditched the idea of going to the police because you can't trust the police, ever or anywhere. And I can't trust this handsome fascist, this possible figment of my imagination, who's breathing down my neck right now, telling me he knows me.

"Well, I don't know who *you* are or what you want," I say, which is probably not the best tone to strike.

It doesn't seem to bother him. The smile stays intact as he says something way too ominous for my liking. "That's okay. I know all about you. We all do."

"You *all* do?" I ask, and I must sound terrified because I feel terrified and I look at the back seat and my backpack and the Heart.

His eyes follow mine and linger for a moment on the Heart, then turn back to me.

"Have you been drinking?"

"No, sir."

He raises his fingers to his mouth to pantomime smoking a joint.

I shake my head.

Smiles again. "Good. But do you know why I pulled you over?"

"No, sir. Was I speeding? I don't think I was speeding."

He shakes his head and says, "No, but you should really wipe the snow off your car. Visibility is bad enough out here."

"I'm sorry, I'm . . . tired."

"Working too hard?" he asks, and he puts a hand on the frame of the open window. The other hand pulls out a . . . thank God . . . a flashlight.

"It's been a long week."

"It's Tuesday," he says with a little laugh, and then drums his fingers on the door. "I'm not here to give you a ticket, Logan."

He *does* know me. He knows my name.

"Okay."

"But I do want to advise you to be careful and get some rest. Also, I want to thank you."

"Okay."

I should ask what he's thanking me for, but all I want to do is get this conversation over with and move along.

Again, his eyes move to the back seat, where they land on my backpack and the Heart. He flicks on the flashlight to get a closer look. "Is all the important stuff on that?"

I spit out an "Excuse me?" and it's way louder than I intend.

"The Strawberry," he says.

The what?

This isn't real, is it? This is my brain rebelling against my body. This is all a warped fantasy, a world of ghosts. Lack of sleep. Death all around. It's taunting me. Destroying me. I have to touch him. I need to confirm that he's not real. I reach my hand up, and—

A car passes slowly behind him. The police officer turns to check it out, giving me a view of the passenger.

It's Holly.

Oh no.

No.

Crap.

It's her, Holly. And there's Meeka too. She's driving. And Grayson in the back. I wasn't imagining it. They *were* following me. And on their faces? Pure disappointment.

The police officer watches as the BMW recedes into the swirls of snow up ahead, and I pull my hand down to my lap, where I can hold it with my other hand to hide the trembling.

Okay. I saw them and they obviously saw me and the police officer. Unless I'm hallucinating them and the trees and the snow and everything else around me, that proves he's real, doesn't it? But this conversation doesn't feel real. It feels like I should be driving away.

"Can I go now?" I ask. "You don't have a warrant, do you?"

He cracks up and I immediately wish the words could go back into my mouth.

"Kid," he says between laughs. "Don't worry so much. I was only admiring the Strawberry you got there. Rock-solid, but an expensive piece of equipment. I hope you're not wasting all those Logan's Heroes donations on a server."

He knows my name. He knows Logan's Heroes. He said "thank you" earlier.

Of course.

"You read the article in the paper, didn't you?" I ask.

He nods and says, "It's nice to see a young man focused on improving the world in tangible, achievable ways. Everyone at the station thinks so. And we don't need young men like that messing themselves up by falling asleep at the wheel on a snowy night. Get home, Logan."

"I will," I say, and I spark the ignition.

He takes his hand off the window and says, "Hold up for a sec."

He steps away from the car and circles around to the back. He uses the sleeve of his jacket to wipe the snow off the back windshield. Then he gives the bumper a tap with his flashlight.

"Keep up the good work," he says.

And I put the car in drive, and I drive, away from the police officer with snow swirling around him. Goodbye to the flashing and accusing lights. I keep my eyes on the road, on the future.

GRAYSON

THAT SON OF A BITCH.

I don't know why Logan is talking to that cop, and I don't know what he's telling him, but I can't imagine it's good for us.

"Keep driving," Holly says to Meeka. "Don't look back."

"Logan isn't stupid enough to say anything, is he?" I ask. I know the answer is *Yes, he is that stupid,* but I want someone to convince me not to trust my gut.

"I saw it," Holly says. "The Heart. In his back seat."

"You didn't?" I say.

"I did."

"This is so fucked," I say.

"None of this is making sense, none of it," Meeka says, and I watch her eyes in the rearview. How freaked is she right now? As freaked as I am?

We bailed on the restaurant a few minutes ago. Meeka slapped down a wad of cash that would more than cover the bill and tip, then we followed her to the BMW.

That text from Cole said, **DID YOU STEAL MY HEART? GOOD THING I'VE GOT ANOTHER.**

It still has us reeling. He's alive! ALIVE! That motherfucker is living and breathing. The message confirms it. We each called Cole's number, hoping he'd answer. But the calls went straight to voice mail. I figure it's because he's hoping to string us along a little more before revealing himself.

Holly wants to go to the gravesite to confirm that the Thule has been dug up. She likes to tick all the boxes and prove, as always, that she's right. Seems like a waste of time. The kid is clearly out there somewhere. I want to go to the trailer, because if he knows his shit is stolen, then that's where he probably is. But Meeka wants to go to Gus's house and talk to him, because it's all about that kid for her.

Meeka is driving, so she has the ultimate say.

I crane my neck to see what Holly is doing on her phone. She's got Twitter going.

"Why the fuck are you tweeting right now?" I ask from the back.

"I'm not tweeting," she says. "Since he won't answer his phone, I'm sending Cole a DM. If this is how he wants to play his game, I'll play. But the game is over. Police are involved now. Time to make a deal. He won't tell the police what we did, and we won't tell the police what he was planning to do. Quid pro quo. We'll all be back to square one."

Meeka cranks the wheel to turn down Garrison Street and at the same time she turns to Holly and says, "Cole is dead. Will you just accept that?"

"Dead guys don't DM," Holly says, and I watch her type the same thing over and over again into a Twitter message:

RED PILL RED PILL RED PILL . . .

"Please listen to me," Meeka says. "I don't know who you're messaging with, but it isn't Cole. The key to everything is Gus. And we have to pick him up before the police talk to him."

I wouldn't usually say this, but I'm with Holly. And here's

the reason. We checked the timestamp on the original DM that Holly got from Thedlom (aka the Dank Lord of Memes). It was sent while Gus and I were in the workshop. There's no way he's the person behind that Twitter account. Another flashing sign that Cole is very much alive. And still very dangerous.

Where I don't agree with Holly is on the visiting Gus front. She thinks it's worthwhile to talk to him, so she's okay with Meeka bringing us to his place. Someone helped Cole, and he seems to be a likely suspect. *Seems*. To her. But not to me. I was the only one in the shop with Gus and I could tell, like I can always tell, that he wasn't giving me even an ounce of bullshit. Digging someone up in the woods? Please. The kid isn't that fiendish.

But what can I do? Meeka gets what she wants. Holly gets what she takes. And once again, I'm along for the ride.

"How are we planning to get Gus to come with us?" Holly asks Meeka.

And Meeka says, "Gray is gonna convince him."

That's some bullshit.

"I'm not convincing him of anything. If you think it's so important, why don't you do it?"

"Because I'm not the one who owes the kid an apology," Meeka says. "That'll be your excuse for stopping by. Besides, he probably thinks you're too stupid to really suspect him anymore."

Low blow, considering I'm the guy who found where the meme started, and I'm the guy who's gotten us closer to the bottom of this than anyone.

"He doesn't think I'm stupid," I say. "I had that little shit cornered, and I could tell he respected my strength and my smarts."

"He was playing you," Meeka says. "So play him. Tell him

we're going to a party. To make up for what you did. See how he reacts."

"He'll turn me down," I say. "Then what?"

"Then—" Meeka starts to say.

And Holly fills in the blank. "You grab him."

"Fuck no."

"It might be our only choice," Meeka says.

"It might be *your* only choice," I tell her. "Because I'm not saying shit. I'm not doing shit. Let's just go to the trailer."

"No, we need Gus with us," Meeka says.

"We need Gus with us," Holly echoes.

I swear, if these two try to grab him, then things will get real bad real quick. But I'm not about to win this argument with words. My best option is to sit here and do nothing until I have to step in and handle shit. Bide my time.

Meeka stops the car. The snow is coming down harder, so I open my window to get a better look at where we're at. We're parked in front of the town houses on Garrison Street, at the edge of the golf course. Seems nice enough, if that's your idea of a home.

This is where Gus lives and—wouldn't you know it?—Gus is here right now. He's stepping out onto the front porch of town house number three. He has a coat and boots on and he's staring at his phone as he closes the door behind him.

Meeka taps on the horn.

BEEP!

It makes me and Holly jump, but all it makes Gus do is put his hand to his forehead like a visor. "Hello?" he calls out as he steps off the porch.

Holly opens her window, and yells, "Hey, Gus. Isn't this the best luck? You're here!"

With his hand still on his forehead, he walks slowly toward the car. "Oh . . . it's *all three of you,*" he says when he sees me. Disappointed? You bet.

"Great to see you, Gus," Holly says in her sunniest voice. It's amazing how she can turn it on so fast.

Meeka can too, and she leans over from the driver's seat and flutters her eyelids. "We were out for a ride and Grayson mentioned that you two had a bit of a misunderstanding yesterday."

"About the meme," Holly says.

"That silly, stupid meme," Meeka says with sigh.

"I'm sorry things got so confused," Holly says. "Can we make it up to you?"

The two of them are a perfect team. Both so damn charming. I can't compete, but I feel obliged to play along. Baiting him into the car is better than grabbing him, that's for sure.

"Hop on in, my man," I say, and I flash him a thumbs-up, which is something I never do. Feels false down to the core.

It isn't surprising that he doesn't bite. He waits, snow sticking on his shoulders, and then he says, "I'm . . . not so sure that's something I want to do."

"And I don't blame you," Holly says.

"Ditto," Meeka says.

"We've been working on Grayson, however," Holly says.

"Civilizing him," Meeka says.

Please. Another bunch of bullshit. But I see what they're doing, and it might even be working. Gus smiles.

"Is that true?" he asks me. "Are you civilized now?"

Having the girls on his side has boosted his confidence and I don't like being the butt of his joke, but I'm not falling into the trap of getting all worked up about it. I shrug like it's no big deal.

"All I can say is that I'm sorry. I was emotional yesterday. Took it out on you."

"But you looked at the Cavalry?" he asks me. "You saw where it all started?"

I nod.

He nods.

"I should go back," he says.

"Oh no," Meeka pleads. "But then you'll miss the party."

"What party?" he asks.

"It was Holly's last game," Meeka says. "We're having a few cocktails. Private party."

"But you're welcome to join us," Holly says. "Our way of paying you back . . . for the misunderstanding."

His eyes don't move from the girls' faces. "It's a school night," he says.

"That's what makes it *fuuuuun*," Meeka says.

I have absolutely nothing to add to this. If the girls can't convince him to sit, then I'm not about to try.

"I appreciate the invite," he says, then he points over his shoulder with his thumb. "But homework awaits."

He's lying. He's dressed like he was about to go somewhere. Not that the lie proves anything. It's the sort of lie we all tell every single day, but it's still suspicious. Where was he going?

He turns back to the house, and right when I think we've lost him, Holly jumps up, gets out of the front seat, and says, "Excuse me, Gus. I wanna switch seats with Grayson before we leave. Give the caveman a bit more leg room up front."

Again with the abuse, but I deal, follow her lead, get up and out, circle around the car to the front seat.

Right away, Gus's face changes. "You're sitting in the back?" he asks Holly.

As she slips in, she pats the seat. "Come on. Anyone who's anyone will be at the party. That includes you."

Gus looks at his house, looks at me, looks at his phone, looks down the road. Then he says, "Fuck it, right?"

The way he says "fuck it" is like he's never sworn before, but Meeka echoes him.

"Fuck it!" she says.

"Fuck it," Holly adds.

"Yeah, fuck it," I finish up.

And then, like that, Gus is in the car, in the back, with Holly.

I'm not sure where Meeka plans on taking us, but I'm making a suggestion. A place where I feel comfortable and safe. Where I can control this madness, and maybe even pull Logan back into the mix. Never thought I'd say this, but I could use him on my side.

I shield my phone with my hand as I type out a text that I don't want the girls to see. Then I tell them, "To the sugarhouse."

LOGAN

"ARE YOU EXCITED?" Dad asks me.

"Sure," I say, though I don't know what we're talking about.

"Good," he replies. "You look it."

If being absolutely terrified that you're going to unravel at any moment looks like excitement, then I must look excited. I got home a few minutes ago and I've been standing at the kitchen counter, tapping my foot on the cabinet and eyeing the driveway through the window, waiting for . . . I don't know what.

Something not good.

Because I just got a text from Grayson. It said:

The fuck? A cop? Keep quiet and get your ass to the sugarhouse and all will be forgiven—we need to talk and I need your help. Girls got Gus Drummond with us. Onto something big.

I keep looking back at the words, hoping they'll disappear. I'm surprised I haven't fainted. They must already know about Gus. But they probably don't understand, or empathize, like I do. Things have gone from really bad to entirely terrible.

Dad walked in a few seconds ago and he's all proud smiles. He's wearing his pajamas already, which he slipped on after an extra-long day at the office. Right now, he's standing next to me, mixing himself a rum and Coke.

"I can't say this enough, but I was so impressed by how you handled yourself with Senator Barnes on Saturday," he tells me as he takes a test sip. It isn't strong enough for him, so he adds another splash of rum.

I squeak out a "Thank you."

"Lots of work still to be done, right?" he says. "I have a feeling Logan's Heroes is only getting started. Speaking of. How'd your little *encounter* go?"

Wait. He doesn't mean the police officer, does he? Or . . . ?

"My . . . my . . . my . . . ?"

Dad slides his glass from hand to hand across the granite countertop—like he's playing tennis with his cocktail—and says, "With the girl. Emily?"

"Oh, you mean Esther?"

"Right, right. Old-lady name."

"It's not an old-lady name."

Dad nods. Then he walks over to the cabinet and takes down a bag of almonds. He drops a few in his hand, then slides the bag across the counter to me. He says, "My grandma's best friend was named Esther. They played canasta. Trust me, it's an old-lady name."

It's a beautiful name, for a lovely girl who broke my heart. That's what I want to tell him, but instead I grab a few almonds and say, "She's a good person."

"I'm sure she is," Dad says. "Is she the adopted one?"

I don't put the almonds in my mouth. I rattle them in my hand like loose change. "No, that's Meeka," I say. "Esther is more . . . down on her luck."

"Does she have a business that Logan's Heroes can help out?"

She should. Esther has the potential to start a tech company and make enough money to do exactly what she wants, namely leave this town and start fresh. In fact, if I gave her some of the

Logan's Heroes funds, she'd probably create a billion-dollar behemoth and become a—

That's when it hits me, a notion so absolutely invigorating.

Esther doesn't need Logan's Heroes. She's bound to find her way on her own, without my help, as she's already made abundantly clear. But what about *me*? What if *I* used the money? What if *I* got out of here? Because I'm the one who's truly suffering. And isn't that the point of Logan's Heroes? To help out people in their time of need?

I cashed out the Indiegogo over a week ago. All that money should be in the bank by now, ready to be withdrawn. All I'd have to do is take it and then . . . go.

I've got a passport. That's enough to get me into Mexico. I'll have fifty-eight thousand dollars to work with. How long would that last in Mexico? I'm guessing years. I could start a new life there. Maybe even an NGO. Or farther south, in Argentina, where people look more like me. I take Spanish. I bet I could get a fake passport in Mexico for extra cheap and then move on to Argentina. Once the authorities come looking for me, they'll never be able to find me. Because I'll be a new person.

But I'd have to go now, before it all comes completely apart. They already have Gus. There's no saving that kid. I can only save myself.

This *can* work. This *will* work.

"Esther is helping me with some IT," I tell Dad, which is essentially the truth. Then I say, "And I actually have an early morning meeting with her tomorrow," which is essentially a lie.

He points at me and makes a clicking sound with his mouth, then winks, which isn't helping my nerves right now. I keep talking.

"I should go to bed. I'll probably be gone before you leave for work."

He takes the almonds back, grabs another handful, and tosses it in his mouth. He pulls his phone out of his pajama pocket—he's never without it because he's obsessed with the fitness app that counts his steps—and sets it on the counter as he chews. He taps away at it for a few seconds, sips his drink, and taps away a few seconds more.

"What are you doing?" I ask.

He raises his drink and says, "Making a note to remember this day. Tuesday, November the Eighth, Two Thousand and Sixteen."

"Why?"

"It's the day I toasted my son," he says. "The man."

I have nothing to toast with, so I tap my knuckles against his glass. He gets a kick out of it. He smiles and sips, lowers his drink, then walks into the living room to watch TV with Mom.

"My son, the man . . ." he says, his voice trailing off.

My hand is clenched into a fist. I've been squeezing on to those almonds. I open my hand to find they've left indentations all over my palm. It looks like I have scales.

HOLLY

I WORRY ABOUT LOGAN. Worry, worry, worry. How could I not? He stole the Heart. I saw it. He had it. There in his back seat. And even though I don't know exactly what was going on with that police officer, I can guess.

It was a confession. An exchange. A deal. Maybe Logan stopped by the restaurant to check if we were still there. Then he called the police and arranged a rendezvous along the road. To turn us in. The traitor.

Good thing we left. But before long, the police will show up here at Grayson's sugarhouse. They'll see that Gus is our hostage. And then what?

Not that Gus knows he's our hostage. We haven't explained that unfortunate reality quite yet. For now, he thinks we're only hanging out, celebrating. And we're doing a pretty good job selling that reality. On the outside, everything is casual. On the inside? Another story. We have to get this solved right now, though. Of course, the others are taking their sweet time.

Meeka is poking around, examining the sugaring equipment. "You're gonna have to tell us how to make maple syrup someday. Always good to know a trade."

"What's to tell?" Grayson says. "Tap the trees right on the cusp of spring when the nights are cold and the days are mild.

Drain the sap into tanks. Get some of the water out by putting the sap in the RO machine."

"RO machine?"

"Reverse osmosis," he says, and he points to some contraption made of tubes and cylinders. "You plan on becoming competition or something?"

She snorts.

Gus is sitting on a bench near the window, and his feet don't touch the ground. He's tapping his heels against the wood behind him. He's obviously nervous, so I smile at him.

Which prompts him to smile back and ask, "Are we getting our drink on, or is everyone watchin' their carbs?"

God, he's trying so hard to sound cool and it simply isn't working. The more I watch him, the more I'm sure he's hiding something. Or someone. Namely, Cole.

Grayson reaches behind a stack of boxes and pulls out a bottle of gin. He holds it by the neck and points it at Gus.

"You first," Gus says.

"Why not?" Grayson replies, and he unscrews the top. He takes a big swig and I can see he's successfully fighting the urge to wince. When he's done, he thrusts it toward Gus again, but Meeka intercepts it. She takes an even bigger swig. And definitely winces.

She looks at me. I shake my head, because no thank you. Gin is so not my thing; it tastes like how I imagine pine tree air fresheners would taste. Besides, someone needs to keep their head on straight.

The bottle finally ends up in Gus's hands and he sips the tiniest of sips.

"Come on," Meeka says. "You can do better than that."

Gus gives me a sideways glance and says, "She's not drinking."

"*She's* going to be driving you home later," I say.

"You let her drive your fancy car?" Gus asks Meeka.

Meeka shrugs. "We're all friends here. We share. I trust her."

A creepy little smile curls up on Gus's face, and he says, "Maybe you shouldn't." Then he takes another swig, this time a bigger one. It hits him hard—his face tightens like it's in a sandstorm—and that pleases me. Because, really, what the hell was that?

"Why shouldn't she trust me, Gus?" I ask.

He gulps and breathes and says, "Because you're you."

"And what's that supposed to mean?"

He hands the bottle back to Grayson and replies, "You're a win-at-all-costs sort of person. That's a good thing."

He's damn right it's a good thing. "But you don't trust me because of that?"

He shrugs. "A lot of times I don't trust myself."

"Cheers to that," Grayson says as he takes another swig.

Meeka has made her way over to the firebox, which is what Grayson's family uses to heat the vast quantities of sap they turn into maple syrup. It's wood-fired—in other words, old-school—but that's part of their gimmick. In March, tourists will show up to watch sugaring demonstrations. The more authentic, the better. My parents still bring Oran and Carter for "Sugar on Snow" days, though I'm no longer obliged to tag along.

"Can we get this thing going?" Meeka asks. "It's chilly as fuck."

Grayson sets the bottle down and grabs a cardboard tube full of long matches. He unsheathes one and he opens the door to the firebox.

"Filled it with paper, kindling, and wood this morning, in

case I wanted to work out here tonight. This is a lot more fun, though, huh?" he says, the comment directed at Gus.

When Gus doesn't respond, Grayson sparks the match. Then he bends over, cupping the flame, before dipping it onto a knot of newspaper.

The fire bursts to life.

"I'm not stupid, you know," Gus finally says.

No one responds right away. Grayson simply shuts the door to the firebox and steps back from it. There's a glass window on the front, so we can all see it's already raging. But Grayson isn't watching the flames. He's staring at Gus.

Meeka, on the other hand, is crouching down next to the glass, warming her hands. She smells like oranges. I noticed it earlier, but in here, with the fresh air coming through the cracks in the wall, it smells even stronger. That and the smell of smoke remind me that winter is around the corner. There's also the snow, of course. Through the window I can see the flakes coming faster. I know some had been forecast, but no one thought it would stick. A couple of inches have built up already. Probably more on the way.

"We know you're not stupid, Gus," Meeka finally says. "Quite the opposite, in fact."

"So why exactly am I here?" he says. "It's not really about a party, is it? Or an apology?"

"No," Meeka admits.

"It's about that meme, right?" he asks.

"It is," she says.

And I want to get it all out there. I want to ask, *Where's Cole? Where's he's hiding? What's his plan?* But I'm also curious to hear how Gus spins things.

I once saw an interview with a documentary filmmaker. He said his subjects would reveal themselves a lot more when he *didn't* ask them questions. They gave themselves up when he gave them silence. And they felt the need to fill the silence.

So I give Gus silence.

And he fills it.

"Cole started it," he says. "He posted the picture on the Cavalry. Just like all the other pictures he posts."

"See, we don't know about any other pictures, because that site doesn't work anymore," Grayson says.

Gus nods, like he knows that already. Then he says, "Pictures of you. I figured you'd catch on at some point. Cole is always posting pictures of you on the Cavalry. A steady stream. He's hoping they'll inspire memes. This was the first one that actually worked."

"And where did he get these pictures?" Meeka asks.

Gus pauses. He surveys the room and our faces. "He steals them from Logan."

"And how do you know that?" Grayson asks.

"I helped him," Gus answers, but he doesn't sound so sheepish anymore. He sounds proud.

And things are fitting together for me. "You created GOTCHYA?"

Gus nods a big nod. "It only worked on Logan, but that's all Cole cared about. I created everything for Cole. The programs. The site. His beacons."

"Beacons?" I ask.

Instead of telling us what he means by that, Gus looks down at his phone for a moment. Then he looks around the room, as if he's expecting someone to pop out at any moment.

"Where is Cole right now?" he asks.

LOGAN

COLE IS DEAD.

Gus is the Boyatee and the Boyatee knows Cole is dead.

The police have seen the Heart.

The others have seen me talking to the police and they're going after Gus.

Everything and everyone are closing in.

But I have money. Thank god for that. Because it's time to run.

I'm sitting on my bed. I have my backpack loaded with my passport and a few days' worth of clothes. An account summary from TD Bank is on my laptop screen. The grand total is $58,481. It would be a crime to withdraw the funds and use them for my own purposes, but in the grand scheme of crimes I've already committed, it's relatively minor.

I send a text to my parents: **Early to bed, early to rise. Getting picked up by Esther before dawn to work on LH stuff. See you tomorrow at dinner.**

Two identical responses ping back: **Sleep tight. Love you.**

I try not to think about how this might be the only communication I have with them in the next few months—maybe even years if there's a lot of heat on my back. Instead, I concentrate on getting out the door. I slip the Heart into my backpack, because I can't leave it here. Then I grab my Marmot puffer and a headlamp, and I sneak from my room to the stairway, which leads directly to the garage.

I'm leaving the Hyundai here. I'm taking my fat bike. No one will notice it's gone, and it handles well in the snow. I can ride it on streets or trails. I can get to town without being seen.

I have to get some quick cash. There's a TD Bank by the library and I can take $750 out of the ATM right away. That'll help until I can withdraw the rest, hopefully tomorrow afternoon from an actual bank teller when I'm in Seattle.

There are a few Uber and Lyft drivers around here, but it's smartest to call the airport shuttle because they probably won't check my phone records right away. I'll have them pick me up at the bank, pay them in cash, and give them a fake name. There's a flight from Burlington that leaves at five a.m., connects in Chicago, and gets into Seattle around noon. I can clear out and close the account there, and then travel by bus over the Canadian border to Vancouver. My passport will be registered as entering Canada and so that's where everyone will assume I am.

But here's what I'll do. I'll ditch my phone there, and then have a cab bring me out to the woods south of Chilliwack. Google Maps shows that I can hike a few miles and sneak back over the Canadian border. I might be back in Washington before anyone even realizes I've left Vermont!

Then my next step will be to use some cash to buy a used car from a private seller. I already checked Craigslist, and northern Washington is swimming with junkers. Which is all I need. A thousand miles of transport.

I'll spend the next day traveling to the Mexican border. I've heard that the border patrol doesn't even check passports when you're crossing over that way. It's only when you're coming back into the U.S. By Thursday, while everyone is looking for me in British Columbia, I'll be on the beach in Baja, completely undetected and with enough money to buy a new identity.

And yes, I realize the plan isn't foolproof and some improvising might be required, but it's so much better than sticking around.

GRAYSON

"WE DON'T KNOW where the hell Cole is," I tell Gus. "And we don't care. When Meeka dumped his ass, so did we. You'd be wise to do the same. That kid is trouble."

I'm actually feeling pretty bad right now. Gus is all hangdog. Honestly looks like he misses Cole. He'd be the only one.

"You're saying you haven't heard from him?" Gus asks. "Because I'm worried about him."

"Are you?" Meeka says. "*Really?*"

"Well . . . yeah. He's my friend."

"He's fine," Meeka says, with more than a little bite to her voice. "In fact, I'll call him for you to confirm. How's that sound?"

This perks Gus up. His head rises and so does his voice. "You're calling Cole?"

"Yeah," Meeka says. "I'll check up on him for you."

"Good idea," Holly says.

It's a move. They're trying to get a reaction out of Gus. I bet Meeka is hoping he'll blurt out, "But Cole is dead!" And Holly is probably hoping for "But how do you know Cole is still alive?" or some shit.

It doesn't work. Because the kid is suddenly juiced. He hops down from the bench and pulls out his phone. "I can call him."

Meeka pauses. "Oh."

"I mean, you guys had a tough breakup, right?" Gus says. "That's what Grayson implied. So why don't I talk to him?"

This throws Meeka for a split second, and she turns to look at the firebox. Then she waves a hand like *whatever.* "Sure, go ahead."

Holly must be thrilled by this. I know I am. Because if Gus calls Cole, then Cole might actually pick up. No matter what Gus knows, we'll have rustled that snake out of the bushes and shown Meeka that we were right.

Gus starts to tap his phone, and it's so quiet in here that I can hear the sound of his finger on the glass from all the way across the room. I look to Holly and she's stone-faced. Meeka too. I know we're all on edge, but we all want to see how this plays out.

But before he places the call, Gus lowers the phone and says with a sigh, "Who am I kidding? I can't do this. I've been trying to get in touch with him for days. He doesn't answer. He doesn't want to talk to me anymore. He won't even respond to my meme. And if he finds out I'm hanging with all of you, he might *never* talk to me again."

"That's not true," Meeka says in a mock sympathetic tone. "He adores you. Because you've done so much for him, Gus. You told us. The programs. The sites. His beacons. It was all you. You controlled everything of Cole's, didn't you?"

Again with the beacons. I'm not sure what that means, but Meeka seems to know.

"We were a good team," Gus tells her.

The fire is really pumping now, and it's getting too hot in here, so I bend down to adjust the intake. The decrease in oxygen calms the flames, and that takes some light out of the room real quick. Shadows dance on faces. Sinister shit.

"But now it's only you, isn't it?" Meeka says to Gus. "Carrying on Cole's . . . crusade? That's what the Cavalry is, right? Memes and misogyny? LOLZ and white supremacy?"

Gus puts his hand on his chest. "I . . . I . . . I . . . well, it's my . . . that's—"

"That's why you're here, isn't it?" Meeka says. "Trying to prove you've got power over us? Rub our noses in Logan's mistake?"

"It's only a silly picture," Gus says. "I'll admit that I wanted some revenge. But I see now that—"

"Strange way to get revenge," Meeka says. "You obviously want something from us. So what is it?"

Gus takes a step toward the door and says, "I mean, I was a meme once too, you know? I know it can sting. People can be cruel. But it passes. I'm sorry I did that to you. I was selfish. My version wasn't even good. It was the others who were mean. Duck, duck, goose? That was my way of saying—"

"I'm not talking about the meme," Meeka says. "Your 'revenge' is about more than a meme. That's crystal fuckin' clear."

"I should go," Gus says, and his hand is on the doorknob.

It's strange. Holly has been pretty quiet for the last few minutes. Normally, she captains the ship. But she's been letting Meeka prod and Gus squirm. Maybe she's been waiting for the perfect moment to ask what's actually a good question.

"Why did you get in Meeka's car?" Holly says to Gus.

Gus pulls back. Not that he's offended. Surprised is more like it. "Um . . . because you invited me," he says to her, like the answer is obvious.

And Holly says, "But you told us that you're not dumb. So obviously you knew something was up. And, still, you got in the car."

It's a fair point. Why *did* he get in? Because he's a little horndog and he hoped one thing might lead to another? That's what I thought at first, but he has to know he has no chance with these girls, right? I mean, I don't even have a chance with these girls.

"Why did you get in the car?" Holly asks him again.

Gus turns away and whispers something. I can't make it out.

"What's that, now?" I ask.

"I'm desperate. And . . . lonely."

It fucking guts me the way he says it. Soft and sad. And so true. He *is* desperate. And lonely as hell. I'm remembering what he told me in the shop yesterday. He said he made the meme because he "thought it might impress some people." More specifically, he thought it might impress Cole. He thought it would bring his best friend back. From the people he believed stole that friend away. But it didn't work—his friend won't even answer his messages—and now he sees his only option is to reach out to the ones he hates. To make friends with his enemies.

Someone dug Cole up. But it wasn't this kid. This kid is too pathetic.

"Go," I say, and I point to the door.

"Me?" he asks.

"Go home," I tell him. "I'm sorry if we freaked you out. It was our mistake. Go on home."

"I'd love to, but . . . *she* sorta drove me," he says as he looks at Meeka. You can tell he's pissed at her and you can tell she's pissed at me.

She glares at me, but she speaks to Gus. "Tell us about the beacons."

Who cares about these beacons she keeps harping on? Gus doesn't seem to. He's not saying a thing.

"Come on," I tell Meeka. "Let the kid go."

"Not until we learn about the beacons," Meeka says.

"Let's go, dude," I say to Gus as I lead him to the door. "Don't sweat it. Meeka doesn't like how she looks in that meme. Isn't all shiny and ready for the gram, you know. Girls will be like that sometimes. Best not to worry about it. It'll pass. I'll give you a ride home."

Gus doesn't move. He stares at Meeka and asks, "What do you know about the beacons?"

"I know everything about Cole," she says.

Gus looks at his phone.

So I look at his phone.

What the . . .

There's a message on it.

And it's from Cole.

One word: **Here.**

And a set of coordinates, like the pin on a map.

HOLLY

"GUS?" Grayson says, like he's confused.

"I-I-I," Gus stutters.

"Gus?" Grayson says again, this time like he's got a broken heart. And he curls two fingers, ordering Gus to *give it over.*

Gus was fidgeting with his phone, but now he's pressing it against his chest and saying, "Not this time."

"Really, man?" Grayson says, his hand now clenched into a fist. "You're getting texts from Cole? Coordinates? And you're acting like you don't know what's up? Don't tell me Holly is right about you. Don't tell me you helped him get out—"

Meeka interrupts me. "Coordinates?" she asks Gus. "To what?"

"All I have to do is hit send," Gus says. "I've already dialed 911."

There are many scenarios of what might happen if the police show up. None of them end well for us. But not many end well for Gus either.

"You're not calling 911," I say.

"I definitely am," Gus says. "You're threatening me."

"We weren't threatening you," Grayson says, then he pulls a horseshoe from his pocket—really, a horseshoe?—and grips it, with the U pointing sideways, so it almost resembles a set of brass knuckles. "*Now* we're threatening you."

I don't know if Grayson will act on his threat. I'm not sure he shouldn't.

"Why did you get in the car?" I ask Gus a final time, because that's the most important question right now, and if he doesn't answer honestly, we might have to take the next step. "The desperate-and-lonely line doesn't work. What do you want from us?"

"To go home," he says, and a tear slips down his face. "Because I'm confused. And I'm scared. And I'm worried about what happened to Cole."

"What happened to Cole?" I ask.

"I don't know," Gus whimpers. "That's why I got in the car. To find out where he was. I was worried. I thought maybe he and Meeka were back together and that's why he didn't want to talk to me. I thought I might see him, and everything would be okay. And we would all be friends and—"

Grayson raises his hand and the horseshoe. His knuckles are bone white. He must be squeezing it so hard. "Stop the bullshit!" he yelps. "Where is Cole sending you, Gus? What are the coordinates?"

The fire pops and crackles. For a moment, it's the only sound in here. And suddenly I have a desire to see the fire break through the glass of the firebox and take this whole place down. Burn it all. Us along with it. Because that's what we all deserve.

But that's not what's going to happen. Because someone has to survive this mess. And that's the person who cleans up this mess. Me.

"We know what you did," I say to Gus. "And you know what we did. So we'll just have to do it better this time. To both of you."

I nod to Grayson.

Grayson raises his horseshoe.

Gus cowers.

And someone says, "Go."

But this time it's Meeka. She's flung open the door, letting in a blast of snow and cold.

"Gus, go!" she shouts.

And Gus bolts through the door. Just like that, he escapes into the night.

Shit.

Shit shit shit.

What now?

Grayson decides what now.

He punches.

He punches wood.

He punches metal.

He punches until his knuckles bleed and drip and cover that horseshoe in fresh red. But thank god he doesn't punch any of us.

"We were so close!" he howls. "He would have led us to Cole! Why would you let him go now?!"

Meeka scurries into a corner to shield herself from Grayson's rage and Grayson keeps rampaging—he's smashing some of his sculptures now. Wood. Metal. Plastic. Cracking and banging and splintering and I have to get out of here. I have to stop Gus. I have to go go go. I dash for the door. I fly after him.

Outside, the snow is coming down hard, in big clumps of flakes. They hit my eyes as I chase Gus away from the sugarhouse and down the hill to Grayson's driveway. Everything blurs. I can't make out much detail, but I know I can catch the kid. There aren't many people who can outrun me. And there aren't many places he can hide.

The ground is slippery, so I should be careful. What I'd give for a pair of cleats. But I try not to focus on that. I don't slow down.

When Gus's feet hit the driveway, my mind hits a realization. I'm the one who will have to do something to him. Physically.

Restrain him? Pull him back to the sugarhouse? I'm not sure. Something.

I haven't thought this through, and I don't want to think it through. Thinking will slow me. I need to react. The time for negotiations is over.

So I chase. And I get closer. And closer.

And his head is on a swivel.

And it's all blurry and white.

And he yells something. "Stop!" or "Help!" or something.

And I don't know, I don't know, I don't know, I don't know what I'm capable of.

He's on the road now. Or next to it. In the grass.

He's faster than I thought he'd be, but I'm closing in.

The snow is slick and I'll use that to my advantage.

I slide.

And foot first, I take him down. Like he has a ball on a breakaway. Penalty box.

And he tumbles into the road, wailing out in pain.

And I'm up and I'm above him, feet planted on both sides of his shoulders.

And he's cowering and it's now or never. I have to—

Lights.

Huge.

Coming toward us on the road.

My only thoughts?

Did he hit send? Did he dial 911?

But my body doesn't care about thoughts.

I lift my foot.

LOGAN

I'M ON MY BIKE, its fat tires ripping through the snow that keeps piling up. Mom questioned the purchase—it wasn't cheap—but I'm not regretting it now. This thing is a monster, and I'm pushing it to the limit. There are a few ways I could get to town, but I don't want to be seen, so I'm taking the long cut.

Not far from here, there are mountain bike trails that lead past Huntington Farm. A private road snakes through the farm and connects to the rail trail that skirts the edge of the Malvern Loop and then bisects the rec path that leads to the parking lot of TD Bank. On a night like tonight, no one will be anywhere near those routes.

So I ride, as hard and fast as my lungs and legs and these conditions allow. And time flashes by.

I've biked these trails, and I've biked in the dark, but never at the same time. My mind can't hold on to much more than the snow and the next rock, the next root. My headlamp is on full blast. If there are any animals in my way, they'll scurry or they'll be stunned. I'm not worried about chipmunks or raccoons, deer or skunk. But it'd be just my luck to run into a bear or a moose.

Or something even scarier. The things I've been seeing in the woods—were they real? Or hallucinations? I sure don't need any more of those.

Somehow, I go a little harder. I go faster. I keep my focus

on the trail and not the surrounding woods. The moonlight is peeking through the trees and the air is swirling with snow. I'd be freezing if I weren't so worked up. My blood is pumping. It's hot. It's fire.

The straps have loosened on my backpack and aren't tight enough, so it flops and twists with every bump. But I don't want to stop to adjust it. I keep going. Pedaling. Head up, head down. On the lookout.

When I hit the roads at Huntington Farm, I get a big boost of confidence. I'm halfway there and the hardest part is over. The road is dirt, but it's wide and flat and I can speed up, even with a few of inches of snow on it.

I follow a fork in the road that leads left. I power up a hill through a patch of pear trees. I spot an old wooden sign marking the rail trail. It's been a while since I've been on this stretch, but I know it's maintained by a land trust. It should be in good shape.

It's gravel, and because of the wind and the height of the trees, there isn't quite as much snow here, so I hit it at top speed. I'm racing along as fast as I've ever gone on a fat bike, which is amazing considering how late it is, how dark it is, and how tired I should be. My headlamp stabs the black—juiced by its endless lithium battery—creating a tunnel of light. The trail is level and wide. It might as well be paved.

I make it far, and fast, and I catch a view of a sign that says the Malvern Loop parking lot is one hundred yards away. Meeka's house and property aren't very far from the lot. And it's the spot where Cole's life ended.

I guess it's fitting that I'm passing this way. One more reminder of what we did before I abandon this place.

I pedal harder, and harder, and I'm wondering if I can outrun this snow cloud. Go faster than the police, and the others, the weather . . . my life. I'm feeling so energized for the first time in more than a week and I don't think I ever need to sleep again.

My phone buzzes.

I'm tempted not to break my rhythm and look, but it could be Grayson again and maybe it's best if I make up some lie so they don't suspect I'm leaving. If it lengthens my head start, I'll take it.

I lift a hand off the grips and reach for my pocket, which makes one of the loose backpack straps start to slip off my arm. I reach back to try to grab it and—

"Crap!"

The front wheel turns and I'm—

Bam! Crrunnccch.

I hear it. I feel it!

"Oh no, oh no, oh no . . ."

In my shoulder. In my arm. Not pain . . . the feeling before pain.

Blood in my mouth. Snowy dirt in my teeth. A tree up against me.

My headlamp? Dead.

It's so black. So dark out here.

"Ohhhh . . ."

The pain comes. Searing. Biting.

I reach with my left arm to touch my right arm. I feel a bump.

Bone.

GRAYSON

MY HAND IS BLEEDING. The sugarhouse is a fucking mess. I have no idea where that came from.

Okay, that isn't true. I know exactly where that came from. There's no trusting anyone or anything in this situation. Especially Meeka. She kept pushing the Gus angle, and when we had him where we wanted him, she goes and . . . sets him free?

If she can't see how fucked up that is it's only because she's too busy staring at my hand.

I swing it behind my back, and I can hear the blood splash against the fire door and sizzle.

Szzzzz . . .

"Gray," she says. "Calm down, please. You're scaring me."

"This whole fucking situation is scaring *me* and I don't know who or what or anything to believe," I say, and now I'm crying. I can't believe it, but I can't stop. I'm blubbering.

"I've gotta go," she tells me. "I've made a terrible mistake."

She moves and I reach to grab her. Fuck. I still have that goddamn horseshoe in my hand. My eyes lock onto it. One side of the aluminum is twisted and dented from my freak-out. Bloody too. In the dim firelight, the blood is maroon, almost purple.

I must be staring at it for longer than I realize, because the sound of the door slamming shut breaks me out of a daze. Meeka is gone and I'm alone.

I don't follow her. Because what am I going to do? Try to bring her back here? Kidnap her? She might as well enjoy the freedom she has for as long as she has it. Who knows how long that will be, the way things are going.

I move to the window. No sign of Holly or Gus, but I do see Meeka climbing into her car. Headlights on and engine on and she's gone.

My sleeve is rough on my face as I wipe away the tears. I'm not sure I've ever cried this much, at least not since I was a kid. To calm down, I sit on a bench and I take in the damage I caused.

I broke a lot of shit. Some sugaring equipment, which Dad will rake me over the coals for, but mostly it's my pieces. A coyote. A raccoon. The fucking stallion. All busted to hell. I destroyed hours of work in, like, one minute. Maybe less.

There's a water jug under the bench and I pick it up and pour it over my hand and the horseshoe, washing blood onto the floor. My knuckles are more scraped than cut, but the blood is still coming. Like groundwater or oil, seeping up through the earth. I let it come.

I try to think like Cole. What's his play? Did he actually want us to see the coordinates on Gus's phone? Is he baiting us into a trap?

When we were at the trailer on Sunday, Meeka talked about all his gadgets and games. Motion detectors and all that. Maybe he's got something set up that will shoot a—

No, it's probably not that complicated. It never is. He's waiting somewhere with a weapon. It's as simple as that. We tried to kill him. We buried him! Why wouldn't he bring us somewhere quiet and do to us what we tried to do to him? Then he and Gus can celebrate. Dance on our bones. Now that's revenge.

Well, I'm not going out like that. I pour water over my hand again. I wipe those last fucking tears from my face. I grab my horseshoe and I head outside.

LOGAN

I'M BROKEN.

I'm bloody and broken and my head is ringing. I could have a concussion, but that's the least of my worries.

My arm hurts so much. I try not to look at it, at the bulge of broken bone. It hasn't pierced the skin, but it almost has. If it does, I might faint. My bike's front rim is bent. Even if I could use both my arms, I couldn't bend it back. The darkness is thick and there's no way I could ride out of here.

The only things that feel okay are my legs. I can walk. But the pain in my arm is so extreme that I can only get a few paces before I have to lean against a tree and catch my breath. Still, I can walk. That's a start.

The headlamp is smashed and I'm using its elastic as a sling. It barely works, so I'm also using my left hand to hold my right arm. Anything to fight the pain. Even gravity is killing me.

There's no one—darkness and snow, that's it. I've abandoned my original route and I'm heading for the Malvern Loop. I reach the dirt parking lot and it's empty, with no tire tracks in the snow.

There aren't many houses along this stretch. I'm guessing most people are in for the night. There might not be a car for a while. The plows will come eventually, but it's getting colder. So very cold.

I sit down with my back to a tree, the snow collecting on my legs. I rest my throbbing arm in my lap and the flakes fall on it too. Maybe they'll numb it. I need something, anything.

This is the spot where Cole died. In a puddle, with us watching. It's so serene now. No one would ever know. There are so many places in the world that must look beautiful but were sites of horrible tragedies. Obvious places like Mount Everest and the Grand Canyon, but also flower-filled fields in the Alps and quiet beaches in Mexico and—

I check my phone—the screen is smashed, but I can make out the message.

It's from Esther.

Grayson lives on Parker Hill, right? What number?

HOLLY

"STOP IT!" a voice yells, and I feel hands on my shoulders.

I also feel a rib cage on my foot.

I'm kicking him. I'm stomping and kicking the ever living shit out of Gus Drummond. I can't stop, even as the hands yank me away.

"What are you doing?" the voice asks, and now I've got a face to go with it: Esther Green's nauseatingly adorable mug.

She pulls me off Gus. I push her away. And now we're both standing in the middle of the road, in the middle of the tepid light that's cast by some busted-up and idling van.

"You don't know!" I shout. "You have no idea what I've had to do!"

She's having none of it. The disgust on her face is palpable. "Get a friggin' grip and stand back," she says, and she rushes over to tend to Gus.

He's bent double on the road, hands protecting his crotch. I don't see any blood, but I can't guarantee I didn't break any of his ribs. I don't know how many times I kicked him. One time would be more than I've ever kicked anyone on purpose. Which is surprising, considering I have two annoying little brothers.

As I watch Esther whisper "*It's going to be okay*" to Gus, I remember that they know each other. And they know each other well. They're both in hack club together, so if I think for a second that I can talk my way out of this, I'm mistaken. She will listen to him, and only him.

Which means it's time to run. I turn tail, and that's when I spot Meeka's BMW in the distance. But it's not heading our way. In other words, she's not going toward town. She's headed toward the Malvern Loop, which means she's going home. Without me.

I want to text her to ask her to pick me up and get me away from what I've done, but obviously she has no interest in me right now. Is Grayson with her? Somehow, I doubt it. He's as pissed and dangerous as I am. And she's the one who got us all riled up about Gus in the first place. Now look at us.

Now look at him.

I don't run, because I'm compelled to check on Gus. Out of sympathy? No. Out of a morbid desire to see how bad it is, how much worse I've made things for myself.

He's . . . okay. Good enough to be limping toward the van. That is, with Esther propping him up on her shoulder.

"We don't have room for another passenger," a voice says, and someone climbs out from the driver's side of the van. It's a guy with dreadlocks. A white guy.

"This is my friend," Esther tells the guy. "And he clearly needs help, Tweety."

Tweety, who looks like a Tweety—all floppy-clothed and twitchy—gives me the once-over.

"And what about Abby Wambach over here?" he says.

Esther doesn't respond, simply tosses me another look of disgust. I'd love to snap back with something cruel, about how she *wishes* she had my life. But I can't. I won't. Instead, I stand here frozen by the realization that I don't have anywhere to run to.

"Don't you move a muscle," Esther finally says to me. "I'm calling the cops, you psycho."

"The hell you are," Tweety responds as he rushes up to her. "No cops, no way. Bring the little man to the ER after the deal is done. Or else you're not making your ten percent."

If there was a *deal* presented at some point, then I'm not aware of it. But I certainly appreciate Tweety's "no cops, no way" position.

"It was an assault," Esther tells him. "We can't turn a blind eye to that."

Gus is climbing into the passenger side of the van and he hasn't said anything yet. He clearly wants to get out of here, which isn't surprising. But he isn't chiming in about the police.

"Listen, man," Tweety says, and he puts his hands on Esther's shoulders.

Esther immediately pulls away from him and says, "No, I'm asking you to listen, *man*. Gus needs our help."

"Does he?" Tweety asks. "I mean, does he really? We haven't even asked this lady what's up. Maybe this is, like, a self-defense situation."

Tweety's eyes are pleading with me to cry wolf, and maybe I should. Maybe that's the solution. Because if I cast some doubt on Gus's character, then who's going to believe him when he tells them what went on here this evening?

But no, I can't do it. Lies dig more holes, and I've got too many holes already to cover up.

"There's been . . . a misunderstanding," I say. "I made a mistake."

"Pretty big friggin' mistake," Esther says.

"Which we can talk about in a while," Tweety tells her. "After the deal is done. And check it out. Maybe it'll be done sooner rather than later."

A set of headlights approach, and for a moment I hope Meeka has turned around to come get me. But no, it's Grayson in his Jeep.

"What the hell is this?" he asks as he jumps down. He moves toward us, wincing as he pulls gloves over his hands. His face is red, and when he gets closer, I see his eyes are too. He scans the surroundings. Trying to figure this all out. Trying to find Gus.

Before anyone can say anything else, Tweety is hounding Grayson. "You must be Mr. Hobbs. I'm angling for a lil' tête-à-tête, my man."

"Excuse me?" Grayson asks.

"It's a classy way of saying we're having a sit-down," Tweety explains. "It's French."

"Oh, in that case," Grayson says with a groan. "But I don't have time to sit down. Just tell me what the hell you want from me."

"The kid gets down to bidness," Tweety says. "I like it."

Esther puts up a hand. "Let me preface things first. The only reason I came here is I promised to make an introduction. I tried to message you on Facebook, Gray, but you didn't respond. So here I am, doing as I promised. Grayson, this is Tweety."

"Tweety as in *tweet tweet* like a bird?" Grayson asks.

"Yeah, man, and this bird's got something that's gonna make your wings flap," Tweety says. "Gonna make us all fly."

Then he laughs a horrid laugh. It sounds like he has a dying rodent in his throat.

Is this, like . . . a drug deal? Is this how drug deals go? Grayson does a lot of idiotic things, but drug deals? I've never even heard him mention pot, and that's basically legal.

Esther still has her hand up. "I'd like the record to show that Tweety is talking about maple syrup."

"What else would you talk about outside a sugar shack?" Tweety says, and he points up the hill to where smoke swirls from the chimney and snow whites out the green metal roof.

"Sugarhouse," Grayson corrects him, but he's not looking at him. He's trying to get a look at Gus, whose head is poking up from the passenger side of the van. It's an old van, with manual locks. Gus pushes his lock down.

"You're trying to buy maple syrup?" I ask Tweety.

"You can pick up a gallon at the Mercantile tomorrow," Grayson tells him. "They always have our stuff. We don't sell wholesale to customers."

Tweety picks his teeth with a fingernail and says, "I'm not buying, friend. I'm selling."

Grayson's brow is as furrowed as a brow can get. A skier could catch some serious air off it. "Not sure you know how this works. We make the syrup. We don't buy it. This isn't a middleman situation."

"Why make it, when you can get it cheap?" Tweety says. "Name a price that would make it worth your while."

"So what, you, like, stole a few gallons from the grocery store and you want me to resell it for you?" Grayson asks.

Of all the things I've been a witness to in the last two weeks, I would not have guessed this. But I'm hoping Grayson throws the guy some cash so he'll look the other way about what I did.

"We've got more than a few gallons, my man," Tweety says.

"How much more?" Grayson asks.

Another laugh from Tweety, which is so, so gross. "Three

hundred. Give or take. Six fifty-five-gallon plastic barrels worth. Each mostly full."

"Wait . . . *how much?*" Grayson asks.

"Three hundie gallons of Quebecoise gold, my friend," Tweety says as he circles to the back of the van. "Clean and untraceable, all ready to get up in them flapjacks."

I can't help it. I start cracking up. Not because it's funny, but because it's so weird. And I'm so scared. My laughing, of course, pisses Esther off.

She sighs. And glares. And heads toward the van. "Final thing I have to say is this: I'm outta here. Grayson heard the pitch, and so I've fulfilled my end of the deal. But there is a kid—a friend—who needs my help. I'm giving it to him. This ridiculousness can wait for another time."

Esther climbs into the driver's side of the van to check on Gus. I move closer, trying to stay in the mirror's blind spot. I press my ear against the side of the van so I can hear what he says to her. But I can't hear anything until Tweety opens the back doors of the vehicle. That's when Gus asks Esther a question.

"Can you drive me to Cole Weston's?"

GRAYSON

THEY REALLY HAVE three hundred gallons of the shit. This Tweety guy is showing us these huge plastic barrels weighing his van down so much that the bumper is almost scraping the ground. The van is a total pile. Rust up to its roof. I'm surprised it made the trip here.

"Retail market for a gallon of syrup is about fifty bucks," Tweety says. "Three hundred times fifty is fifteen thousand dollars. It's worth even more than that if you split it up into pints. But of course you know this. Here's what you don't know. I'll let you have it all for the low, low price of six thousand. Which puts six hundred bucks in your pal Esther's pocket for her finder's fee. Everyone's happy. Easy-peasy lemon-squeezy."

I don't know all the financials of the family business, but it actually doesn't seem like a bad deal. If the syrup is 100 percent real, then we could have it in containers and ready to ship by the end of the week. Even if the stuff is stolen, and I'm betting it is, there would be no way of tracking it. Can't microchip syrup.

"Not interested," I tell him, and I slam the van doors shut. It may be a good deal, but I'm not about to stack more shit onto my life.

"Oh, come on, man," Tweety says, and he puts his hand on his chest like he's doing the Pledge of Allegiance. "I know you don't know me from Adam, but you know Esther. She can vouch. And she's making a few bucks on the deal."

Esther doesn't vouch. She stays in the van. Everyone knows her family doesn't have much cash, and a few hundred dollars would probably make a difference. While I wish I could set her up with that, this isn't the time.

"Tell you what," I say. "If you still have some in the summer, let me know. Besides, I bet you'd be able to find someone else to take it off your hands for even more than six thousand."

Tweety is swaying, hands in pockets. "Reason I came to Esther to help make an introduction is because I'd already made the rounds. No luck."

"Wish I had better news for you, but no luck here either," I say.

Tweety seems like a chill dude, so it hits me by surprise when his face gets all nasty and he raises his fists to his bony chest. "What the fuck, man?" he says. "I'm giving you the deal of a lifetime."

A fight with a burnout is the last thing I need, so I start hoofing it back to the Jeep, saying, "I plan to live a long time, so let's put a pause on the deal of my lifetime. Okay?"

Holly sidles up to me. "We have to get out of here. Now."

"Damn straight we do," I say.

Tweety is raving and barking as he follows us to the Jeep. "You're forcing my hand, friend. Esther wants to call the cops on your pal and maybe that's how it's gotta go. I'm happy to say I was the witness to an assault. Or not. Depends."

Holly really went after the kid, huh? I'm pissed, but also impressed. When I lock eyes with her, she doesn't give me any signal to show she's denying it. Opposite, in fact. Her eyes are pleading with me for help.

"So what's it gonna be, ace?" Tweety asks.

My eyes have found their way to the towel in the back of my Jeep, where the back flap is rolled down and letting in the snow. Thinking things through has gotten me in as much trouble as acting, so I'm better off acting. At least then I don't have time to second-guess myself. I grab the towel and unroll it with a yank, sending snow flying and uncovering the rifle. It clangs against the roll bars.

"Get. The fuck. Off. My. Property. That's what it's gonna be," I say, and I pick the rifle up.

The barrel is pointed to the dirt. I don't aim it, because I've never actually raised a gun at anyone. At least not a real gun. Nerf, sure. BB, probably. But with a real gun, you don't have to aim it at someone to scare them. In fact, you're stupid if you do. The mere sight of a gun is usually enough.

Proof is in the pudding. The dirtbag's hands go up and he whimpers. "Oh man, oh man, oh man . . ."

"I'm not buying your shit," I tell him. "And you're not calling anyone. You're going home. All three of you. This night never happened. Make sure the others know that."

"*Gray . . . don't shoot,*" Holly whispers.

Of course I won't shoot, but she thinks I might, so this guy must think I will.

"I was never here," Tweety says.

"Then go!" I yell.

His dreads flop against his back as he runs to the van and his legs are flying all over the place. Goofy as fuck. I'd be willing to bet the guy hasn't run in months, or years even.

"Come on," I say to Holly as I wrap the towel around the rifle and return it to the back of the Jeep. She doesn't say a word, climbs on in.

In one fluid motion, I flop into my seat, pull the key from my pocket, and jam it into the ignition. As the engine roars to life, she asks, "Where are we going?"

Then I tell her, "Where we should've gone before. Cole's trailer."

She shakes her head. "But that's where they're going."

Really? I'm not sure how she knows that, but she seems fairly certain.

"Okay, then I don't know," I say as the Jeep idles.

Then she asks, "Where did Meeka go?"

LOGAN

MOONLIGHT FALLS ON THE PARKING LOT. And Cole falls face-first into the ground.

Snow puffs in wisps, like cold white sun flares around his body. It's horror. He chokes, he cries and curses, and he's gone. He's dying again, here in this snowy lot. And I hear the same song that played the first time he died.

The dog days are over.

The dog days are done.

And I watch him die again, and again, and again. An endless loop of—

No.

Not true.

Stop it. I hate this. It's wrong.

I'm not accepting this reality.

And I can't stay here. My body is broken and so is my mind. It's tricking me. Memories infecting the here and now. And if I let it keep tricking me, I'll die in this lot too. But for real. I don't think that's an exaggeration.

Get it together, Logan. Press on. It isn't over yet. You can do this.

I pull myself to my feet. I drag myself across the Malvern Loop and into the woods. It's excruciating. Good thing I have a destination in mind. It propels me, slowly but surely, through the agony.

Meeka's house isn't far. At least not if I cut through the woods. Following the Malvern Loop will take at least three times as long. It snakes to the west, turns tightly, comes back east. But as the crow flies, it's a straight shot through the woods. Probably no more than half a mile to her house.

I can do this.

No, I can't.

Yes, I . . .

I'm moving. Oh, it hurts so much. I'm struggling to breathe. I don't know how I'm doing this. But I am. Because I have to.

If I get to Meeka's house, I should be . . . okay. Her parents are on vacation. Costa Rica, I think. Even if the house is locked, I can sneak into the barn. It has a fridge, a gas stove, a deep utility sink. Wi-Fi. Oh, that Wi-Fi.

Helpful now, though. It means if I can't get a cell signal and call a cab company, I can still get a ride. I know Uber or Lyft aren't ideal—they leave a digital trail—but they're my best options now. They can get me to the ER, which is only a few miles from the airport. I can be treated. Nurses will patch me up. Then I'll have another driver take me to the departures gate. I'll sleep on the plane. I'll get better. What other choice do I have?

None.

So I move.

I deal with the awful. I cry, I wince . . . I stay the course.

I don't know exactly how to get to Meeka's house, but I know the general direction. My phone is cracked. Bad signal. Google Maps is filled with blank patches. I have to rely on memory. It's not ideal, since I've hardly ever ventured off the trails . . . that is, except in extreme circumstances. This qualifies.

I head toward marshy patches near the creek. I grit my teeth. I trudge up a hill toward the stone wall. It's not steep, but I'm hacking and coughing and . . .

It hurts. So much.

But . . . but . . . but if I follow the stone wall, it'll take me to the gravesite. I can find my way to the house from there. Not that I want to be near the gravesite. It's just the easiest route. My whistle-stop tour of Cole's demise continues.

Look at that. Oh god. Look.

My arm keeps swelling up. I'm putting snow on it, but I don't think it helps. The broken bone is still pressing against the skin, but the swelling hides it. It's like I'm smuggling a small grapefruit in my arm. The pain is . . . it's . . .

I can't move much farther. I slide my backpack off my good shoulder and set it down. I try to breathe deep and slow. I crouch to sit and . . .

Oh no.

No.

The zipper is open.

I rifle through the backpack. I find clothes, passport, everything.

Except the Heart. It fell out somewhere. By now it's probably buried in snow.

We dug that hole.

I still marvel at the fact.

We dug a grave.

The physical act was amazing—the four of us with shovels attacking the ground. It seemed easy at first, but the deeper we got, the more we understood how difficult it was going to be. Rocks, clay, roots, all sorts of things to slow us down. It took us two nights, but we made it.

That first night, when we did most of the digging, we didn't talk much. We sang instead.

"In August, when the team was running for double sessions, I sang," Holly told us. "I made all the girls sing. They worked harder and it took their minds off the pain."

We couldn't agree on any songs until we got to one that Meeka used to sing in Girl Scouts. It was a song about swimming in a swimming hole. We modified the lyrics to be about digging.

Digging, digging, a really big hole.

When days are hot, when days are cold, a really big hole.

Shovel it, pile it up, wipe your brow too.

Don't you wish . . . you never had . . . anything else to do?

We sang it over and over again in rounds, like you do with "Row, Row, Row Your Boat." It seems tone-deaf to the situation, but you have to remember that Cole was still alive at that point. Everything was abstract.

You aren't a murderer until you murder. Then that's basically all you are.

I'm sitting at the bend in the stone wall, only a few yards from the gravesite.

I don't want to be here, but I need to rest.

It's a gorgeous night out. I should count myself lucky for living in this corner of the world.

I'm not lucky. And I can't stay here.

Sure, that's what my mind wants me to do, but my mind is wrong. It's a deceitful . . . spiteful . . . thing.

I have to keep moving, as hard as that is. I can't go back for the Heart. It's lost to me. I have to press on. But any sort of movement seems impossible.

I wince, I groan, I cry. And hyperventilate.

I close my eyes and try to picture my goal: the house, the barn, the warm safe inside, the Uber, the ER, a plane, a plan, a new life.

I keep my eyes closed.

HOLLY

O HOLY NIGHT, *the stars are brightly shining.*

It is the night of our dear Savior's birth.

The only station Grayson can get on his radio is playing Christmas music and for some reason he's keeping it on. Maybe he's trying to drown out all the awful thoughts in his head. If he's got half as many as I do, then it'll take more than some carols.

To go with the music, we have the roar of the wind. It's bad enough that Grayson drives a soft-top in the cold, but leaving the back window unrolled is madness. Grayson is used to it. No wonder he's always yelling.

"How well do you know her?" he asks me.

He's talking about Meeka, of course. And I'm not sure I like where this is heading.

"She's my best friend."

"And you'd do anything for her, right?" he asks.

Frankly, this offends me. "Haven't I already done enough for her?"

"Yeah, but what would she do for you?"

Is it a fair question? No. No, of course it isn't.

"Everything," I say, and I try to say it with as much conviction as I can muster. Which is less than I'd hoped.

"She acted so sure that Cole was dead, when it's obvious he isn't," Grayson says. "And then she put our focus squarely on

Gus. Got us all riled up, had us on the express train to beating the truth out of him . . . until what?"

I shrug.

"Until you basically admitted what we did," Grayson goes on. "Then for some reason, she let the kid go. And she ran for hills too. It's odd, isn't it?"

While I wouldn't say I "admitted what we did," I do have to own up to telling Gus we'd "have to do it better this time. To both of you." Which is vague enough on its own. But when paired with kicking the guy in the ribs, it's not exactly a declaration of innocence.

"Meeka is as confused as the rest of us are. Besides, I didn't tell Gus anything he didn't already know."

"Maybe, but something isn't sitting right with me. She hasn't exactly been helpful. Through any of this," Grayson says, and he jams the wheel left, taking a tight turn onto the Malvern Loop. Normally, I'd tell him to slow down, but we're not in slow-down mode anymore.

O hear the angels' voices.

O night divine.

We're heading toward Meeka's house now. That's become abundantly clear.

What's also clear is that Grayson's rifle, wrapped in the towel, is sticking out from the back of his Jeep. He's already waved it around once tonight. When will he do it again?

"I'll text her," I say. "No, I'll call her. And—"

Grayson stops the car. He points to the woods. "What the hell are those?"

We're at the edge of Meeka's property. And there are footprints on her property. Deep fresh footprints in the fresh snow.

This might not seem weird to most people, but it's definitely weird to us. For a number of reasons. First, it's not rifle season until next week, so we can rule out hunters. Second, the rail trail is nearby. As well as the road. Plenty of perfectly nice places to go for a stroll. There's no compelling reason to bushwhack across private property. And third, it's night. It's dark. And cold. And snowy. And of all the places to visit, this is the spot someone chooses? It's acres away from Meeka's house, about as far from it as you can get on the property. You definitely can't see it from here. Plus, the footprints are leading in a slightly different direction. Specifically, toward the grave. There are coincidences and then there's this.

"They're heading toward the spot, aren't they?" I ask.

"Appears that way."

Suddenly I know what I want to do.

"I'm getting out," I say as I grab the door handle.

And Grayson grabs my arm, exactly as I guessed he would. "You don't know whose tracks those are."

"Maybe they're Meeka's," I say.

"Too big," Grayson replies. "Besides, where's her car? She's at home. Forget the footprints and let's go talk to her. Really talk. Figure shit out."

I'm done talking and *figuring shit out*. At least with them. We could go back to Meeka's together and shout and accuse and I don't know what. Or I could take matters into my own hands. Find out who's heading to the grave.

Following some mysterious footprints into the deep, dark woods should seem scary. But it isn't to me. This is when I thrive. When it's all on the line and I only have myself to count on.

"I need to see who it is," I say.

A thrill of hope the weary world rejoices

For yonder breaks a new glorious morn

Fall on your—

He turns off the radio. "You'll be safer staying with me."

"It'll be safer for everyone if I go."

I open the door. White flakes hit the black dashboard.

"Don't," Grayson says.

I slide to the ground, my sneakers sinking into what's now more than a few inches of fresh powder. "Promise you won't do anything to her," I tell him.

But I don't wait for a response. I slam the door. Then in one quick movement that I'm fairly certain he doesn't notice, I grab the towel and the rifle from the back of the Jeep. Now that I have them, he can't do something stupid.

Cradling it against my chest, I run headlong into the woods.

The land behind Meeka's house used to be so magical to me. We were in kindergarten when we started building fairy houses deep in the woods. The two rules were that you could only use things you found in nature and you couldn't use anything that was still alive. Pinecones and twigs and stones and so on and so forth. All fair game. And since there was so much land, our canvas was huge.

Imagining a world with only fairies can get boring after a while, so we created an enemy society. The stone wall was a border between Fairy Land and Goblin Land. Fairy Land had ferns and trillium. Goblin Land was wet and rocky. Goblin houses were mostly mud and dead leaves. We'd spend hours constructing our worlds, imagining scenarios, dabbling in romance and war.

It was standard "kid stuff," but it endured. The last time I built a fairy house in those woods wasn't years ago. It was barely more than a month ago.

The leaves had started to change and Meeka and I had gone for a walk on a Sunday afternoon, along paths her parents had paid someone to cut fifteen years ago, when they first bought this land off a farmer who had no need for extra acreage of forest.

"Think of the girls who were seniors on the team last year," I told her as we climbed a small hill. "Haley. Nessa. Lauren. They all broke up with their boyfriends within a couple weeks of going to college. There's no reason to have a boyfriend after junior year."

"I know that," Meeka said. "It's just . . ."

"What?"

"It's nice, isn't it? Having someone who's always there for you?"

"I'm always there for you."

"For now," Meeka said, and she stopped by a spruce and crouched down. "Things will change with us too."

I crouched down as well, because I could see what she was doing. It was instinctual. In a spot where the roots split, I placed a piece of bark. Then I covered it with a freshly fallen pine bough to make a roof for our fairy house. Meeka was right about things changing, of course, but I wasn't going to say that. I wasn't going to say anything. I was going to build.

"I know he wasn't the one to start a life with," Meeka said as she made a walkway to the house out of small, flat stones. "I realize I never should've been with him in the first place."

"That's for sure."

"He's angry. All the time. He needs someone to calm him."

"Not you."

"I know."

"Anyone but you."

There was a white feather on the ground, and I picked it up and blew off the dirt. I stuck it in front of the fairy house like a flagpole.

"He could get better," Meeka said.

"Or he could get worse," I said.

"He's not coming back to school, you know?"

"Ever?"

"Officially dropped out. What if I never see him again?"

"What if none of us did?"

He hadn't threatened us at that point. There was no plan yet. As far as I was concerned, he was simply an overbearing creep. I didn't want him dead, but I certainly wouldn't have cared if he, and every guy like him, just up and disappeared. Poof. Gone.

We didn't say anything else for a while. Our focus was on the fairy house. It was probably the best one we had ever built. I didn't have a worry in my head. I didn't focus on anything but how great it was to have my friend, single and free, down in the dirt, there near the stone wall, making something with me.

GRAYSON

IT ISN'T WORTH chasing after her. Like I could catch Holly anyway. She's faster than most guys in school, and I'm not exactly a runner. Besides, it's so dark that as soon as she was out of the Jeep, I lost sight of her.

I drive on.

I'm not noticing any cars on the side of the road. Or any other footprints near, or on, the road. It's hard to say where those other prints came from. The rail trail? The lot where it happened?

Goddammit. It was so stupid for Holly to go out there. So fucking reckless.

But now that I'm alone I can think for a moment.

Gus and the maple syrup gangsters are headed to the trailer. Is that where the coordinates lead? Is Gus going there to conspire with Cole?

No. Because why would Gus need coordinates? He would already know where the trailer is. I think Gus is checking up on Cole, making sure he's okay. He suspected something happened, and Holly opened her big mouth and basically confirmed it. Now Gus is truly scared shitless.

He's guilty. He's innocent.

He's so fucking guilty! He's so clearly innocent!

What is wrong with me? Why do I keep flip-flopping with this kid? I mean, why can't he just show us who he truly is? Like have horns on his head and hoofed feet? Or little angel wings? Why does he have to look so . . . weak?

Because he is weak. And that's why Cole is using him. Those coordinates are a trap meant for us. But Gus didn't design the trap. He's doesn't even know about it. He's a pawn. Cole has obviously been watching us, and he knows we've been hounding Gus. So he sent the kid a text, knowing we'd read it. But I don't have the coordinates, so I'm not falling for that shit.

Something is still missing, though. If it wasn't Gus, then who dug Cole up?

Well, I think I've figured it out.

When I reach Meeka's house, the first thing I see is the tractor, parked next to the barn. And the first thing I notice about the tractor is there's a backhoe attachment on it. Perfect for digging.

You've gotta be kidding me.

The lights are on inside the house. Checking the driveway, I spot fresh tire tracks leading to Meeka's closed garage. Her parents are on vacation, so that confirms it. Meeka is home. And she's alone.

Or is she?

Now's a crucial moment. I have to figure out my strategy. Do I storm in there and fire away with accusations? *Is it you, Meeka? Did you drive out there with the tractor and dig Cole up? Did you have second thoughts about the plan? Is that what this is? Or do you just enjoy fucking with us?*

I could do that . . . but what if he's in there with her, waiting for me? I'd have to get violent, wouldn't I?

Holly made me promise not to hurt Meeka, but that's because she didn't think Meeka was capable of being so devious. *Please.* Look at what we've done so far. Each and every one of us is devious as fuck and getting more devious by the minute. And the most devious among us are the smartest ones. Case in point: Meeka. Not that I want to hurt her. I wouldn't hurt any woman. I'm just not sure what the best approach is.

I need more time to figure shit out, so I loop around the driveway. I park next to the barn, hoping she hasn't noticed me yet. I watch the house in the rearview.

Too late. I'm already spotted.

I notice her silhouette, still and framed in an upstairs window, both shoulders visible, as if she's looking out. It's flawless, but that's the thing about silhouettes. They hide so much. And for the billionth time in the last year, I wonder about another why. Why Cole?

Not why did she dig him up. I mean, why *him*?

I know the chronology. Meeka cared about Teri, and when Teri died, it was natural for her to care about Teri's broken-hearted son. But still, without sounding weepy and jealous and all *why not me*, I have to ask, out of curiosity: Why not me?

I've always done fine with girls. No virgin here, that's for sure. And I've been told I'm not bad-looking. Plus, Meeka likes me. Throughout this madness, I think the girl has trusted me even more than she trusts Holly. It would've made sense to at least hook up with me at some point, right? I'm a natural fit.

But now? Never gonna happen.

Her silhouette moves away from the window. Since I've been spotted, I figure what the hell, and I pull out my phone. I text her.

Meet me in your barn. Alone.

She texts back. **No. I'm done.**

Done with what? With your game?

????

Come to the barn.

No. Come to the house. There are things I need to tell you. I can prove Cole isn't alive. I'll show you something.

I don't want to go into the house and into a trap. The barn feels safer. It's also where this started, and so this is where we should finish it.

Come to the barn.

Her response isn't as quick this time. Her silhouette appears in the window again. She's there for a few moments. Then moves away.

Where's Holly?

In the woods, with who the hell knows. The more I think about those footprints, the more I think they have to be Cole's. Maybe he's not in the house with Meeka. Maybe he's returning to the scene of our crime. And the coordinates he sent to Gus? Maybe those are for the grave. That would get everyone's attention.

Goddammit. Why did I let Holly go out there alone?

Change of plans.

Stay put, I text to Meeka, because I can deal with her in a few minutes. I may not be Holly's biggest fan, but I'm not about to hang her out to dry.

I get out of the Jeep and jog to the barn. First thing I see when I pull the doors open is the dark shape of the Trans Am. How much is this car is worth? Twenty-five K? Fifty K? A hundred K? Knowing Meeka's dad, he wouldn't skimp on parts. And I'm no classic car expert, but I'm guessing this one's a rare model. Why else would he put so much time into it?

I flip on the lights, which hang from the ceiling by braided cords. The whole place is yellow now, like there's sunshine pouring through the windows. The opposite of reality. There's a ring of keys hanging from a peg on the back wall. I pull it down and look for the key that has *John Deere* etched on it. But I stop on the one for the Trans Am.

There are two types of rich people: the type who keep everything locked and secure and the type who don't give a shit if you steal from them because they can always buy more stuff. Meeka's parents are the kind who don't give a shit. Still, the man loves this car. It would break his heart if someone took it.

Now, I'd be lying if I didn't say I'm tempted to be that someone. Drive through the night without a destination in mind. *See ya later, suckas*. But that's not who I am. I don't run. This is home. I'm not even the type who'd take off for a few years and live in a city, only to come back when I'm married and ready to raise kids because I'm afraid to do it anywhere else. That's not to say I'll be here forever. But I'm never leaving only to get out. I need something to chase.

I stop for a moment to catch my breath. Ever since I smashed up the sugarhouse, my heart has been on an absolute tear, seizing and shaking, and it hasn't slowed down. I sit on the hood of the Trans Am and breathe deep.

The barn smells . . . clean. Once upon a time, I'm sure it stank of manure and hay, but it's been forever since this was a working farm. Meeka's parents have held carnivals here, though. Real-deal carnivals with bouncy houses, hayrides, and petting zoos full of animals trucked in from actual farms. They were always fully sanitized and monetized, a way to raise cash for local charities. Food banks, addiction therapy, good shit like that. Tons of these organizations would fail without the Millers.

For most of the year, the barn is basically a guesthouse. There's a fridge and a sink. A futon in the corner. There's a photo of Meeka's mom, Sara, hung on one of the knotty walls. It's one of those printed wraparound canvases. A winter shot. Sara is skiing in knee-deep powder in the backcountry. Her blond hair is fanning out from the back of her helmet and she's smiling so fucking wide.

I wonder what she'd think about how we tried to help her daughter. It'd be a safe bet to say she'd act horrified by what we did. But would she *really* be horrified? Every parent wants to protect their kids. And when they can't do it themselves, they sure as hell want someone else to, right?

Her dad would understand. Any dad would. There's a picture of him too. His name is Mason Miller and it fits. Stubble-faced. Streaks of gray in his dark hair. Always in sunglasses. I know he's a climber and ultramarathoner, but his ruggedness isn't entirely authentic. Handsome, though. I'll admit it, because all the girls think it. His picture is a summer shot. It's from the reservoir and he's smiling, wearing a T-shirt and board shorts. He's sporting sunglasses, holding a beer in one hand, and in the other, a horseshoe he's about to toss.

A horseshoe.

I reach into my pocket. My horseshoe is still there. Dented. Bloody. *Lucky?*

I give it a squeeze.

Then I search through the keys, find the John Deere one, and take it off the ring. I pocket it and hang the ring back on the peg. I flip off the lights and pull the doors shut and step back out into the snow.

No more silhouette in the window or response from Meeka on my phone. I can deal with her later. As I walk past my Jeep, I stop to look in the back. The rifle is gone.

HOLLY

I'M MOVING AS FAST I CAN, my phone in an outstretched hand casting a bouncing light on my snowy path. The towel-wrapped rifle is over my shoulder. I feel like a soldier. And I don't hate the feeling.

A text arrives. It's from Meeka. **Where are you?**

I don't answer, but it reminds me I'm glad I have the rifle. Grayson was definitely suspicious of Meeka, and I'm not sure what he's willing to do. Because I'm not even sure what I'm willing to do. And I might have to do more awful things before the night is out.

I keep moving, following the tracks.

After a few minutes, I'm in the orchard, which means it's not far to the wall. There are still a couple of wrinkled apples hanging on to the branches. They've survived the wind and frost all the way into November. I doubt they can hold on much longer. The snow will eventually bring them down. Or the freezing rain that's inevitable this time of year. That'll finish them off, leaving behind the icy fruit-shaped shells known as ghost apples.

This is the first real snow of the year, so there's no crunch of my footsteps on any icy stuff beneath. It's all soft. Feathery. Silent. I bet there are people waxing their boards and skis, getting their skins ready to earn their first turns tomorrow morning. This is what many live for: fresh powder.

Right now, I'm not among those people. My feet are freezing, and I pause to dig snow out of my sneakers. That's when I notice drops of blood. I check myself to make sure I'm not hurt. Nope. It's the person who made these prints who's hurt. They say that injured animals are the most dangerous animals. I wonder if the same is true of people.

I hold my phone in my mouth as I unwrap the rifle. I toss the towel to the side and I get a good grip on the weapon. I place the back of the stock firmly under my armpit. I raise the barrel and point it out in front of me, like I've seen people do in movies so many times before. I hold my phone against the front of the stock with my left hand. The light will follow wherever I point the barrel.

I disengage the safety. I take a deep breath. I follow the footsteps.

LOGAN

THERE ARE BOYATEES EVERYWHERE. They're identical. They're dancing in a circle in the snow, like a cult or a coven, and they're singing.

Walk like a man, talk like a man, walk like a man, my son.

It's lovely. So I'm humming along as I sit . . . my back to the stone wall, my body . . . getting covered in flakes. No, I'm not walking like *anything* anymore.

My legs are buried. My torso might be buried soon. For the moment, I feel . . . okay. I'm not sure if the pain is receding. Or if I'm numb to it.

I'm at peace, possibly?

Hypothermic, probably.

My mind isn't all gone. If it were, I might give in completely, accept this world around me as . . . real? I could live in a world like this. Or die in it.

Cole is underground, only a few feet away. I'll probably be joining him, sooner rather than later. Especially since Holly is pointing a rifle at me.

"Logan?" she says as steps out of the trees, enveloped in a globe of light cast by her phone. The barrel of the gun is like an accusing finger.

I wave my good arm. "Here to finish me off?" I ask, only half joking.

She lowers the rifle and raises the light. "Of course not. Are you okay, Logan? Did someone do this to you? Is someone else here?"

She checks the forest, head darting back and forth like she's on the soccer field. I simply check in front of me. My boyatee friends have . . . escaped into the ether.

I take as deep a breath as I can and say, "Sadly, no."

"What are you doing out here?" she asks.

"Long story. You?"

"Short story. I saw footprints and I followed."

"Don't worry. I'm not here to . . . to dig him up," I say. I cradle my arm against my chest. I doubt I'll ever have the strength to dig . . . or do anything with it again.

Holly sets down the rifle—Grayson's rifle?—in the snow. She says, "I'm not worried about that. I'm worried about you." Then she approaches me with an outstretched hand. I don't want to get up, so I don't take it.

"I'll be . . . I don't know . . . what I'll be," I say.

"Did Cole do this to you?" she asks.

I laugh. Or try to. My lungs feel empty.

Maybe Cole *did* do this to me. What if Cole's ghost knocked me down? One more gotchya before he descends to the fiery depths. Wouldn't that be something?

"Fell off my bike," I tell her, and I shake my head. "That's funny, though. Cole. Will he . . . ever . . . ever stop haunting us?"

Holly places a cold hand on my cheek. "I'm not joking. Because he's out there."

Sure. Why not? With everything that's happened so far, I'll accept that too. Zombie Cole is in the forest with us, growling and stomping . . . ready to eat our brains. In fact, he's so loud, I can hear him from a hundred yards off.

"That him?" I ask.

There's a rumbling and grinding sound in the woods. It's getting closer. Headlights too, which doesn't make much sense. Closest road is hundreds of yards away. But hey, maybe Zombie Cole can drive a zombie car . . . through these zombie woods.

Holly jumps up and she paws at the ground to find the rifle. But she placed it in the fluffy snow and now it's buried. Lost . . . like a detached ski.

The noise gets louder. Holly gets more frantic. She doesn't find the gun, but she tries to find a tree to hide behind. They're all too young and thin, so she dives behind the stone wall.

I stay put and through the swirl of flakes I watch it appear. A big green tractor. A John Deere . . . Meeka's tractor.

My muddled mind goes back to the night we did it. We held that tractor tight. We let Meeka drive us away from our greatest sin. I wish I'd never seen that tractor. I wish . . . I wish I'd never met Meeka. I'd like to warp to some alternate reality, where her parents adopted some other unfortunate kid, a person who wouldn't end up messing up the lives of good people . . . like me. Maybe even Cole would be at peace in that reality. Perhaps his mom would be alive too. I hate that I'm thinking this . . . but it's honest thinking. That's not my brain playing tricks. That's the curse of being . . . an exceedingly honest person.

I'd like to tell Meeka what I'm thinking, to . . . to . . . to get it off my chest. But I can't. Meeka isn't driving the tractor.

Grayson is. And no, Esther isn't sitting on his lap, twirling a finger through his hair. That's the one silver lining in this sky full of storm clouds. Grayson arrived alone . . . holding something in his hand.

GRAYSON

I CLING TO THE HORSESHOE. It's the only real thing I have left to hold on to. My rifle is gone. Must've fallen out of the back of the Jeep while we were hauling ass toward Meeka's. Call it karma? I don't know. It's something.

My fingers are aching and I didn't even realize it. I've been gripping this thing so damn hard. And I'm holding it up, like it's going to protect me. I feel like a fool, because what was I afraid of? It's only . . .

"Logan?" I say.

And as soon as I say it, Holly is here too. She pops up from behind the stone wall. "Oh, thank god," she says, and she rushes over to the tractor.

"Is he nearby?" I ask.

Holly shakes her head. "Just Logan."

Logan is looking beat to hell. Blood and snow all over him. "Who did that to you?" I ask him.

"Would it surprise you to hear that he did it to himself?" Holly says.

It would not.

"You okay, man?" I ask.

He shrugs, and snow slides off his shoulders into his lap, which is completely buried. He takes a breath and asks in a soft voice, "What's the . . . horseshoe for?"

Like it isn't obvious. "Luck," I say.

"We all need that, but you're supposed to . . . to . . . to hold it the other way around," Logan says, because even in his sorry state, he has to get a word in.

"I hold it however I want to hold it," I say.

"The two ends have to be . . . pointing up," Logan says, and he coughs and winces, and then smiles. "Horseshoes collect luck. Like, like, like rain. Luck falling down from the sky."

Only thing falling from the sky is snow, and it's been the opposite of lucky.

"Believe whatever you want, but it doesn't make it true," I tell Logan. I don't tell him the devil story, because I don't need another earful of his bullshit. I hold this thing the way I want. Tight.

Logan mumbles something that I don't hear and don't care to hear. And Holly takes another step closer.

"Where's Meeka?" she asks.

"The house," I say. "She's fine. For now."

"What's that thing?" Holly asks, and she cocks her chin toward the backhoe attachment on the tractor.

"You noticed it too?" I say.

"It wasn't on the tractor before," she says. "I would've remembered."

She's right. We were standing on the back of the tractor the night we buried Cole. We were all holding on to the frame. Would've been impossible to do that with a backhoe attached.

I climb down and circle around to the backhoe. I tap the bucket with my horseshoe, which knocks some snow and dirt off the teeth. I look at them closely. "There's rust," I say.

"Metal rusts," Logan tells me.

"You think I don't know that? What I'm trying to tell you is that the bucket isn't brand-new. Odds are, her family didn't buy it in the last week."

"Which means Meeka owned it when we dug," Holly says, catching on. "But she never told us. Makes you wonder."

Makes my back wonder too. It ached for days after we dug that hole. When this thing would've made easy work of it.

"You'll have to . . . to get me up to . . . to speed," Logan says. "I'm not following."

"Meeka made us dig with shovels when we could've dug with this," Holly says, and she's obviously annoyed. "Why would she do that?"

"So that after we left, she could use the backhoe to dig that son of a bitch up," I say, though I hardly need to say it. Holly knows this shit is true. She has to.

She's probably going through all the evidence in her head right now. How Meeka has never really been on board with her plan. How when it came to actually getting shit done, Meeka did next to nothing. Like when we were digging, she was constantly taking breaks, sitting on a log with her chin in her hands, watching us sing and bust our asses. We let her, because she's the smallest and weakest. And because she's Meeka. Her only job was driving the tractor. So she obviously knew what the rest of us didn't. That the goddamn thing had a backhoe attachment!

"Hold on," Logan says. "You've actually seen . . . seen Cole? Alive?"

"We haven't seen him," Holly says. "But he's been posting things. Texting. And I've been messaging with him."

Holly taps on her phone and starts to crouch down next to Logan so she can show the screen to him. But she stops midway. Springs right back up when she notices something.

"What is it?" I ask.

HOLLY

IT'S A DICK PIC.

And it's not Cole's dick. That's clear enough.

The wait is over. The guy who goes by @THEDLOM on Twitter has sent me a DM. It's been there for the last thirty minutes, but I didn't notice it. Which is understandable, given the circumstances.

The message reads *BEHOLD THE TRUTH*. Then there's a picture of a bespectacled, pasty, absolutely hairy dude. He's probably in his thirties. He's naked. And he's, well, he's holding it. And it is . . . *it*. I don't have enough experience to say whether it's big or small or weird-looking or what. It's simply . . . *it*.

At the bottom of the pic, there's a signature.

The Dirty Lova of Minneapolis

Not *the Dank Lord of Memes*. Not even close. The penis—and the body that goes with it—belongs to *the Dirty Lova of Minneapolis*. In other words, there's more than one Thedlom out there making the world an uglier place.

Jesus. It never once occurred to me that whoever was behind this Twitter profile didn't know what I was talking about. But now that I'm looking through his feed, I see that it's filled with memes, sure, but they're all filthy. And when I scroll back through our message thread, I realize that it might not seem all that threatening. It might even qualify as . . . flirty? For a pervert.

"What did you wanna . . . wanna show me?" Logan asks.

"Nothing," I say, shielding my phone.

All at once, my "Cole is alive!" argument begins to crumble. Like a wall coming down. Crash. Boom. Gone. But is it a load-bearing wall? And what about the other walls? The Cavalry and the text messages? The fact that whoever took the screenshot of the video knows what we did, but hasn't told the police yet? It still points to Cole being alive, right?

I think so. But now I don't *know* so.

We all keep fighting over who did what, and I'm starting to wonder if there are other possibilities we haven't considered yet. More logical scenarios. It's certainly conceivable, but I'm not about to throw another theory into the mix without confirming some facts.

"We should dig," I say, and I point to the backhoe. "With that."

"Hell no," Grayson responds.

I stomp over to a spot next to Logan. I'm fairly certain this is where the grave is. If someone did dig Cole up, then they also filled the grave back in. And now the ground is covered in snow. At this point, it's difficult to tell exactly what happened.

"Hear me out," I say. "I could show Logan the messages and tell him about the texts, and we could all freeze to death tossing accusations around. But if we dig, we'll have no doubts about Cole. Plus, we might even find some evidence to implicate his accomplice."

"We have all the evidence we need," Grayson says. "Meeka dug. Isn't that obvious? Now she's back in the house with Cole and they're laughing their asses off. They've made fools of us all."

I'm used to being seen as a fool. Not that I'm stupid. That's impossible, of course. But I've always been surrounded by fools. Guilt by association. Because the teams I've been on have never been better than mediocre. We haven't had a winning record since I was in eighth grade. And even then, we were barely above .500.

But there was one game. One game this September. My *best* game. We were down two to nothing. Only fifteen minutes left. We needed a comeback, something we hardly ever pulled off. Except this time. We ended up winning four to two. No overtime. No last-second goal to win it. Four to two in regulation.

And the reason we scored four goals? I took control. I didn't expect any of the other girls to handle a thing. Was I passing? Hell no. I might've even challenged some of my teammates to fifty-fifty balls. Thrown a few shoulders to get them out of my way. Who cares? Because I scored *four* goals in the final fifteen minutes and we won decisively. Didn't even need that fourth goal, but I scored it anyway.

What I'm saying is that a game can feel entirely lost, and then turn around in the most striking way possible. You simply have to separate yourself from the fools.

So how about this?

"If we dig, and what we find confirms that you're right about Meeka, then I'm through with her," I tell Grayson.

"Your friendship?" Grayson asks.

"Through in *every* way," I say. "I'm tired of speculation. We need action. No one will make a fool out of me. All I need you to do is assure me you know how to operate this thing."

Grayson stares at me. "My uncle has one."

"Good," I say. "I'll show you where to dig."

LOGAN

I HAVEN'T MOVED. For the last however many minutes, I haven't had to. Grayson has been handling that backhoe with more skill than I ever could. He's not a pro exactly, but he's been doing an admirable job. Trade school is probably the best route for him in life . . . if we're being honest. Nothing wrong with that. Manual labor is a noble path . . . for some people. Go Gray Go.

I'm having trouble keeping my eyes open. It doesn't feel like sleep. It feels . . . different. I want to close my eyes. But I'm scared to keep them closed.

It helps to watch Holly. She's been pacing around the crater Grayson has been digging. She's like a hyena. Back and forth . . . looking in . . . snarling orders. He's not always listening to her, but he's listening enough. She hasn't taken over yet.

The Thule is in there. Or so they tell me. I can't it see from here. The bucket hit it, cracked the top . . . but didn't open it. And Grayson isn't skilled enough to scoop it out. So he's digging around it. Not once have they asked if they should pause . . . take me to the hospital. Shows exactly what type of friends . . . and people . . . they really are.

"Stop!" Holly calls out with a hand up. "I think there's room now. I can probably get it open."

The box was more than gently used when we bought it. It was missing the lock. That worried us when we were driving it away from the lot. But now it's a good thing. Means they don't have to unlock it . . . or smash it open to . . . to find what's inside.

Holly slowly lowers herself into the hole until I can only see her head. Grayson turns off the tractor's engine but keeps the lights on. Then he climbs down from the tractor and stands at the edge.

It's quieter now. I can hear Holly's breathing. It's long and deep. Almost meditative. I try to copy her rhythm . . . but I can't. I'm fading.

"Anything seem weird?" Grayson asks.

"The bottom is stuck in the ground, so I can't move it," Holly says. "And the handle is jammed because there's dirt and stones where the lock should be."

"Use this to clean it out," Grayson says as he tosses her a key.

I can hear the key against the Thule. *Scrr, scrr, scrr . . .*

The sound of metal scraping plastic makes me think of . . . fingernails. I imagine being buried alive.

Horror. Awful. Nightmare.

Even with someone planning to dig you up, how do you stay calm? The lack of air. The cold. You can't even begin to . . . to sit up. Forget about trusting a person to save you. Think of the . . . the . . . of the darkness.

"Almost got it," Holly says.

There's no way we buried Cole alive. No way. No one would do that to themselves. Doesn't matter how sick in the head you are. Or whether you're determined to . . . to trick someone. You wouldn't do it.

So when Holly opens the box, she'll, she'll, she'll . . . have to look at . . . Cole. Cold. Dead. A lifeless, soulless thing. Because of . . . us.

On the night we buried him, I told her that she would get over what we did. If she hasn't gotten over it already, now would be a good time. Though I wonder if it ever really affected her . . . the way it affected me.

I close my eyes. I shouldn't . . . but I do. I wait for . . . for . . . for . . .

The hinges on the Thule box creak and . . .

"It's . . . wow."

"I fuckin' knew it."

"What are you doing?"

There are three voices talking. I recognize the first two. Holly and Grayson. The third one isn't my voice . . . I think. It's grumbly and low.

I open my eyes.

There . . . standing in front of me is . . . a creature.

That's the only way I can describe it. Not a boyatee. Those were cute. This thing is ugly. It's like some mythological beast. It has the body of a man . . . and the head of a horse.

It must be here to bury me in that hole.

GRAYSON

THE THULE IS EMPTY.

No body, no phones, no tarp, nothing. It's as empty as the day we bought it. I was already sure it would be empty, but it still surprises me. All that arguing and wondering and digging and here we are. We buried Cole. And Meeka dug him up. All the proof we need.

And there's more proof in the woods. They're full of snow, and dark, and a guy wearing a rubber horse mask. Seriously, there's this guy (at least he sounds like one) and he's standing there in one of those stupid rubber horse masks.

"Don't move," I tell him.

He doesn't. Just asks in a gruff voice, "Did you find it?"

Holly climbs out of the hole. Then she almost falls back in it when she sees the guy.

"I don't th-th-think it's buried that deep," the guy says, his gruff voice now stuttering. "It's prob-prob-probably in the wall."

He starts to walk toward Logan and I shout, "I told you not to move!"

He doesn't listen. He moves faster and becomes more frantic. He's saying, "I need it. You don't, don't, you don't need it. I do. I do."

It's like he's Gollum or some shit, and I'm thinking this is Cole. It's got to be. But what's he after? And what's with the fake voice and goofy mask? I'd assume he'd want to reveal himself and laugh his ass off. "Ta-da, suckers!"

But no, he goes straight over to the wall, and starts brushing off the snow and pulling rocks away.

"Stop him, Gray," Holly says, as if the thought hadn't occurred to me. But I don't know if he's got a weapon on him or what. Because this is Cole we're talking about. And all I know is that this spot—this spot we're at right now—it means everything to him.

This is where he and Meeka first kissed.

This is where he threatened Meeka. And us.

This is where we buried him.

This is where Meeka dug him up.

And this is where he's reaching into the stone wall and pulling out . . . a metal toolbox?

That's right. There's a hollow section in the wall, a chamber where a dirty metal toolbox was hidden. Damn. I'm impressed. It's like a book with a hole cut out in the middle of the pages so a kid can hide his weed.

Logan is closest to him and he's looking up and saying in a soft voice, "I wish you two could see . . . Mister Horse Man. He's really . . . something."

Fucking Logan. Is it terrible to wish that he was in that hole? Looks all set to go, why not roll him in? Not because he's annoying, which he is, but because he's so hypocritical. He thinks he's such a selfless, innocent soul. *Please*. He may not be violent, but he'll be hurting plenty of people for years to come. Count on it.

Right now, his glassy eyes are fixed on that toolbox, entranced by it like it's the sword in the stone. Maybe it *is* the sword in the stone. Or in this case, the gun in the stone wall. The toolbox is big enough to hold a .45, or even something bigger.

"What's in the box?" Holly asks, her voice quivering in a way I've never heard it before.

Horse head doesn't answer. He doesn't open the box, either. He wraps his arms around it, like it's a girlfriend he's trying to protect. And that's when I realize I'll never understand how Cole and Meeka's relationship worked. How a guy can treat a girl like such shit, how she can dump him, and then . . . well, I'm not about to dive into Meeka's mind. She was never like the rest of us anyway.

Holly steps toward him and he makes a growling sound to keep her back. I grip my horseshoe tight and my thoughts shift to the devil and how that story isn't actually about a blacksmith beating the devil, is it? Because the devil lives on and still gets to do his devilish things. All that the blacksmith did was protect his own. The rest of the world is fucked, right?

And as he starts running, I remember that meme, the one with the DUCK, DUCK, GOOSE. A game like that doesn't have an end, does it? Everyone runs in circles over and over again until someone says, "I'm sick of this shit."

Yeah, I'm not chasing him. He can run away, and he can try to keep torturing us, but I'm—

Bam!

A gunshot.

Shit.

He's down.

HOLLY

HE TRIPPED OVER THE RIFLE, causing it to fire. My bad. I should've put the safety back on.

We're all frozen in place for what feels like a lifetime. Until he slowly stands up.

He's not hit. None of us are. But he's patting his trembling body to make sure. Everything is intact. (The only broken one among us is Logan.)

The rifle is still hidden in the snow. The toolbox too, because the guy dropped it when he fell. The horse mask flew off his head and now sits atop the snow. Crumpled, deflated.

"Am I . . . the only one . . . who heard that?" Logan says with a wheezing breath. "Am I . . . the only one . . . who sees him? It was the Boyatee . . . all along."

The boy-a-what? Logan's body is in bad shape, but I fear his mind might be worse. Because all I see is Gus. As in GUS! The kid who keeps coming back for more.

"I'm sorry. Plea-plea-please don't shoot. Is it Meeka? Why does she keep . . . ? Is she? Is she hiding somewhere?" Gus whimpers. Whatever weird gravelly voice he was using under his mask isn't necessary now. His identity is clear.

But he clearly doesn't know he's the one who triggered the rifle. Maybe he thought he tripped on a stick and then Meeka fired a shot at him. Like she's a sniper. It's a bit extreme, but that's the last few weeks in a nutshell. Extremely extreme. And, honestly, Meeka is probably capable of it. At this point, I'm wondering if I could put anything past her.

The best thing for me to do is play along. Keep Gus afraid and in place, until we can figure out why he's here. So that's what I do.

"The butt of Meeka's rifle worked wonders on Logan, didn't it?" I say, motioning to the googly-eyed mess resting against the wall. "Just think about what one of her bullets might do to you, Gus. That was simply a warning shot. But she has you in her sights. So it's probably best for you to stay put and tell us what's in the box."

He checks his flanks. He folds his arms across his chest and brings his heels together, making his body as small as possible. He asks, "She might shoot again?"

I shrug.

Grayson looks either puzzled or pissed, but he's not paying attention to me. He's eyeing the ground near Gus. He knows that's where the shot came from. Maybe he already knew I took his rifle, or maybe he's figuring it out at this very moment. If he finds it—when he finds it—there will be hell to pay. One way or another.

As for Logan . . .

"Look at you," he says to Gus between gasping breaths. "You're . . . okay. When I heard these guys had you . . . I thought . . . I thought . . . I thought . . . they'd toss you in the firebox. Kill you . . . like we did to Cole."

For Gus, these words might as well be another gunshot. They nearly knock him over. "You did wh-wh-what to Cole?" he says, his body shuddering but staying put.

"It's all good, Boyatee," Logan says. "We got your . . . your revenge. Made the world a . . . safer place. If you have the . . . the . . . the . . . stomach for it . . . look in the hole. It's your old frenemy. Not pleasant but . . . but . . . but necessary."

Gus's eyes are so wide right now. He looks so scared, even more scared than he was in the sugarhouse. A tear slips down his face.

"Settle down, everyone, there's no one in the hole," I say, because Logan must not be able to see what Grayson and I see. Which is pure and utter emptiness.

"Sure there is," Logan responds, and he closes his eyes and smiles. "Cole's . . . in the hole. It even . . . rhymes . . . rhymes . . . rhymes . . ."

As Logan's voice fades out, Grayson's busts in. "Holly's right. Cole isn't dead, and he sure as hell isn't in that hole."

Grayson is holding the horseshoe in his hand and he's shuffling his feet through drifts of nearly knee-high snow. Clearly, he's searching for the rifle. I should probably look for it too. Grab it before he does. But I'm too focused on Gus. What is he doing here?

Gus's head slowly turns until he's facing the hole, which is illuminated by the tractor lights. When I last saw the kid, he was in that van, heading in the opposite direction from where we are now.

"I thought you went to Cole's trailer," I say to him.

He nods, but he doesn't look at me. He wipes the tear from his face and keeps his gaze locked on the hole. His voice is soft and distant, almost like he's in a trance. He says, "Cole wasn't there. And that didn't seem right. The server was gone. Stuff was rotting. Esther was worried, so she called the police. Tweety didn't like that, so he left. I asked him to bring me here."

"Esther called the cops?" Grayson says, stopping his search for a moment. "Why would she do that?"

"She didn't say anything about any of you," Gus says quickly. "It was about the smell. And the server."

"You mean Cole's Heart?" Grayson asks as he glares at Logan.

But Logan doesn't do anything. His eyes are closed. His body is slumping.

Gus, on the other hand, nods and says, "Cole called it his Heart, yeah, but it was more important than that. It was the server for the Cavalry. He had me set up a device to send texts if the server was ever disconnected. Twenty-four hours later. Distress beacons. That's how I got those coordinates. They directed me here. So if anything ever happened to the server, the Cavalry's legacy would live on."

"The Cavalry isn't just Cole, though. It's your legacy as well, isn't it?" Grayson says. "You posted on that trash site too, didn't you?"

Gus doesn't answer.

And I see another one of my "Cole is alive!" walls crumble. If the texts from Cole went out automatically twenty-four hours after the Heart was disconnected, then that means Cole wasn't actually sending them. It was a failsafe. Like a dead man's switch on a train. The conductor dies, the train stops; the server is stolen, the texts are sent. Which leads me to wonder about what other mechanisms Gus might have set up.

"How is content uploaded to the Cavalry?" I ask Gus.

He doesn't answer.

So I peer into the dark woods behind him, hold up a hand, and call out, "Meeka, if you want to take another shot, then—"

"Cole has full control of the server and the Cavalry," he blurts out. "He puts some content up manually, like the stuff I send him. The Emperor Augustus posts. But a lot of it goes up automatically. I built a system for him. Whenever something new landed in certain folders on the server, it posted to the Cavalry with the Dank Lord of Memes watermark. It was supposed to inspire memes and lead traffic back to the site. Put a bunch of content out there and hope that a small percentage of it catches on. Sort of like panning for gold. Most of it was mud. But a tiny bit was shiny."

"Is that what happened to Logan's GOTCHYA?" I ask.

Gus nods again. "His pics went into a folder. Then went online with the watermark. Like I said, 'panning for gold.' "

"And his videos?" I ask, because that's what this is all about, isn't it?

"Too big to upload automatically," Gus says. "They live on the server, but only screen caps go online. Like the thumbnails on YouTube videos."

"Jesus," I say, because *Jesus!* There goes another wall. Crumble, crumble, crumble. If the screen cap was an automatic post, then it's possible that no one else has actually seen the confession, especially if Gus didn't have access to the Heart. It's possible that he's as clueless as he's always claimed to be.

It still doesn't explain why the Thule is empty, though. Cole is still out there somewhere.

"Can I get what I came here for and go?" Gus asks, though he's not asking me, or Grayson, or Logan. He's asking the woods, where he thinks Meeka is hiding with a rifle.

Of course, she doesn't respond.

But I do. "Depends. What's in that box, Gus?"

At this point, he probably realizes he has no other choice but to tell us everything, because he sighs and says, "It's the backup for the server. It's the only one. Cole didn't trust clouds, for . . . obvious reasons. So he made a physical backup once a week and hid it. I should've guessed it was in the wall. This place is special to him."

"*Did you steal my Heart? Good thing I've got another,*" Grayson growls. He's quoting the beacon, the text that was sent to Meeka, and he's looking at Logan.

Again, Logan doesn't respond. Either he's passed out or he's ignoring Grayson. In either case, I'd be willing to bet he lost the Heart.

Lost the Heart. Boy oh boy, isn't that a perfect metaphor for everyone and everything right now? I've lost the heart too. I don't care about these people. They don't care about me. Why not let Gus have the backup to his nasty little website? What does it matter? Unless Cole came back here and replaced it in the last week, it's probably too old to have our confession on it. And even if it does, that confession doesn't mean anything. Some walls have come down, but my argument still stands. Cole is out there somewhere. Probably conspiring with my former best friend. Like Grayson has been insisting. I hate that he's right, but he is.

"Stand down, Meeka," I shout into the woods.

And relief crashes over Gus. His shoulders fall. He puts a hand on his chest.

"Wait a sec," Grayson says as he sweeps his foot through the snow again. "I don't think we're done here."

"I think we are," I say. "Take your precious little box, Gus."

Gus pauses for a moment. Then bends over to pick up his mask. Which . . . whatever. I don't even care why he was wearing that ridiculous thing. He's a weird kid. We'll leave it at that.

Gus shakes off the mask and stuffs it in the pocket of his jacket. Then he reaches back into the snow to search for the toolbox.

Ding.

Ding.

Ding.

Ding.

Logan's phone is hidden by the snow that covers his body, but messages light it up. It's like a fallen star in his lap.

He doesn't reach for it. He doesn't move at all. Neither do the other two. So I go for it.

I grab Logan's phone because I need it to be messages from Cole, telling us the game is over. No one wins. It's a tie. We can all walk away.

It's the opposite of that. The messages are from Esther Green.

I'm not sure how to tell you this.

But you were his friend so I think you should know.

Cole Weston is dead. The police found his body behind his trailer.

I'm so sorry, Logan.

As my last wall crashes down, I notice Gus's hands stop searching.

Grayson's foot stops too.

Gus bites his quivering lip.

Grayson drops his silly horseshoe.

They both found something. And I'm going to have to do something about that, aren't I? I pocket the phone.

"What is it?" Grayson asks.

I don't know if I can tell them, but they're going to find out soon enough. "They found Cole," I say. "He's . . ."

"He's what?" Gus asks.

"I don't know what Meeka did, but we're . . . we're—"

I can't finish my thought because, suddenly, someone is laughing. Loudly.

It's Logan. His eyes aren't open, but he's awake. And he's laughing and coughing and sounding like he's completely lost it.

"We're fucked, aren't we?" he says. "Fucked, fucked, fucked . . . Gus. Get it? Get it?"

We stare at him.

And he keeps laughing and laughing and laughing.

MEEKA

NO ONE CAN SPEAK FOR ME.

Not Logan. Not Grayson. Not even Holly. Sure as hell not Cole. They try. *He* tried. Failures, each and every one of them. They think they know what I want. But have they ever truly listened to me? Of course they haven't. It's not that my voice isn't loud enough. It's that they choose not to hear. They assume they know better, and so they try to speak for me.

I'm sitting in my dad's Herman Miller Aeron chair, at his desk, with the lamp and the iMac filling the book-lined office with a soft yellow glow. Cole's Heart sits on the desk but it isn't beating. It's blinking. Its little light flashes on and off. Blue, then black, blue, then black. I plugged it into the iMac as soon as I got home.

It was a fluke that I found it. Some people might've called it fate, but fluke works fine for me. As I drove, slip-sliding my way home along the snowy Malvern Loop, I saw a splash of red in the middle of the white, like blood on a clean sheet. I got out, reached down, and picked it up. I held the Heart in both hands, fingers wrapped around it, dumbfounded by my dumb luck. *Well, lookie here, isn't that something?*

I set it on the back seat and drove it home, as if it were a stray I planned to nurse back to health. Plugging it in didn't scare me, because I wasn't afraid of Cole. I never have been. Maybe I should've been, but that doesn't matter now. It was the others who feared him, and that's why they murdered him. They like to say they did it for me. But come on, who are we kidding?

The Heart is a server. Duh. The brand name is on the bottom; it's called a Strawberry microserver. To gain access to it, I needed a password. It took me about five seconds to crack it. The name of the server is "MY HEART BELONGS TO" and its password is "ME."

Short, maybe not so sweet, but oh so obvious. At least to someone who knew Cole.

Cole used to tell me, "My brain belongs to the world, my soul belongs to you, but my heart belongs to me." I always figured he was trying (and failing) to be poetic, but what he was really doing was grasping for the last word.

You see, that's what the beacon was about. When we were in the sugarhouse and Grayson saw those coordinates on Gus's phone, I put it all together. Logan unplugged the Heart, and after a designated amount of time, automated messages fluttered out into the world. Like pigeons with messages on their feet. Flappity-flap. One to me, blaming me and telling me that stealing his server was a useless endeavor. Another to Cole's former best friend and partner-in-slime, sending him to find . . . the backup?

Make sense? Sure it does.

So what's on the Heart? The Cavalry, obviously. That's why the site hasn't worked since it was disconnected. Within the Cavalry is GOTCHYA, which is nothing more than a folder containing Logan's pictures and videos. The apps and site that Logan used as a cloud did nothing more than redirect his data here. Simple.

Beyond that, there are some programs designed to capture and steal information, to post and share the mountains of garbage

Cole put out into the world. All lazy and instant, the way he liked things. And there are plenty of other files and photos here too.

I'm looking through a slideshow of pics right now. It's called *Cavalry Leaders,* and it's scored to classical music, the type with lots of drums that plays in movies when soldiers shuffle off to war. But the pictures aren't of soldiers. They're of Cole and Gus, from when they were awkward, and slightly more innocent, freshmen. I'm guessing Cole's mom, Teri, was the photographer.

The two boys are trying out a variety of poses as they stand near the woods next to the trailer. They're both aiming for manliness and landing on ridiculous. In half the pictures they're wearing rubber horse masks. It's beyond embarrassing.

Cole loved those horrible masks; he even asked me once if he could wear one while we were fooling around. That was a big "no" from me, thank you very much. The Cavalry was a part of his world that didn't interest me, in any way, shape, or form. Why open that can of worms when life was wormy enough as it was?

But obviously the Cavalry was important to someone. Earlier today, when we were in the sugarhouse, Gus mentioned he was trying to get revenge, and so he made and spread the meme. It makes sense. It *made* sense, and that's why I thought Gus was behind *everything*. That was my mistake.

He wasn't behind *everything*. Hell, he was hardly behind *anything*. Only the first meme that sparked our paranoia. But he certainly had the motive to torture me and the others. Because he hates me. He hates everyone I associate with. He believes I stole Cole away, and ruined his silly little site. Which is a bunch of horseshit. The reason the Cavalry was never popular is because it sucked ass, with or without Cole. And I suspect Cole realized that. Though I don't know for sure.

The one thing I do know for sure (because it was a point of pride for Cole) is that the whole Cavalry thing started when they posted a humiliating video of Gus. It was from when he was a kid. He was a singing a song. Oh, my goodness, it was terrible, so bad that I've never been able to watch it all the way through. It was far more sad than funny. But it got views. It went viral to a degree. And they tried to ride that wave by becoming . . . I don't know. *Political?* They were never skilled at it. They could never capture the world's attention unless it involved humiliation. That's why Gus tried to humiliate me, with his weak-sauce meme. All the while, he didn't understand the power he was actually wielding. Because he didn't know the awful thing my friends were guilty of. Kinda tragic, come to think of it. But here we are.

Here I am. I didn't ask for this, any of it. Decisions were made and carried out without my express written or oral approval. If actions speak louder than words, then the others were screaming on my behalf. What I wanted was whispers and solutions that didn't involve parking lots and drugs and vomit and death and burials and interrogations. Yes, I *wanted* out. But they saw to it that I'm thoroughly and completely still in this shit.

And I might be even deeper in now. I sincerely hope not. A few minutes ago, I heard a gunshot coming from the woods. A single gunshot—*Bam!*

One gunshot usually means an accident or a warning. Maybe a suicide. You don't shoot once if you intend to hurt another person. You make sure you finish that job. And as far as I know, there's only one person out in those woods. Grayson.

When he stopped by earlier, he "borrowed" the tractor, with the backhoe attached. I watched him drive it toward the grave. That backhoe is probably cutting into the ground and searching for Cole's body right now. Maybe Grayson has already found the Thule, and out of frustration, he shot his rifle into the air, or into the ground, or into the plastic. (I hope not into himself, though that would be very unlike him.)

But frustration fits. Frustration makes sense. Especially if he dug, which means he didn't find Cole's body. Because that's not where I left it.

The night after we buried Cole, I attached that backhoe to the tractor, and I returned to the stone wall and unearthed the Thule. I used the tractor to carry the whole thing and dropped it into the bed of my dad's pickup. Then I dumped Cole's body where it should've been dumped in the first place—behind his trailer.

I erased the phones (including Cole's!), smashed them to bits, and scattered the pieces on the bottom of the hole like I was planting silicon seeds. I wasn't sure of the best way to get rid of the Thule, so I tossed it back into the hole too, buried it once more. I never thought anyone would have any reason to dig there again. Because I always figured the police would've found the body by now. It's not exactly hidden. It's near the propane tank I made a point of emptying. Maybe it's half-eaten by animals. It's certainly rotting. We could already smell it when we went back there on Sunday.

When they do find the body, the investigators will perform an autopsy. They'll conclude that Cole ODed, just like his mother. They'll notice the propane tank is empty and maybe they'll come up with a theory. Cole got high, decided to cook something, or turn on the heat, and when those things didn't work, he went outside to check on the propane, and that's when the drugs hit him. Down he went.

They'll assume he died alone, because why would they assume otherwise? He's got a little dirt on him? So what? He's been outside for days. If they find fibers from the tarp on his body, that'll be easily explained by the tarp I put in the trailer.

Our confession exists on the Heart and only the Heart. Gus never watched it. I'm convinced of that now. Like everyone, he only saw the screen cap. I don't know how and don't care how, but I'm guessing that picture was automatically uploaded to the Cavalry. Another of Cole's lazy-but-instant approaches to life.

And what's that picture anyway? It's a meme, a joke, a nothing. No one will ask where it came from, because origins rarely matter. And if they do ask, who will speak up? Logan? Holly? Grayson? Not a chance in hell.

I worry a bit about Gus, because our behavior around him has been worrisome. But we can explain it away by saying we were bothered by the meme and worried about Cole and full of emotions and blah blah blah. We never confessed in Gus's presence, though Holly came close. And without a confession, who's actually ever going to suspect murder? The police will forget about it. So will everyone else. Eventually.

For the moment, I'll deal with the inevitable blowback from the others. I'll probably get an angry message from Grayson, accusing me of conspiring with Cole. Yes, I do realize that finding the empty Thule will only strengthen his conviction that Cole is still alive. So I'll get Gray on the phone. Holly and Logan too. I'll put their stupid fantasies to rest once and for all.

I'll explain that I never thought they'd be so callous as to *murder* someone—holy living fuck, right? Call me naïve, but even the night before they did it, when we started digging the grave, I thought the whole sordid affair was pretend. Posturing. Cosplaying at crime. Playing a game of chicken to prove who was the better friend and citizen.

Still, I was ready for the worst. And when they went and actually did the worst, the only thing I trusted them to do next was ignore my original advice. They wanted to bury the body, so I had them bury it on my property. That way I could get it the hell off my property and put it where it should've gone in the first place. Sure, I could've let them in on this secret sometime in the last ten days. (Specifically, when their batshit brains were convinced that Cole was alive.) But they probably would've insisted on burying the body again.

You know what? Forget *probably*. Let's go with definitely.

Will they accept the truth gracefully now? Fat chance, but they'll have to learn to live with it. This is one instance where they can't speak for me.

I'm far from a genius. I didn't predict GOTCHYA, the Cavalry, all the beacons. But it's handled, because I handled it. Just like I'm going to handle Cole's Heart.

Here it sits, on my father's desk, my ex-boyfriend's most treasured possession. I plan on destroying it. I'll delete it, bash it with a hammer, toss it from the ferry, and consign it to the bottom of Lake Champlain. I know that in Cole's beacon he bragged about a backup, but I'm not going to worry about that. Because any backup doesn't have our confession on it. It's a time capsule that was sealed away while Cole was still alive. And no one was a murderer.

Gus can have it. Snuggle up with it and make out with it for all I care. He can continue on with his pathetic memesturbatory alt-right revolution. Maybe he'll even dedicate that trash site to Cole's memory. Not that Cole deserves a memorial. I'm not sure *what* he deserves. Or, deserved. Was he dangerous to me, the others, the world? Maybe, but I don't think I'll ever know for sure. I have to stop asking myself that question.

It's time to move on. Which, for now, means getting some fresh air. So that's what I'm doing. I'm standing up from this desk and walking out to the back deck, where I can feel the snow on my hands and my cheeks, the cold flakes on my hot skin.

It's tranquil on the deck, and the moon is sneaking out from behind the clouds. I can see the forest, dancing in white. It will all belong to me someday. My parents plan on living here until they're through, and then they'll pass it on to their one true heir. It's nice to know, but it's wild to think that Holly, and Logan, and Grayson would all believe I would want to live on this beautiful stretch of land with a body rotting on it. They were all born around here, and so they don't understand how much a place like this can mean to someone who wasn't.

I stare for a while, and I pray for more stillness and silence, the type that lasts for as long as you need it. But I don't get it for more than a few seconds. Because I hear another gunshot—*Bam!*

Followed by another—*Bam!*

Then—*Bam! Bam!* Two more, screaming through my forest.

It tells me that Grayson is not the only person out there. And probably rules out accidents or warnings. I could run into the forest, arms up and hollering, trying to help. But I'm not going to do that. I know how little my voice matters to them.

So instead I step inside, I lock the door, I pull the blinds, and I turn off the lights. I pick up my phone. Whatever happens next, I'm making sure of one thing.

The last word is mine.

ACKNOWLEDGMENTS

Without three groups of people, this book would still be a muddled mess existing only in the back of my mind. And you certainly would not be reading it. Those groups are . . .

The brilliant folks behind the scenes: heroic editor Julie Strauss-Gabel, fearless agent Michael Bourret, vigilant copyeditor Regina Castillo, talented designers Samira Iravani, Theresa Evangelista, and Anna Booth, and the rest of the dedicated team at Dutton Books for Young Readers who whipped this story into shape.

The supportive and loving family on the front lines: Dad, Mom, Toril, Tim, Dave, Magela, Jacob, Will, Matteo, Mauro, Jim, Gwenn, Pete, and all the members of the Starmer, Amundsen, Wells, and Evans clans.

And, of course, the three kind and wonderful souls who encourage and inspire me every day: Cate, Hannah and Rowan. I love you so.